An Old Fashioned Murder

❖

By
Laurie Pooler-Pelayo

Copyright © 2006 by Laurie Pooler-Pelayo

All rights reserved. No part of this book shall be reproduced or transmitted in any form or by any means, electronic, mechanical, magnetic, photographic including photocopying, recording or by any information storage and retrieval system, without prior written permission of the publisher. No patent liability is assumed with respect to the use of the information contained herein. Although every precaution has been taken in the preparation of this book, the publisher and author assume no responsibility for errors or omissions. Neither is any liability assumed for damages resulting from the use of the information contained herein.

This is a work of fiction. Names, characters, places, and incidents either are the product of the author's imagination or are used fictitiously. Any resemblance to actual events or locales or persons, living or dead, is entirely coincidental.

ISBN 0-7414-3579-9

Published by:

1094 New DeHaven Street, Suite 100
West Conshohocken, PA 19428-2713
Info@buybooksontheweb.com
www.buybooksontheweb.com
Toll-free (877) BUY BOOK
Local Phone (610) 941-9999
Fax (610) 941-9959

Printed in the United States of America
Printed on Recycled Paper
Published November 2006

Dedication

This is dedicated to:
Judy Harris – Who gave me my murder weapon. Peace.

Aunt Mil for her support and love through the years.

The Jane's (Richmond and Terry) – For giving me encouragement and being my cheerleaders.

Ed, Shawn, Claudia & Kerry – For putting up with me.

Christian – For his editing expertise.

And most of all for my family – Alden, Lessa, Alec and Alyse
Without whom I could not survive.

And finally to my Mom who started the genealogy bug – I miss you.

Chapter One

Lydia Proctor collapsed onto the couch in her family room with a woosh. Leaning forward, she picked her laptop up off the coffee table and placed it on her lap. She had decided to multi-task by running upstairs to put a load of wash in while waiting for the information she had just entered into her genealogy program to file.

It was the first ten minutes she'd had alone to herself all day. With the kids upstairs doing homework or playing on their respective computers, and the household chores taken care of, it was her opportunity to get something done without any major interruptions.

Recently her job flow had increased ten fold so her day just seemed to speed by. The on-order books were finally starting to arrive at the community college library where she was employed, now that funding had been approved. Lydia liked being busy but for her being busy meant sitting in front of a computer all day either downloading information, or cleaning up information. There was very little getting up and down anymore unless it was to get a copy from the laser printer. The days of card catalogs and filing in them had ended long ago.

Being busy at home was a different story—at least as of late. Lydia's husband, Lance, had recently taken a job that required a lot of traveling, so she was pretty much a single parent more often that she would have liked, and much to Lydia's chagrin, this was one of those weeks he was out of town.

She found out the hard way over the last few months that tasks performed on a daily basis—ones that would take just minutes to get done when he was home—now took far (far) longer when he was away. But, if one wished to pay the bills, one learned how to suck it up (as Beth her oldest would say).

Lydia's outlet, when Lance was home, came in her trips to work on her family history with Faye Carter her best friend of twenty-five years at the local Family History Center in Los Angeles.

It was hard to imagine sometimes that she and Faye were even still friends after all these years since they were such polar opposites in personality and backgrounds.

When they had been in high school, she and Faye had been dubbed "Laverne and Shirley" after the old television show. Part of that branding had come from the fact the two of them had bickered incessantly, and the other because of their physical appearance.

Back then Faye had been a stocky five feet two, with dishwater blond curly hair and green eyes; and like Laverne her Italian heritage was quite apparent both in appearance and mannerisms.

Lydia on the other hand was taller at five six with straight black hair, fair pale skin, blue eyes, and thin as a rail; and like Shirley her Irish (and French Canadian) heritage was pretty dominant. Lydia, through the years, was quite surprised at how many people clued in on her "black Irish" side just from getting a look at her.

Things had changed over the years. Faye had straightened and then darkened her hair; whereas Lydia had highlighted hers—mainly to hide the encroaching gray—and then cut it shoulder length to keep up with her busy lifestyle, namely chasing her children around. Faye had lost weight, and Lydia had finally gained a little. Lydia was pleased that so far she had escaped her mother's curse of gaining pounds and then never losing them.

Even after all their physical changes and twenty-four years, people still called them "Laverne and Shirley," which made Lydia laugh, and Faye groan.

After high school their lives diverged for a time as well. Faye went directly to a four-year college where she received a degree in business administration, which took her only as far as being an administrative assistant at a medium sized law firm in town.

About four years ago Faye "suddenly" decided she didn't want to be an administrative assistant anymore, announcing to the world that police work was what she truly wanted to do with the rest of her life. Her family had been shocked by the idea but Lydia knew that the decision had not come lightly. Faye had always been the outdoorsy, sports minded of the two, so it only seemed fitting that a job with an option of working away from the traditional office setting would be more suited to her.

Lydia knew for a fact too, that Faye's decision had been influenced somewhat by a very successful blind date. The object of that date—a seasoned police detective—later became her husband, a tidbit that no one but Lydia knew about. No matter how the decision had come about, it had been the right one for Faye, and Lydia was happy for her.

Lydia on the other hand had gone to work right away at the local community college where she was also taking classes. She had fallen into the job at the library by accident, and was still there in the same department after twenty years. She had met Lance at the same college in one of her classes. It wasn't too long after meeting that they married and started their family right away, which forced Lydia to set her studies as well as her genealogy aside.

Lydia had started working on her own genealogy, now also known by the trendy term "family history," while still in high school. The five generation pedigree chart assignment had been part of a home economics course called "home and family."

The trend/hobby/pastime was also beginning to take off due to the popularity of Alex Haley and his *Roots*, which helped to drive Lydia's interest. But long before Alex Haley had come along, there had been Lydia's maternal grandfather. Raymond Day had been one of those people who felt that history and family were the most important things in life. The man had recorded on paper everything he knew, saving it for future generations. It was that forethought that had initially started Lydia on her quest, long before the class in high school. Besides her grandfather, Lydia was enormously grateful to her mother, who had been wise enough to pass those pieces of history on to Lydia many years before she died.

Lydia found that her major in college, which had been history, tied in exceptionally well with the pursuit of genealogy, giving her an extra insight into events that affected her ancestor's lives. It provided her with new ideas that opened up paths to finding information that others might not consider. Working within a library setting had its advantages too, by affording her the opportunity to explore and use many different resources.

As for Faye, during high school, playing sports was what consumed her interest. Lydia had tried to get Faye to join her—even taking a stab at teaching her how to start her family tree but being the narrow minded sports person she had been Faye never gave it a chance. It wasn't until the death of Faye's grandparents and later her father, that she decided it was time to pick the brains of those living and had sought out Lydia's help to begin her journey. So at last Faye, like Lydia, had been bitten by the genealogy bug; both knowing there was no going back.

As Lydia and Faye spent more and more time together, they found that they also worked well together. Faye supplied the analytical cop insight, whereas Lydia tended to rely more on her gut. They were comfortable bouncing ideas off of each other, no matter how strange they seemed.

Although Faye was content with her foray into the realm of genealogy, Lydia felt it wasn't enough for her. She had been active on the board of the local genealogical society in town for a number of years, and when a vacancy for the society's librarian became available four years go, Lydia had jumped at the opportunity. She found it fun and challenging, letting her do things that she wouldn't have the opportunity to do at work, since she didn't hold a masters in librarianship.

In addition to the volunteerism, Lydia did some freelance genealogy work on the side—nothing too elaborate since she didn't always have the time. She saw it as an opportunity to help people, as well as to broaden her horizons while she learned something new. Making a little extra spending money didn't hurt either, since it gave her a slush fund of her own for copy and travel expenses.

An Old Fashioned Murder

This particular Family History research trip was supposed to help Lydia focus on colonial Virginia, in an area where she was having a hard time finding a several-generations-removed aunt. Usually she was organized, keeping a list of items that she needed to follow through on. But at that particular point in her evening she hadn't written a line, a note—nothing. It was just as she was about to call up that pesky relatives' family information and start making those notes, that the phone rang for the umpteenth time.

Normally the phone wasn't an issue but that had all changed when her son turned fourteen. That magic number had brought him a growth spurt of three inches, a pesky girlfriend, and a mustache; which today when Lydia passed him, she could have sworn he had finally shaved off.

She quickly laid her laptop down and ran across the room to grab the phone before it went to voicemail. Lucas was always the first one down the stairs running for it (that pesky girlfriend Lydia assumed) but whatever he was doing at that moment (probably not homework—but online gaming) must have taken precedence over answering the phone. Sometimes Lydia was sorry they had gotten DSL.

"May I speak with Ms. Proctor, please?" Since the voice didn't sound familiar she hesitated in answering immediately.

It seemed as if every time she picked up the phone lately it was a crank call, obnoxious sales person or wrong number—never anything relevant. And for it to happen now just seemed wrong, considering she had just started hunkering down with her to do list.

"May I ask who's calling?" Lydia asked trying not to sound too rude.

"This is Davis Jackman from the historical society, and there's a situation I need to consult with her about." He sounded friendly enough, but very matter of fact.

It must be a client referral, Lydia assumed. Sometimes they passed problem people on to her when they weren't quite sure what to do with them. Darn, she thought, just what she didn't need right at the moment.

"This is Mrs. Proctor, how may I help you?" she responded, waiting for what she hoped was something simple.

"I'm sorry. I should've said who I was right off. It's been a long day," he said, sighing. So he was having a long day as well—that she could relate to. "How do I begin? A patron has brought in a genealogy here that involves her family..." Lydia waited through another pause. "...Apparently there is something not quite working out for her and she would like some advice, if you don't mind." He seemed hesitant to ask that part for some reason. Lydia got the distinct impression that he was unsure about what he was doing. "We simply aren't equipped to provide that kind of help—genealogy I mean—and one of the other volunteers suggested you."

Well, that was easy, Lydia thought. Why had that been so difficult for him to spill? Since the name Jackman didn't sound familiar, and after many years of the historical society and the Tri-Cities library working together, she knew just about everyone. Lydia wondered if he was new, which might have accounted for the uncertainty.

Lydia had given out her personal business cards, some to the historical society, and some to the local library in case there was anyone who needed help and didn't know what to do. Since the genealogical library was only open a few days a week, with limited hours, and the society meetings were just once a month, she was the back-up just in case.

She was always afraid though that an oddball might get her card by accident. If they did Lydia told herself, then that's just what she got for putting her name and number out there, even if it was in what she considered safe territory. One took chances, she'd been told by her mother, if the results were worth the effort.

"Would I be able to speak with her to get a better feel for the problem?" Lydia asked. It would have been easier for him just to pass the phone to her, instead of relaying the conversation back and forth between the two of them. But then the distance may not entirely have been because of him; it could be that the person was simply shy, or elderly. Quite a few "arm chair" genealogists were not only shy, and elderly but recluses as well.

"I'm sorry... nice lady...just a little worried about talking to someone, afraid you might think she's batty," he paused. "She said that not me..." He whispered the latter statement into the phone. Wonderful—Lydia thought—it isn't going to be simple either.

"Would it be possible for me to take a number and call her then?" Lydia suggested. The whole conversation was starting to feel a lot like pulling teeth. The sooner he got to the point the better, not only because of the irritation she was beginning to feel, but also because at that moment the two oldest had started screaming at each other. Their echoing screeches were making it hard to hear.

"...She says she would prefer to meet you in person. Is there a place she can? Somewhere in town maybe?" Lydia wanted to say duhhh but decided that was probably unwise, and obviously rude. She wasn't sure who had referred him to her, or if he knew her position at the library but she decided to play it safe and explain anyway, as she offered a place for them to meet.

"Sure, I'm librarian for the Tri-Cities Genealogical Society on the corner of Main and Carson, can she meet me at our society library on say...Sunday at noon?" That would save her Saturday at the Family History Center with Faye, and the meeting would be during her volunteer time at the Tri-Cities library.

There was another long pause, Lydia gathered they were conferring. "That would be fine. She will see you then," he said. Before Lydia could respond, he had hung up. Suddenly she realized he hadn't provided her with the person's name, a contact number or had he asked for the specific address of the library building. She hoped that somehow, someone at the historical society would show that poor soul how to get to the library and not get her lost.

Lydia knew she should call back, just to be sure that the woman was taken care of...But first things first, break up the fight, and then start dinner. Her file could always wait until after dessert.

That Saturday Faye picked Lydia up as usual. Since Lydia only lived a couple miles away from Faye, and her house was on the way to the Family History Center in Los Angeles, Lydia usually got to ride along—which suited her just fine.

Lydia hated freeway driving but then again, she hated Faye's driving almost as much. From shutting the car door to parking the car in the library lot, it was a contest to see how high Lydia's blood pressure could climb before her head burst: Changing lanes, tailgating, stopping on a dime (sometimes more like a penny), Faye's driving hadn't improved one iota since high school. But then Lydia conceded—one did what one must, if one wanted to do research.

She had thought about calling Faye during the week to tell her about the peculiar phone call but then decided it could wait until Saturday. What could Faye do anyway besides remind Lydia that she read way too many mystery novels and was, as usual, overreacting?

Once they had hefted their fifty-pound bags containing their laptops, binders and other paraphernalia into the back of Faye's truck and had settled in their seats, Lydia brought up the topic. Faye tended to be pretty levelheaded, though sometimes a bit opinionated. Either way, Lydia knew she would get an honest observation no matter what.

"I got an unusual call the other day from someone looking for help with their research," Lydia started.

"Business is picking up then? I wish I could do more of it but not now. Work just doesn't allow me enough time for things like that anymore."

"Well...it seemed strange. The woman wouldn't talk directly to me. She went through some guy at the historical society...Jackman I think his name was." Lydia thought about how to phrase it so she didn't sound paranoid. "It was odd, that's all. I guess it just bothers me when people can't express what they want. I mean, is she a nut, or is it that complicated she couldn't explain it to me over the phone?"

"It could have been too complicated to explain on the phone. Or, she may be shy," Faye tossed out. "Aloof...Doesn't like to talk to people? You can be like that you know. It has taken you years to answer the telephone."

An Old Fashioned Murder

"True but then that's why I have children, so I don't have to answer telephones, take out the trash, bring in the mail, or mow the lawns. Usually the calls are for them, anyway."

Lydia laughed thinking about the last statement. It had taken her years to get her kids to help around the house. She tended to cut her oldest daughter, Beth, some slack because she was such a good student, and was willing to help around the house and with Sarah, the youngest, without being asked. But with Lucas, her middle child, Lydia made sure that he worked his butt off around the house, since his grades needed *lots* of work. Since he was the one on the phone all the time now, she figured she had a built in receptionist for free.

"Sometimes people are uncomfortable making contact with strangers," Faye continued. "I bet she's elderly and needs help, and just didn't know how to ask, that's all. I wouldn't worry about it." She paused on that thought. "You're just being paranoid. I think you've been around me too long."

"Okay, I thought about all of the above, to be honest. It just bugged me that's all. Lance told me I was being paranoid too when I talked to him on the phone last night." She thought about her suspicions. "But, in this day and age...as *you* know, one can't be too careful who they take on as a client. Right?" Lydia asked.

"Yeah but I wouldn't worry about it. The lady either legitimately needs your help or she's looking for an ear to bend. Either way, I think you're safe." Faye smiled. "I promise I won't tell any more stories that might cloud your judgment of the human race. It probably wouldn't hurt to take your can of Mace with you, though," she added.

"What a nice thought. Thanks." Lydia responded, not at all encouraged.

"Anytime. That's what I get paid the big bucks for...taking action."

Chapter Two

Overall Lydia's day had gone well. She had been able to find a few useful items regarding her Virginia family. Although the information didn't take the line much farther, it did help cement what facts she already had.

Lydia found from experience that there were some research trips when information seemed to come easily and in large quantities, and other times where it was more like beating your head against a wall. She was pleased that this trip had been more of the former, instead of the latter.

After arriving home, Lydia made a list of the things she needed to work on the following day at the Tri-Cities Genealogy Library. She knew the list would keep her occupied until her mystery client made her appearance.

In the South Bay there were four larger genealogy libraries in the Southern California area. Lydia had been to all of them at one time or another over the twenty years she had been doing research on her family. Three of them were sponsored by other genealogical societies (this included the Family History Center) and the fourth was the main branch of the Los Angeles Public Library, downtown.

The Tri-Cities Genealogical Society library was a smaller version of the Family History Center that she and Faye had been to that day. The beauty was that each library, no matter its size, had something for everyone. The Family History Center contained books, some microfiche, and the main resource for genealogists; microfilm, resources that Tri-Cities could not offer.

Microfilm provided the opportunity for researchers to view original records: births, marriages, deaths, wills and the like, something that the books could not always do. Books tended to contain only abstracts of those items (although that had started to change with the advent of scanners and computer technology), in addition to family and town histories, family genealogies, and so on. Each library served a specific purpose, and Lydia's goal was to make sure that their genealogical library served its purpose, too.

She could proudly say that the library contained almost two thousand books and hundreds of periodicals, many of which were not available locally in any other repository. The Tri-Cities library's diverse collection kept them in the spotlight as a good research facility, which with donations—although few and far between—kept them open and afloat.

Lydia noted, while making her ever growing mental list, that she had some cataloging that needed to be done, as well as some final processing of a few books for the shelves, which were growing a little too tight. A few years ago, the Tri-Cities Genealogical Society, after much finagling with the city for a permanent location, finally gave up and bought a rundown old house on the "other side of the tracks" for a permanent library.

After time, and what seemed like a million city council meetings, the society was able to persuade the city to move the house to the local park near downtown, as a show of good faith and support for what the genealogical society was doing for the community. It took two years but the house had been converted into the small genealogical library they now had. Since the bigger libraries closer to Los Angeles were forty-five minutes or more away, their little library was perfect for doing light research and analytical thinking in a quiet atmosphere.

After she fed the kids, loaded the dishwasher, threw in a load of clothes, and then called Lance at his hotel, Lydia poured herself into bed. It was not as early as she had planned but not as late as it could have been either. She found it was easier to get certain chores done when Lance wasn't home, since it seemed like he followed right behind her making the same messes all over again. Sometimes Lydia thought he was worse than the kids.

Lydia woke at eight, dressed, and then fed herself and the kids. Just before noon, she dropped Beth off at work, leaving Sarah with Lucas since she would only be gone for a couple hours. Even with the nine year age difference, Lucas and Sarah didn't fight as much as Beth and Lucas did when they were alone. She tended to come home to a messier but more peaceful house on days when he had babysitting duty. As long as Sarah had her Nickelodeon and Lucas had his computer games, all was well.

When Lydia arrived at the library, she was pleased to see there weren't any other cars waiting in the lot. Because of their limited hours on Sundays, many patrons arrived a bit before opening in the hopes of taking advantage of the short time frame. Due to a survey the society had taken at one time (pre Lydia), the decision had been made to open for only a couple hours in the afternoon on Sundays, in order to accommodate the church going patrons. It had worked so far but Lydia felt an extra hour or two would be helpful, especially for those beginners who were just starting to get their feet when it was time to shut the doors. Lydia and her family attended church too but when Lance was gone she took that one selfish advantage of being able to sleep in, even for an hour.

Lydia unlocked the door, turned on the lights, and looked around. She remembered when they had moved in. It had taken a lot of work to get the building into shape to house the collection. The floors had been stripped of carpet and refinished, wall paper removed, windows replaced, walls stripped and painted, and the roof re-done.

Inside the door to the left they had an old card catalog—which was very rare, especially now with the universal reliance on computers. Five huge oak tables dominated the middle of the room. They had been donated by an old home-style Italian restaurant in town and refinished by their current society president Jack Tyler. Each table could seat up to twelve people at a time, which worked well during workshops and seminars. Along the wall were some beautiful antique oak bookshelves donated by a retired lawyer, who ended up becoming one of their volunteers. The back wall held a fairly nice sized collection of periodicals and newsletters in both Princeton files and displayed on magazine racks.

To save space, the library was leaning towards eliminating the card catalog. Lydia had mixed feelings about this idea since many of their users were what were considered "old timers," or "pre-computer." After an impassioned plea, the board had decided to keep it for a little while longer.

An Old Fashioned Murder

Staffing consisted of a number of volunteers, mostly retired. Lydia was quite surprised to learn when she took over librarian duties, that many retirees were busier retired than they had been while working, and could only help for short spans of time.

Because of cost concerns, the library was open three days a week, Tuesday, Thursday and Sunday. The board had hoped to expand to five days but that would take more money, and volunteers of which they didn't have enough of either.

Through the years Lydia found that a number of library patrons, as well as members of the genealogical society who'd died, would will their books to the library but leaving their money was rare. There were always supplies to buy, books to purchase, utilities to consider, and of course what they had to pay the town annually in rent. Although the amount wasn't much since it was a community service kind of thing, they still had to pay two hundred dollars a year for the lease of the land. That had been the trade-off for the town putting out the cost of moving the house, which had been quite expensive. The society obtained their income primarily through dues and fundraisers, and more than half of that income went to the running of the library. Lydia knew there were so many things that could be done to make the place better but those costs were above and beyond what the budget and additional resources allowed. Lydia hoped to start supplementing the income by trying her hand at grant writing, to see if she could bring in more money towards special projects.

Since Lydia worked a regular Monday through Friday job she was not available to work at the society library during the week. The volunteers who worked those days were under the guidance of Lydia's assistant, a fun loving widow named Muriel Grant. Muriel was a sweet woman in her early seventies, who was very active and very busy. Because of Muriel's schedule, Lydia tried to pick up the slack on weekends when she could. It had its pluses since it provided Lydia the opportunity to work on her genealogy as well but a lot of that depended on the number of patrons who needed her assistance. They always came first no matter what.

Interruptions from patrons were different than the ones at home where many of the problems could be solved if people simply (and calmly) explained what they needed or just asked for help instead of screaming at each other. Patrons, as Lydia found, asked for help because they truly needed it and many times would return the favor if they could—that could not always be said of her children.

Lydia found the volunteers to be an eclectic group of people. Besides the lawyer, the volunteers consisted of retired policemen, businessmen, housewives, teachers, and librarians. There was even a minister, and a retired doctor at one point. In talking with them over the years, not only as volunteers but as friends, Lydia found that genealogy not only helped fill their off time but it also provided them with something to pass on to their families after they were gone. Thankfully not too many of them had passed to the great beyond in the ten years that Lydia had been involved with the group.

As Lydia wandered about, turning on lights she contemplated the reasons why genealogy appealed to her so much.

Genealogy, for Lydia was the organization of a life, one that encompassed both the past as well as the present. Even though the ancestor in question may have lived anywhere from seventy-five to two hundred years ago, their blood still flowed through the veins of the person doing the research. Every piece of information a genealogist found on that ancestor, helped to make them a real person again, flaws and all.

Lydia divided the process of genealogy into two parts: Collecting and documenting the facts of an ancestor's life was the "genealogy" portion of creating a family tree. It not only formed a structure to work with, it was the fact-finding portion of the mission; the documentation of life events through vital and other recorded events.

To her the second part of creating the tree was the "family history" portion. It was the part genealogists called putting the "meat on the bones of the ancestor." The meat included the gathering of the circumstances they had been born into: being born in a log cabin, the back of a wagon train crossing the prairie, or on a steam ship crossing the Atlantic. It also included how they lived: a small farm on the prairie, a business in a city, running from drought and poverty. These were the stories that gave that person a full life, making them once again flesh and blood, more than just names and dates.

One also learned while creating that tree that death was simply another part of that ancestor's life.

Lydia had learned through family diaries and letters that although her ancestors accepted birth as a joyous, although painful event; so too were they forced to accept death, especially before the advent of modern medicine, because there was no other alternative. She also found that death caused by disease wasn't new, nor was death caused by accident or murder, although murder tended to be a little rarer.

She found most people, who didn't understand genealogy, would think the excitement in finding a death date for someone to be morbid but it was just a part of the process. It made that ancestor's circle complete.

As she reached her desk, sitting her purse on top, Lydia sat those thoughts aside as she glanced at her calendar to see if anything important had been scheduled for the day. The only volunteer due in other than herself, was Muriel who looked to be doing some clean-up work of her own, in addition to making the new volunteer schedule for the month. Lydia noted she wouldn't be in until one.

Lydia put her purse away and then walked over to the copy machine by the wall next to the entrance to the kitchen. She turned it on, checked the paper tray and then put out the change jar for the copies. The library committee had established an honor system for patrons when paying for copies, instead of messing with a change machine and the hassles that went with it. Overall most people were honest in chipping in what was considered the average price for copies, which basically covered the cost of paper and some of the toner. Some patrons weren't as honest as others but those were few and far between.

Once she was back at her desk Lydia opened the door to the cabinet beside it and pulled out the container of books that needed attention. There weren't too many, which was good. The stack was just enough to keep her busy, until her appointment.

Lydia glanced up at the clock and then down at the door reminding herself it was still a bit too early for her mystery client to arrive. Thankfully she was way beyond her stupid paranoia of the other day, and had started to speculate what the woman would want from her.

Even though she hadn't gotten any clues from the conversation with Mr. Jackman, that hadn't stopped her from letting her imagination run wild. Lydia started going over her mental list: Maybe it was a date conflict, an adoption problem, a child out of wedlock, a run away spouse, or a slave in the family. It was surprising sometimes to learn what would shock or puzzle someone when they worked on their genealogy.

As the clock got closer to half past noon Lydia became a tad concerned. Maybe the woman had changed her mind and decided whatever the issue was, wasn't that important after all. Or poor Mr. Jackman really had sent her somewhere else. When Lydia had gotten a chance to make a call back to the historical society it was right before their closing. She had been able to talk with her friend, Maggie King who was a volunteer there, as well as a member of their genealogical society. As Lydia had suspected Mr. Jackman *had* just started the day before and unfortunately the person in charge of volunteers had put him on the desk first—a sort of trial by fire kind of thing. Maggie admitted she had been the one to pass him Lydia's card.

Just then the door opened and the bell rang. It was a tiny one, not too loud but enough to let someone back in the kitchen, who might be eating lunch or making a cup of tea, know that there was someone in the building.

At the door Lydia spotted an older woman, close to Muriel's age but frail looking. She had short silvery-gray hair, and a very fair complexion. Lydia walked over to join her at the door and looked into the deepest green eyes she had ever seen. The pantsuit she wore was a deep copper color that seemed to make her eyes even more vivid. Lydia noticed her no-nonsense black flats didn't add a whole lot of height to her already petit frame so she barely came above Lydia's shoulders.

She was carrying a box that was bigger than anything Lydia had ever hauled to Salt Lake City when going on one of her serious research trips. Lydia was surprised—from looking at the lady's somewhat petit stature—that she could even lift that huge box; and even more so, that she was able to get it up the stairs and inside the door.

A dainty hand shot out, flashing two plain gold rings, and a pretty bracelet with charms dangling all over it. Her hand seemed tiny within Lydia's, her grip not too firm as she made an attempt at a handshake.

From the looks of things, Lydia was pretty sure there would be no need for the Mace.

"Hello, my name is Julia Franklin, and I am here to get some help."

Chapter Three

"**W**elcome, my name is Lydia Proctor. I gather you are the lady I have been waiting for?" Lydia said, flashing her most accommodating smile.

From the look on Julia's face, Lydia got the feeling that she was embarrassed for having to ask for help, and Lydia didn't want to make her feel any worse.

"I'm so sorry I'm late but I took a short nap and overslept, and then carrying this box tends to slow me down as well," she chuckled. It was a nice lilting sound that made Lydia like the lady even more. "My granddaughter was supposed to drive me in but she had an emergency to take care of at her work, so I was on my own. Where can I sit this monster down?"

Shame on me, Lydia thought, for not having helped her right away. "I'm so sorry, let me take that," Lydia offered, taking the box from her hands. "Please, have a seat over there at one of the tables, we can sit and chat a bit, and then you can tell me what you're looking to find."

Lydia found it easier to pose the statement like that since genealogists were always *looking* for something, be it a vital record, a will, an obituary, or even for some, a place to start. Looking at the box that Julia brought, it appeared she had enough to start with, so Lydia guessed her quest was more specific.

"Thank you. I know that kind Mr. Jackman didn't explain much but he really wasn't sure what I was talking about, and he hoped you might be able to help me better." She seemed like she was beginning to feel at ease, which was a good start.

"I'll do my best," Lydia assured her. Before they settled down for the long haul, Lydia offered Julia a cup of tea or

An Old Fashioned Murder

coffee. Julia graciously accepted the offer of tea, and Lydia then escorted her back to the kitchen.

Lydia placed Julia at one of the lunch tables and then put the tea pot on to boil. As they waited, they chatted a bit about the library. Lydia explained what the society did and the purpose of the library, as well as society membership and their library volunteer committee. At the teapot's signal Lydia poured water into their cups and then encouraged Julia to tell her story.

"Let me briefly tell you about my mother's life, and then what I am looking for may make more sense," Julia began. "My mother, Amy, was raised by her maternal grandparents, Jack and Carrie Stowe. Her mother Katherine, their daughter, died when she was just a little thing, and they didn't trust her father to raise her." Julia took a sip of tea and closed her eyes for a moment. It looked like she was reflecting on some long ago story that had been told to her, and she was trying to picture it in her mind so as to explain more clearly. "Apparently my grandmother was the Captain's third wife. They called him Captain for some reason I'm not too sure of..."

Lydia waited patiently for Julia to continue. Many older people would diverge on other thoughts, which took them away from the original one; but if left alone they would come back to the topic on their own. Sometimes though, you had to steer them back to the subject with an open-ended question, which worked the best. After a few moments though, Julia re-grouped without assistance and started on her path again.

"...Anyway, all of his wives died very early within their marriage, except for his first... and the last wife, she outlived him. And each of them, except the last wife, left very small children to be raised by the next one. For some reason, my Grandmother Katherine's death struck an odd cord with her parents, and so they took my mother and her brother Cyrus away right after their mother's funeral."

Lydia added more water into their cups, and then motioned for Julia to continue.

"The other children by his first two wives and the son from his fourth wife remained with the Captain." Julia took a breath and then continued, this time with pain in her eyes. "My mother, growing up, would listen in on family gossip. She got the impression that they thought the Captain killed her mother somehow. My mother shared that knowledge with her brother first, and then a couple years before she died, she told the story to me. She asked me to find out the truth. I tried doing it while she was living but I didn't know enough then. Now that I have something to work with, I'm not sure what to do next, and that's why I'm here. I want to see if there is a way to find anything to back up my grandparent's suspicions."

"There are a few things I can suggest. But I must ask you honestly, after all these years, are you sure these are bones you want to dig up? Are you sure this is something you really *need* to know?" Lydia felt it was a fair question. She wouldn't hesitate to say yes, she took her family as they were, warts and all; but she knew of people who had spent years working on their genealogy, found a nasty skeleton, and burned the whole thing in the fireplace, or shredded it and threw the scraps in the trash. She learned from experience that each person took the truth a little differently.

Lydia returned to the question at hand, did Julia really want to know?

"It started off being a promise to my mother but after all these years...I guess I need to know." She looked heavenward, patting her chest for emphasis. "It isn't a burden I want to carry anymore, and I don't want to pass on such a huge uncertainty like this to the following generations. They need to know the answer, good or bad, while I'm alive to soften the blow."

Lydia was impressed with her resolve. It was at that moment Lydia decided she would help Julia Franklin any way she could.

"Where did the story come from originally?" Lydia asked as she refilled their tea cups.

"From what my mother told me, no one ever said anything directly to her. She picked it up in passing, her grandmother Carrie, talking with an aunt, or her grandparents sitting at the table after dinner thinking she was out of earshot. They would say what a terrible shame it all was...things like that. Hearing them talk got her to worry, and wonder."

Lydia thought that maybe Julia's mother had misunderstood what she'd heard, maybe taking the information out of context. Back then, women died in childbirth, as well as from hundreds of other diseases; from scarlet fever, to small pox, to diphtheria, to the measles, to the flu, no one was immune.

"Let me show you my pedigree chart and group sheets, and then you can see what I have pieced together so far," Julia said, as she began removing file folders and papers from her box.

Lydia was impressed with how neat and well marked they were. There didn't seem to be any organizational issues with this woman, at least from what Lydia had seen so far. Unfortunately the same could not be said for herself. She had been trying to get organized for years.

The folder was identified as "Captain Andrew Bower Family," and from there Julia pulled out a hand-drawn pedigree chart which she laid on the table. Lydia leaned over in order to take a closer look. The family was drawn with Andrew being the head, and then to the right of him there were listed five different women; Melissa Stewart, Amelia Brown, Katherine Stowe, Mildred Wells and Priscilla Drake. She noted that he wasn't married to any of them longer than five to seven years, except for the last one. The first wife had three hildren; the second, Amelia, had two; Katherine, Julia's grandmother, had another two children, and the fourth wife only had one. The final wife had none but then she looked to be about fifty-two when they married. All the others had been around age twenty-five when he married them.

Lydia wondered if there was a hidden agenda behind the Captain marrying such young women. Did the fairer sex, being young, keep him feeling that way? Now, in the twenty-first century, they would be considered trophy wives. Back then they were most likely spinsters; and Lydia had to admit even that was an unfair assumption.

"That is some chart. He married just the five and had eight children total, correct?" Lydia was working out the scenario in her head.

"Yes," Julia replied as she pointed at the first wife, Melissa. "Family history says that he married his childhood sweetheart first, and then later she died of diphtheria."

"Where did you find the cause of death?" Lydia asked, curious as to where Julia was getting her source information from. Depending on the type of information, it could be second hand and therefore not necessarily accurate.

"My Uncle Cyrus worked with my mother on the family history for about forty years until he was hit by a car and killed. When he died it became my mother's to continue. I believe my mother told me that when they started filling out the family information, there was a great-aunt still alive and in her nineties, on the Stowe side, who told Uncle Cyrus that Melissa had died during a diphtheria epidemic along with their youngest child, Clarkson." She smiled that lopsided embarrassed simile that many people get when unsure of what they are telling. "I never thought about which aunt he got the information from, there are lots of papers in here, and I have only glanced at them. Maybe it is in a letter or something." She patted the pile with her hand. "None of my siblings are interested in the family, so it became mine. As you can see I am still learning what to do. I am still not even sure what is in this box, other than it's supposed to contain all my family lines. Maybe you can show me, so I can better understand what I am looking for." Lydia then realized that the organization had been her mother and uncle's work. They had thought ahead, trying to make it easy for who ever took over the job; but the ultimate question was—how well had they documented it all?

"If it isn't in there, that piece of information should be easy to prove, through courthouse death records, obituaries, cemetery records. Don't worry about it." Lydia smiled reassuringly. "Now wife number two, Amelia, do you know anything about her?"

"Once again, family history says that Amelia and Katherine, my grandmother, simply collapsed. Mildred supposedly passed in her sleep, no trauma that the doctor could find…so I was told. I think my uncle said there was some kind of an inquiry into Katherine's death. That might be in here, too. My grandmother just keeled over in the kitchen while cooking dinner." She shook her head at the thought. Such huge amounts of cooking over hot suffocating flames, in small, semi-enclosed rooms wouldn't happen much anymore now with microwaves and fast food. "She supposedly hadn't been feeling well for some time, and they just attributed it to the fact she was raising six children ranging from teenager to infant. Now, Amelia was found in the barn lying in a pile on the floor." Julia once again shook her head at the mental image. Lydia could imagine what she was thinking, because she was thinking it too; three, probably healthy women, all gone with no real apparent cause of death. Since they didn't die from childbirth, or from any contagious diseases—in that day and age, it probably would have been considered very strange.

"I can see he followed the usual pattern of a widower with young children. He appears to have waited the required six months to a year for mourning, courting, and wedding, in order to secure a mother for his younger children." Lydia remarked sarcastically.

Historically it had been proven that most men re-married as quickly as they could, especially if young children were involved. The majority of men born before the end of the twentieth century were not raised to care for infants and children. This was traditionally the duty of their wives, so most men were ready to re-marry anywhere from six months to a year in order to secure a new mother for their child.

Lydia had always thought that to be unfair. The male was always able to re-marry and start over but it wasn't as common to see a widow do the same—especially if her deceased spouse left her with very little income, or property. And the men most often remarried someone younger, usually a lot younger. That would never happen with a widow, since for her, it would have been considered the ultimate scandal.

"I was really appalled at first when I saw the chart. But then after looking at other family lines, he wasn't alone in doing it, he just seemed to do it more often," Julia said while looking at Lydia and rubbing her hands on her lap. It looked to Lydia like she was trying to rub a stain away. "So how do I prove what I need to? Where do I start?"

"Okay…" Lydia began. "Lets look at names dates and places, and then we can make a research strategy." It was then she realized what a sad situation this was. How in the world did this poor woman hope to prove that her grandfather was or wasn't a killer? It was then Lydia realized the real question was more like...how would she? She decided it was time to ask what Julia wanted of her.

"I guess I should ask this before we continue...Do you want me to guide you, do the research for you, or assist you?"

"I really can't do it alone. I'm getting too slow to move around quickly, and the brain doesn't always process as it should." She laughed again and then tapped her forehead. What was it called senior moments? Lydia had those now. "I don't want you to do it all alone, not because I don't trust you, you seem like a nice young lady but I want to be a part of it. So I guess I would like to work with you...help when I can...do anything you need me to."

"That sounds fine. My feeling is that most people have a better feel for their own family anyway, so if I am giving you information you have reservations with, we can cross that bridge together." Lydia got up and walked to the desk. She opened the middle drawer and pulled out some business cards.

"Ms. Proctor..."Julia began.

"Lydia, please Ms. Franklin..."

"Julia, please..." she responded in kind.

There was an awkward moment of silence. Lydia waited knowing Julia would eventually share with her whatever concerns she might have.

"I didn't truly think what my mother told me was possible until I actually sat down and looked at those names and death dates, and ages. It was then that I decided I needed to know." Julia placed her hand over her heart as she looked at Lydia imploringly. "Lydia, do you think there could be some truth to my great-grandparent's suspicions?"

Lydia could tell by her expression that Julia wanted assurance that those deaths were just a coincidence, that her grandparents had simply been overly cautious. But Lydia was beginning to have her own doubts. It was then she decided that no matter how the research progressed she would try and make the process as easy as possible for Julia, regardless of what the outcome might be.

An Old Fashioned Murder

"Julia, I am going to give you my personal business card. It has my home number and e-mail address. I am also going to give you one of the library cards too with our hours and phone number," Lydia handed her the card. "To be honest, now that I've had a chance to look at your charts, I feel it wouldn't hurt just to fish around a little and see what we can come up with. Let me play with it for a few days...roll it around in my head, and then I will call you with some ideas of what we can do, and how. How does that sound?"

"Perfect, thank you." Julia got up from her chair and stretched. "Getting older isn't any fun. I find I have joints that ache I never thought existed." She began scooping the papers up and putting them back in the folder.

"Just leave the Captain's family information that you have, with any documentation your uncle or mother may have supplied. I may take this from the point of view nothing has been searched, just to see what I come up with independent of them." Lydia thought that might be best. Then there wouldn't be any influence to steer her one way or the other. The documentation would be helpful though, if they were primary records.

"That's fine. I'll take the other members of my family home then." Julia gently closed the box and began to pick it up. "I hope I am doing the right thing. Now I guess I just need to find someone who wants it all after I pass on." Lydia knew many genealogists and family historians felt that way as well, Lydia being one of them. So much work...who would take it and continue after they were gone?

"Here, let me carry that for you." Lydia reached over and took the box. "Also is there a way I can contact you when I need to ask questions or confirm something?" Lydia asked remembering that piece of information was something that had been missed during initial contact. What good was doing the research if she couldn't ask questions and get feedback? Julia grabbed a piece of scratch paper from the desk and wrote her name, number, and address on it.

"I personally don't have a computer or e-mail, so the phone is my ear to the outside world. I tried playing with my granddaughter's computer—she's an accountant and a part-time student at the university, working on her business degree—but I just couldn't get the hang of it. I did like the games though!" Julia started for the door. Lydia followed behind.

"Not a problem. We'll keep in touch the old fashioned way," Lydia assured her as they headed down the stairs.

"Thank you again," Julia said, turning back to Lydia and smiling. "I truly do appreciate this."

Chapter Four

When Lydia arrived home she put her bag away, fed the kids the leftover chicken and rice she had prepared the night before and then made a quick call to her spouse at his hotel. Normally when she made phone calls she locked herself in their bedroom because it was the quietest place in the house. And because it was the only phone in the house with a cord she didn't have to worry about the handset dying while she was talking. None of the kids could put the phone back in its cradle to charge downstairs, so more often than not she found herself running through the house for a non-moveable extension.

Lydia actually caught Lance in his hotel room, although he was in the midst of preparing to go out for dinner. Before Lydia could even ask about his day, he immediately began grousing about his dinner plans. The group at the conference was going to eat at another buffet, this time a barbeque, as opposed to the normal Chinese that they all seemed to enjoy so much. It had become a running joke that every time he traveled with his boss they ended up at some kind of a buffet; and more often than not, it was some version of an Asian cuisine since his boss was of Asian descent.

Lance who was a Pacific Islander mix on his paternal grandmother's side didn't have the urge to spend every meal eating something exotic. Rice, eggs, and Spam were his basic foray into his genetic cuisine traits, with an occasional detour into something more complex like laulau or kalua pork.

Since his dinner was at six, and it was now going on five-forty-five, it didn't leave them much time to talk. Even though dinner was in the lobby restaurant, a short elevator ride away, he was going to be meeting some other corporate executives and she didn't want to keep him. Lance worked for a travel magazine as an advertising coordinator, so while Lydia got to sit at home and keep the peace, he got to travel the world, taking pictures of places Lydia would probably never see. She decided not to be morose and shook the negative thoughts from her mind. She had to remind herself she hated to fly anyway, so what difference did it make?

Trying to get back on topic, Lydia reminded him about the call from the historical society and her meeting with Julia at the library. She decided the kids' adventures could wait until he called her back before they went to sleep.

"Sounds interesting... do you know how much work is required yet?" he asked her. There was a buzzing in the background. Lydia figured he was shaving while talking to her. She was pleased to learn he was finally learning to multi-task. Lydia then wondered if that would translate to chores at home—doubtful.

"Well I took a quick look at the small pile of folders she left for me. It looks like there isn't a whole lot of documentation on the Bower line. If they did spend forty years working on their family they must have worked on the other branches first and saved this one for last," Lydia commented. "Possibly due to the situation, it doesn't look like either of them knew where to start." Lydia was chewing on a piece of chocolate bar. Chocolate always seemed to help her think better.

"What are you eating?" Lance asked knowingly. "Almond or toffee?"

"Almond...Okay, there is something like a coroner's inquest in the box, which helps. Unfortunately it doesn't go into great detail since it looks to be an extract. The process seemed to have been more of a formality since Katherine's parents forced the issue, otherwise I don't think there would have been anything done." Lydia could hear feel the vibration of the door slamming closed downstairs. Beth must be home.

"Anything else that might help?" Lance asked. She could tell by the muffled noise and the dropping of the phone he was dressing for dinner.

Boy wouldn't it be nice to eat out? She wouldn't think about that right now. It was hot dogs and chips for dinner tonight. Since Lydia wasn't a fantastic cook, she cooked what was easy and stuff that she couldn't burn too badly. She and Lance shared cooking duties when he was home. Reluctantly Lydia had to admit he was by far the better cook but since he was gone more often now, she was working on bringing up her culinary skills. At least she could say the kids hadn't gotten sick from anything she had cooked yet.

"There's an obituary for the Captain, which I glanced at, and an obituary for his last wife, some letters which I will need to read, a few newspaper clippings, an accounting journal for his mercantile, and not much else. So it looks like I will literally be starting from scratch." She noticed the shower was running; that was probably Beth.

Through the wall from their bedroom to the study she could hear Sarah begging for the computer from Lucas the computer whiz. That confrontation was on its way to a fight in about five minutes. He wouldn't give it up without an act of God. Lydia realized that their conversation would need to end fast or the hysterical crying and whining would be starting soon—from both of them.

"I should let you go. You need to leave for dinner and I need to break up a war," Lydia said. The scum spouse he was, just laughed. Yeah, he could laugh since he was four thousand miles away. She figured even though he was gone on business, he still enjoyed the break from the house. Soon she would have one but unlike him, she just had to schedule it.

"Remember, I'll be home in three days, then you can show me what progress you've made. Did you talk with Faye about it? A rookie cop perspective?"

"No, that's tomorrow after dinner. We are meeting for coffee and donuts." Both Lydia and Faye liked Krispy Kreme, and it was just a stones throw from Lydia's house. There was no better excuse for getting together, and out of principle they both avoided the joke about cops and donuts, since it truly was a universal food.

"Okay, good luck. Love you."

"Love you, too." Lydia hung up the phone and headed for the bedroom door…Off to break up the Alamo.

❖

"Okay so 'esplain Lucy," Faye began as they sat down at one of the booths. She had gotten a cup of coffee and a sprinkled donut. Lydia had gotten coffee as well but just a plain glazed since it was her favorite. Sarah, who was in red with a bow clipped on her brown ponytail, had come with her. She was over at the big glass window watching the donuts being made, which gave Lydia and Faye a few minutes of uninterrupted talking.

"Well apparently from what I can tell, this man, Captain Andrew Bower, married five times, three of the four wives dying 'mysteriously.'" Lydia did the quotations in the air with her fingers. "Back then it could have been anything, I suppose but the manner of death for two of them, including Julia's grandmother, not only seemed irregular but also somewhat similar in that there was no definitive cause of death. So, according to Julia, her grandparents became suspicious and took the grandkids from the father."

Lydia was trying to explain the scenario to Faye, in the hopes that she might be able to give her some additional ideas of places to look, besides the usual sources. "Their daughter Katherine was the third marriage. Why they thought something was off when she was only the second that died from collapsing, I don't know. The one he married after Katherine died in her sleep." Lydia sighed in exasperation. "Oh, I don't know, maybe it does sound bad."

"In my humble opinion, it does seem a little strange. One I could see but two…eh, might get me thinking. By the third unresolved death…no question, I would have been calling the inquisition," Faye remarked. "It sounds to me like the grandparents did know something that didn't get passed to the grandchildren, probably deliberately, too. They obviously didn't want the kids to know what they suspected, and Julia's mother by eavesdropping, heard something she shouldn't…It's always possible she took it out of context, too." Faye looked out the window, stirring her coffee as she was thinking.

"Yeah, I thought the same thing." Lydia agreed.

"No…they had to have had a damn good reason to pull those kids, they just couldn't walk in and do it without the law behind them…I'm positive. Too bad she waited to start this until after her mother died. Maybe she could have learned more," Faye said as she finally took a sip of coffee. "You may find something or nothing. What were you planning on doing?"

"I'm going to try vital records first, birth, marriage and death. It was late enough in the century that those should be recorded. They were near Athens County, Ohio at the time, so I should have pretty good luck. The area's near some of my family's stomping grounds, so I've had some experience with how to use the records." She took another bite of donut. "Then I'll try the newspaper, for a report on the inquiries, and any obits that I don't already have, and then court records, just for fun. The best part is there are some photos, so I can visualize what these people looked like as I'm searching for them. Maybe help me bond with them since they aren't my own family." Lydia rubbed her temples. She started thinking maybe she had bit off more than she could chew.

"Well, if you need help holler. They might still have some sheriff's records from then, assuming it even involved them enough to make a report. If you end up at a dead end it wouldn't hurt to try, and they might be more inclined to talk with another police person than a complete stranger, and non relation on top of that." Faye winked at Lydia. Lydia knew Faye liked throwing her newfound weight around; she also liked a good mystery, too. She agreed with Faye that the chances of there being any police records still around were pretty slim. "And remember you can always bounce stuff off me too if you need some insight. That always helps as you know."

"Okay. My job tonight after I get her to sleep..." Lydia pointed across the way to the small girl holding a glazed donut in her hand, completely entranced by the conveyor belt of donuts dropping into the hot cooking oil. "...Is to go through those files and start putting a family together. Then see what I have, what I need, and then start searching the Family History Library catalog for microfilm." Lydia had pulled out some paper and started making a list. "I'll also check and see what newspapers were being printed then and start searching."

"Sounds like you have the beginning of a good plan. You know, you should have been a detective. If you had, we would've made one hell of a team."

"Aw, that's the nicest thing you have ever said to me. Want another donut?"

❖

After Lydia had gotten Sarah to sleep, she sat down at the kitchen table with a bag of chocolate kisses, her trusty legal pad, a pencil and the information that Julia had supplied. She began looking over the myriad of items, making a list of the additional documents that she would need to look for.

In theory all genealogists were advised to work backward in obtaining information, death to birth and so on. That was done so it prevented the researcher from jumping to conclusions by working forward, therefore making false assumptions. Something similar to a person with the surname Washington, thinking they were related to George and working from him down. Since George didn't have any children, legitimate or otherwise, that assumption would lead to a dead end. The same with someone like Custer, and so on. By working backward, and proving each generation, it was more accurate and complete. And then if you hit a snag, you just tried to work the problem from a different angle.

Sometimes depending on the situation, there was no other choice than to work down and meet somewhere in the middle but those instances were few and rare. Lydia had two lines like that, and no matter which end she worked from, she was still missing the middle.

Since this family already had names, dates and so on, it would be more like filling in missing puzzle pieces. Sometimes proving information already provided was almost as challenging, if not more so, than locating the names, places and dates.

So Lydia started with the main man in this drama, which was the "Captain." According to the information Julia provided, he was born on, 10 July 1851, in the town of Saylesville, which was about eighty miles or so east of Chillicothe, Ohio. He lived there until his death on 10 March 1920 and was buried in the Methodist Church cemetery a few blocks from his home.

He married Melissa Stewart first on 5 November 1883 in Saylesville. The location of the ceremony was not noted, so Lydia wasn't sure if it had been in a church or not.

Lydia jotted down on the legal pad that there would not be a birth record for Andrew. She knew from experience that most of the Midwest states didn't start keeping vital records until at least the 1870s, so his birth date would probably come from his death record, tombstone, or obituary.

Lydia figured the marriages would be easier to locate since many states and counties had marriages in the courthouses back to the early 1800s. According to Julia, Melissa was the supposed childhood sweetheart, and mother, of his first three children. Also according to Julia, Melissa and one of her children died of diphtheria sometime in 1893. Lydia knew that would be easy to prove since death records in Ohio started at the county level sometime around 1870 as well. Lydia also wanted to prove that Melissa died of a good, old-fashioned disease, therefore eliminating any leanings toward something more sinister.

Since all the marriages, all the children's births, and all the deaths took place in Ohio, Lydia would be able to start ordering microfilm from the Family History Library in Salt Lake City. It was the largest repository of genealogical materials in the world, owned and operated by the Church of Jesus Christ of Latter Day Saints. The library was open to the public year round, and free of charge, except for a small fee when loaning a roll of microfilm to their satellite centers. Lydia was pretty sure she should be able to get whatever she needed up to 1909 from them, and then anything after that would have to go to the historical society in Columbus. It would put everything into black and white or sepia tones, depending on the copy.

Lydia saw a library trip in her future. Now she just needed to call Faye.

Chapter Five

"The films are ordered, I just need to wait for them to come in. It usually takes around a week to ten days," Lydia explained over the phone to Julia, who was home with a cold. If it hadn't been for that little bug, Julia had planned to meet Lydia at the library for a run down on what was going on. "I really just wanted to call and let you know what I was doing, since we couldn't get together."

"That's fine." Julia said, her voice sounding rough. "I just wanted to let you know too, that my granddaughter is flying to Ohio for some business and will be near Columbus. I thought maybe she could do something while she is there."

"That's fantastic, how soon?" Lydia asked.

"She leaves next Friday and will be there for four or five days. She told me the conference ends Friday and she can stay an extra day, maybe two, to look some things up if we need her to." Julia sounded almost as excited as Lydia.

"Well...if she's willing and since it isn't that far of a drive, she could go the historical society in Saylesville and see if they have any written or oral history on the family that might give us some more leads...Also while she's there, maybe she could locate the Methodist church and visit the cemetery, it would be nice to get photos of the stones. They might even have some records there if it's still an active congregation," Lydia's brain was running at high speed. She didn't want to overwhelm Julia and her granddaughter but this was a one-time opportunity for them and they needed to take advantage of it.

"Could she do all that in a day?" Julia asked in awe.

"Whatever she could get to would be fine. I'll make a list and then rate them number one down. Most things are just to back up what we already know but the cemetery and church could be important. I'm interested in who is buried where."

"Can she just pick up the list from you at the library? I came across some more pictures that might help you put a face to a name, and she could leave them with you the Thursday before she leaves for the airport, and then pick the list up then." Julia was starting to cough again so Lydia decided not to drag the conversation on. She was sick after all, and Lydia was giving her a laundry list over the phone.

Lydia liked that proposal since it would give her a chance to speak with Julia's granddaughter in person, mainly to feel out how much she could handle. Many times people mean well by offering to help, thinking it will be something quick. But then once they see the amount of work involved, are instantly put off.

"That should be fine. I'm usually not there on Thursdays but I'm due some vacation time from work, so I'll take a couple hours off so I can be there."

"Wonderful. Her name's Karen. She's a brunette, looks like a young me." Julia laughed in between coughs. "You're open two to five, so she will be there about four or so. She's leaving work early to pack, and it's on her way home...She'll see you then."

❖

Two days later, Lydia dashed from work and drove to the Tri-Cities library. She had tried to finish up some work items before leaving, one of which was running downstairs to circulation so she could place an order for newspaper microfilm from the Ohio Historical Society. There was only one paper in Saylesville, aptly named the Saylesville Gazette. She wanted to get a few rolls from around the time of Katherine's death and maybe the other wives too, just to see what might have been reported. Some newspapers had sections devoted to township gossip and specific news to that area. She was hoping that maybe the inquiry Julia had mentioned would be in one of the issues.

It was because of that she had lost track of the time, and being on the road even five minutes late made getting from point A to B in their town somewhat of a chore. Even though the town was no more than seven or eight miles in either direction, it could take twenty minutes to get anywhere. There had been a huge growth in new home development, as well as the traffic that came with it. She couldn't complain too much since her home had been one of the many that had been built but the increase in congestion did impede the flow of traffic at rush hour and on the weekends.

Lydia's hometown of Rancho Camino was seven miles in from the ocean, in one of the smaller communities that flanked the beach cities. The location was wonderful on warmer days as it provided a terrific cooling breeze, but it also served up some nasty cold snaps when the fog rolled in. Since it was the end of June, the "June Gloom" as everyone called it, made the day miserable. The cooling snap would dissipate for about two hours during the day, usually around lunchtime; otherwise the rest of the day was nothing but fog, fog and more fog. Because of that, Lydia had turned her car heater on in order to warm up her feet and hands.

Lydia disliked being late, as well as making people wait. She hoped that Julia's granddaughter was smart enough not to freeze outside and had gone into the library to wait. Muriel would be there today, so if Karen had gotten there already, Muriel would keep her entertained until Lydia arrived. She knew Julia's grand-daughter had packing to do, which only added to Lydia's guilt. On top of that, Lydia had to be at the day-care center to pick Sarah up before they started charging extra after five-fifteen, so the meeting would have to be brief.

The drive was shorter than expected, and she flew into the building just after four. Sitting at the table was a small brunette, with big blue eyes and a fair complexion. Even if Julia hadn't said so on the phone, Lydia would have recognized her granddaughter right away. She did look like a younger version of her grandmother. Karen was dressed in a pair of casual tweed pants and a beige silk shirt. Her brown hair was loose but shaped to fit her face. She appeared to be about Lydia's height and probably in her mid to late twenties.

An Old Fashioned Murder

"I'm Lydia...I am so sorry I'm late..." Lydia threw her jacket on one of the chairs just inside the door and strode over to the young woman. "I know you have a ton to do."

"Not a problem, I actually just got here myself. The traffic was bad. I work about five miles from here but you can never judge just how long it'll take," she said standing up, and at the same time laying down the large manila envelope she had been holding when Lydia walked up to the table. Just then, Muriel flew out of the back room with a stack of books in her arms.

Muriel was dressed for the cold weather in warm running pants and a gray sweatshirt that read: "Genealogists Shake the Nuts from their Family Trees." Lydia almost started to laugh but stopped herself. She decided that it wouldn't be such a good first impression for Karen to see the person she was supposed to be having an intelligent conversation with, rolling with laughter on the floor. Lydia then noticed that Muriel had gotten her hair done accenting the gray with some additional highlights. The combination was now more of a salt and pepper than pitch black. It had finally gotten to the point where Muriel's jet black hair made her look far older than she really was; the salt and pepper was much more flattering. Lydia planned to tell her so later.

"There you are. I knew you'd be here soon. I have some more stuff to do in the back, so you two can talk." Muriel laid the pile of books down on the table by the desk. "These are for Mr. Tuft. They're all on North Carolina history, so if he comes while I am in back, just set him down in front of the pile and tell him I'll be right with him."

Muriel then turned around and trotted back to the storage area; which when it had been a house, had been a small child's bedroom. The tip off had been the "little lamb" wallpaper which was found beneath some old paint after it had been scraped off the wall. They had preserved part of it as a reminder of the house's beginnings. Besides, it was cute.

"I think I can do that..." Lydia called to Muriel's retreating form. "Have a seat again, and then we can go over the stuff. It shouldn't take long; the list is small and pretty straight forward."

"Let me formally introduce myself since my grandmother just did a short explanation on the phone." She put her hand out to shake; Karen's grip was firm and steady. Lydia hoped that this meeting would be easy. Finally they sat down.

"I'm Karen as you know, and for the last few years I have been taking care of Grandma. I decided to help her out with this project since it seems so important to her but she really hasn't told me too much." She looked right at Lydia, her hand resting on the folder, almost clutching it. "I hate to botch anything up, that was why when I told her where I was going I did so thinking what I needed to do would be minor but then she started rambling on about courthouses and cemeteries and I started getting worried."

Lydia smiled in an attempt to reassure Karen, even though Lydia wasn't feeling very reassured herself. It was just what she had been afraid of; Karen was having second thoughts about the whole thing. Not meaning to—and thanks in part to Lydia herself –her grandmother had started to scare her off, and Lydia's list wasn't going to help the cause any either. It wouldn't be the end of the world if she backed out but it would sure help if she didn't. Lydia decided to try some damage control.

"I'm sorry, I tend to forget that not everyone is as enthusiastic as I am, or I guess as your grandmother, for that matter. Many times we do this and think that everyone shares our drive for knowledge of family and history, and they usually don't," Lydia stated.

Lydia could honestly see where Karen was coming from. She knew first hand how family members didn't always "get it." Lydia would try and share with her husband an exciting find she had made, and he would stare at her with that glazed donut look he was famous for. She had tried to get him interested in genealogy for years since his parents enjoyed it too, but to no avail. And since none of her husband's siblings were interested either, Lydia was sure that when his parents were gone she would inherit their family tree too. She only hoped and prayed that she would have someone to pass all her hard work on to someday, since at the moment it looked like the apathy had passed on to her own children.

"I understand your hesitation but just doing this little bit of research will help your grandmother so much," Lydia entreated.

"I guess I just don't get why she needs to do this. They're all dead, what difference does it make?"

Lydia had heard that one before, too. She realized that was a hard concept for people to understand, the interest in researching "dead people."

"I'm sure that she has told you there is something not right about the relationship of her grandfather and his wives. It's something she needs to settle for herself, and she feels for you, her grandchildren as well. What we would like you to do will help in her desire to close this chapter in her life that needs to be closed." Karen was looking lost. How could Lydia explain something that was so simple to a genealogist? "Let me put it this way, many times we are missing a part of ourselves, and we need to fill that part to be whole. In your grandmother's case, she was given something to solve, and she needs to solve the problem in order to feel whole. To understand how her mother lived, and why she became the person she was, and in turn, how your grandmother became the person she is. So she needs your help." Lydia thought it sounded like psychobabble, and maybe it was. But that's what finding these lost, dead people were, filling a hole, learning about, and knowing who your family was, and why they did what they did.

Karen sat there for a few minutes thinking. Lydia could tell that she was deciding how much she wanted to put herself out for this project of her grandmother's.

"Okay, I'll do what I can for the day I have promised, since I am going there, and since I already volunteered I can't let her down. I understand the part about closure, and I see that this would be important to my grandmother since it involved her, and not by choice," Karen pulled the envelope Lydia had brought to the table towards herself. "So, tell me what I need to do. I love her and she's my grandma, if this will help her to be at ease, then I'll give it my best shot."

Lydia smiled, so far so good.

"...So you're saying that I'm looking for the arrangement of the head stones in relationship to each other, correct?" Karen clarified.

Lydia had pulled out the pictures, and the list from the envelope. They had then started going over the finer points; starting from one to ten in importance. Once again Lydia reiterated that *whatever* Karen was able to find would help immensely. Taking some of the pressure off seemed to help Karen relax.

"Yes. Many times the arrangement will tell how a particular person felt when a loved one was buried, and can also explain the wishes of the deceased too," Lydia explained. "Case in point...my great-grandmother despised her husband. So much so, that she made sure she was buried on the other side, next to his brother, so she wouldn't have to lie next to him through eternity."

That statement got a look of surprise and then a laugh out of Karen. She was finally starting to get it. Lydia felt that having a sense of humor when doing genealogical research was important, considering there was so much disappointment that also went along with it. Laughing at the situations that those long ago ancestors got themselves into helped to keep it all in perspective. The deceased had been human after all. Karen just needed to lighten up some and enjoy the ride.

"Fine, so I need to cover as much as I can, and not stress if I don't get to everything. I think I can do this," Karen sighed and brushed the hair from her eyes. She had made notes in the margin of the list that Lydia gave her, so she wouldn't forget anything. "I have a camera, and I will take a notebook with me."

"And remember change, dimes and quarters to make copies, in case you come up with something that you think might help. Remember nothing is too trivial, and if someone tells you something you don't get, ask them to repeat it, explain it clearer, or write it down for you." Lydia stood and stretched. "Don't worry you're a smart woman, you'll know when you need more information. Just go with your instincts and you'll be fine."

An Old Fashioned Murder

Karen stood too. It was getting late and Karen needed to pack, and Lydia needed to pick-up a child. It was almost five. She would have to fly.

"I have a cell phone; if I get into trouble can I call you?" she asked. Karen seemed a lot more relaxed that when she had first walked in.

"Sure. I'm alone in my office during the day, so call anytime except between twelve and one our time, that's lunch for me." Lydia gave Karen her work number, and then walked her to the door. "Good luck and take it slow you'll be fine."

After Karen left, Lydia scrambled to pick up the pictures. She placed them back in the folder, and then slipped the folder into the envelope, and then into her canvas bag. She called to Muriel as she was starting to run out the door. Muriel popped her head out.

"No Mr. Tuft huh? He must have forgotten again. Poor man, his memory is just leaving him. Alzheimer's isn't a nice disease. He'll probably show up tomorrow and we won't be here." Muriel shook her head. Lydia thought to herself how lucky Muriel was to be so active and happy, so many older people weren't. Sometimes she reminded her a little of her mother who had passed several years ago. It was a nice feeling.

"Well he still has fifteen minutes," Lydia assured her. She knew Muriel worried about some of the patrons like a mother hen. "I have to go and pick Sarah up, and then run home and make dinner." Lydia looked out the window and watched as Karen's car pulled onto the street. "I hope she does all right. We shouldn't have dumped this on her," Lydia pondered out loud. Muriel walked over and put her hand on her shoulder.

"She had the choice not to. I think sometimes that young people are so busy they forget they have a past or family, maybe more of them need to have a chore like that *put* on them. Show them where they come from, and that if it weren't for those before, they wouldn't be here in this time of medicine, electricity and flushing toilets." Muriel sighed as she started to turn around. Lydia knew she was right

Just as Lydia started to head out the door Mr. Tuft pulled in and parked crooked in the handicapped space. She looked back at Muriel to see if she needed any help.

"Don't worry I'll stay late. He doesn't have anyone, and it's good for him to get out…now you scoot. I'll call you later and we can talk more if you want."

Thank God for Muriel.

❖

Lydia sat down that evening and re-evaluated the information Julia had provided. There was so much that she still needed to prove or document, it was almost too much, and without strong documentation the whole thing could simply languish. She hoped that Karen would have some luck. Until the microfilms arrived, and Karen returned, there was nothing she could do.

But like any good mystery Lydia kept dwelling on it, and going over the information she did have, looking for clues. So much so, that she was letting the stuff around the house, and her own genealogy slide.

What ifs started forming in her head. What if he did do it, would the family like knowing they had a murderer in the family? What if it appeared he didn't do it—without positive proof—would they still continue to wonder? That doubt always remaining. How had the family of Lizzie Borden felt, the not knowing?

She had just a few minutes before getting Sarah ready for bed. Lance would be home tomorrow, so that would take a little pressure off of her. She would be able to hide in the study and think, while he distracted everyone else. It was nice having a college student living at home, but her studies came first, babysitting second, and only in a pinch. So when there was only one parent, it was a little harder to get things done.

So for the few minutes she had, she pulled out the file from the inquiry and started to read it. She made detailed notes, so if Karen was able to bring the original back from the courthouse she could add to them and not have to start all over again.

Julia's uncle had asked for it in the days before copy machines because it was extracted from the original by hand. From the opening statements Lydia learned it had been a sheriff's case, but the sheriff in the area didn't know what to do with the Stowe's accusations, so he enlisted the help of the town mortician who handled all the deaths, and later a Judge from the county court. The family doctor was also consulted, and they all met at a special session of the court to talk about the issue; it was set up similar to what is now known as a coroners' inquest.

As a courtesy they invited the parents of Katherine Stowe, the Captain (obviously), as well as anyone else who was interested in the incident. From looking at the scrawl of the clerk who copied the information, they seemed to be the only people who attended. For the fact it looked like no one else thought it was important enough to show up, Lydia thought that in itself was strange. She got the feeling something was missing from the file, and hoped that Karen would be able to bring the missing pieces home. But first things first, Lydia began to examine the papers in front of her.

Lydia wasn't sure whether they were in the order they testified or not; and in the grand scheme of life, it really didn't matter. According to the notes the clerk took that day, the doctor who was named MacKay reported:

"Katherine had been seeing me consistently since the birth of her son. She had symptoms of being tired, thirsty and feeling out of sorts, and was complaining of heart palpitations. I examined her and questioned her about her home life. She was honest in telling me that she had six children to take care of, and the baby had been colicky, and she wasn't sleeping well for various reasons."

Lydia figured the sleep depravation wasn't just the baby it was also the Captain, too, who was once again asserting his manly duties. Lydia and Faye, on more than one occasion had pondered how, with that many kids, and small homes, that the couple even found a time and a place to do anything?

Lydia continued to read the doctor's statement.

"She told me she had been taking a patent medicine called Mothers Helper, which was supposed to help her feel better. She told me that the Captain had been bringing it from his store for her. I then asked her how long she had been taking it, and she told me since just after the birth of the last child. She told me she had complained to the Captain about her malaise, and that was when he brought the medicine home. The Captain assured her it would give her energy. She admitted she had started feeling better right away but then about a month or two ago, she started feeling poorly again; and her heart started acting funny. She thought maybe the medicine had stopped working, or she was expecting again. I made a full examination and determined she wasn't with child, so I figured the medicine was either too powerful for her, or it had simply run its course."

Funny Lydia thought. She was pretty sure that patent medicines were full of alcohol and herbs and stuff. Lydia assumed the alcohol alone would take the edge off of any stress she was feeling, that was why she felt better after taking the doses. Katherine wasn't constantly worrying over every little household thing anymore. And from the sounds of it, the Captain, although doing well monetarily, didn't seem to feel the need to provide the poor thing with any household help. But whatever the reason, whether the tonic had changed ingredients, or she was really ill, only the doctor seemed willing to believe her symptoms.

So it continued:

"I (Dr. MacKay) told her to go home and rest, and not to do anything for a minimum of two days. I told her if the Captain had a problem with that, he was to come by and see me. I then advised her to ask a female relative to come and help take care of the household while she rested. If she didn't feel better by then, I was planning to refer her to a women's specialist in Columbus that might be able to help."

Well, Lydia thought, at least the man was more sensitive than the average doctor back then. Many of them, being men, would tell the woman to stop complaining, go home, buck up and work.

Lydia found it strange that Dr. MacKay's testimony didn't continue beyond that point. There was nothing mentioned of the condition he had found Katherine in, or any thoughts whatsoever in regards to her cause of death. Great, Lydia thought, another missing link, in a chain of missing links.

The next testimony given to the inquiry was from Katherine's mother, Carrie Stowe. As Lydia began to read her testimony, she wondered what must have been going through Carrie's head as she spilled her daughter's confidences in front of the man she distrusted, and perhaps blamed for her daughter's death. Lydia read Carrie's report.

Carrie stated that:

"I had come for a brief visit to town for items for the household, and decided to stop in and see Kate since she had been writing to tell me how awful she was feeling. I could only visit for the day since I still have small children of my own at home. Kate then asked me (Carrie) if either I, or her sister Emily, might come back the next week to let her have the two days the doctor recommended. She told me that Andrew was going out of town on business, and she would be alone, except for the children of course. That way she could rest, and she wouldn't have to worry about him needing anything. I told her I would find a way to do it. I planned to leave Emily, my next oldest at home, and Jack (her husband) with the younger children. I assured Katherine that I would be there the following Monday. I knew I could take better care of my daughter, since I'd had more experience with womanly problems."

Katherine's mother's reaction seemed legitimate. She had a family still at home to worry about in addition to responsibilities to her married daughter. Carrie Stowe must have been terribly torn between her duty as a wife, and her duty as a mother.

Katherine's mother continued:

"When I arrived at the house the following week, I walked toward the house and the older children were outside in the yard playing. The oldest girl, Lissa, she's sixteen or so, was holding baby Cyrus. She told me that Kate hadn't been feeling well all morning, and was in the kitchen working. When I walked inside, I found her lying on the floor, fainted. I started to yell for Lissa to come right away. The oldest boy, Elias, came in at the same time. I think he had been in the barn cleaning the stalls. I told him to run for the doctor, as I sat there on the floor holding my child. She was barely breathing, and the kitchen was so hot. Lissa took the children to a neighbor three doors away. I understand she was the employee of Andrew's who worked at the mercantile. I later learned she was getting ready to leave for the store when the children arrived."

Lydia sat staring at the writing. How sad for a mother to find a child like that, to go through something like that. Even though the Captain's absence had been expected, was Katherine's death, at that time—a coincidence, planned in some manner, or just a sad state of events?

Carrie Stowe's testimony just stopped. There was nothing after it. No details of the doctor arriving, the reaction of the other children, not another tidbit. Lydia wondered if they cut her off for fear of her saying something about the Captain that she shouldn't, or they felt she would only re-hash what the doctor had testified to.

The last person to testify, if you could call it that, was the Captain. Lydia noticed a distinct change in tone when reading his testimony. It was cold, almost removed from the situation. Matter-of-fact was how Lydia could think to describe it. But then it was a transcription, he could have been crying when he was giving his statement but for some odd reason, Lydia couldn't picture it.

He began:

"Katherine had been ill, but she was always sickly. I figured she was complaining to get out of work. My first wife, Melissa, had been a sturdy, hard working woman. Nothing could tire her. To be frank, Katherine and Amelia before her, had been such a contrast. They always had a complaint, the kids did this, and there wasn't time enough in the day for that…I wasn't sure what to do with them, to be honest. Melissa had not only been able to work at home but was also a part-time clerk at our store when the need arose. Never complained a day in her life. She was the mother to my first three children. Melissa even trained the clerks who worked in the store. She always had breakfast and lunch on the table at the same time each day…"

Geez, what an ass, Lydia thought. Here he was giving testimony on the death of his current wife, and he was supplying a detailed list of merits for his deceased first wife. That kind of praise made it sound like he was still *very* enamored with Melissa, revering her almost as a saint. Comparing the two women and their skills at home-seemed un-necessary, as well as un-called for, nor did it have anything to do with the fact his current wife was dead, with no apparent cause.

Lydia shook off the disgust she was feeling. She continued to read a couple sentences further down, skipping the additional list of virtues that he continued to heap on the assembled group. Eventually she arrived at something a little more relevant to the issue at hand.

An Old Fashioned Murder

"But the more she (Katherine) complained the more I thought there might really be something wrong. So one day when I stopped in the mercantile to check the inventory, I asked Silla, my clerk, what she would recommend. Silla suggested the tonic that I had taken home to Amelia (The brand was Mother's Helper), the same one she had taken off and on when she had felt poorly. She reminded me how well it had worked for her, so I decided to try it with Katherine. I was pleased with the results."

Someone must have asked him the brand, because although the exchange wasn't recorded the name brand was written in parenthesis under the word tonic in the previous paragraph.

"I noticed that she had started feeling better right away, and was very pleased. She continued to improve until right after the town's founding celebration, and then started feeling bad again. I thought she might be expecting a babe, so I advised her to visit the doctor to see."

Well, Lydia thought, at least he had the decency to tell her to do that. But Lydia was sure that if she had come home with, "Honey, the doctor told me to take a couple days off." He would have blown a gasket. That had to have been why she asked her mother to come and help while he was gone. It had just been a little too late.

Lydia continued to read his testimony, which she hoped would be a bit more insightful:

"At the time of Katherine's death, I had business in Chillicothe that had to be attended to. I was horribly shocked and saddened when I received the telegram at my hotel from my father telling me of the sad event. My oldest son, Elias, was sent out to me by coach, and he arrived at my hotel the following evening. The next morning he helped me to pack and load the wagon. We both then rode home. He was a great comfort to me on the ride back."

And that was where the transcription ended. There were two things Lydia thought strange. One was the fact that he didn't leave immediately for home when he did get the telegram, and instead waited for Elias to join him. It wasn't like the wagon wasn't parked somewhere waiting for him. Lydia wondered if maybe the telegram from Elias came at the same time, so he had been forced to remain and wait.

47

And why did they send Elias to accompany him home? Did they think he was so distraught he wouldn't make it? Or were they afraid he wouldn't come home?

The other thing Lydia was shocked at was the fact that they *had* sent him a telegram. What a cold way to announce something life changing like that! Lydia felt something so personal, so potentially devastating, should have come from his son, another relative, or a close friend. Since they sent the son to accompany him home, the whole unpleasant chore could have been done in person, not over the telegraph wire. Lydia didn't get it.

Oddly enough the court declaration, the morticians report, and the decision on Katherine's cause of death were not included in the extract. Was there something in the original file that shouldn't have been and therefore ignored? With luck Karen would get a true copy of the whole package, and then Lydia could see what wasn't there. It might prove extremely telling.

Chapter Six

A week later things were relatively back to normal. Lance had returned home and the house was running smoothly again. Lydia was notified through e-mail that her films at the Family History Center had arrived, which prompted her to make an immediate call to Faye to set a date for a trip to the library. Unfortunately though, the newspaper rolls had not arrived yet, but Lydia was expecting them at any time. Julia was beginning to feel a little better and seemed more willing to go over the few things that Lydia had been able to extract—at least over the phone. The best part was Karen had returned from her trip to Ohio, and according to Julia, had been able to accomplish at least five things on the list, which pleased Lydia greatly.

The end of the school year activities and deadlines were starting to pop up for the Proctor household. There was eighth grade graduation for Lucas, pre-school graduation for Sarah, and finishing up some final book orders at work. The one nice thing about genealogy, and in this case working with Julia's project especially, was that working on it would take some time. So although getting the information was crucial to what they were doing, getting to those research items on their list could be melded and merged into what was already going on. The world wouldn't come to an end if the film didn't come tomorrow but not getting a dress shirt and tie for Lucas' graduation could be a catastrophic event.

Lydia planned on meeting with Faye before their trip to the library to show her the complete inquiry report, since one of the items Karen had been able to get, was a copy of the full file from the courthouse. Lydia hoped that maybe Faye could give her a little enlightenment on the subject. Court records could be interpreted in a number of ways, and she might catch something that Lydia might miss.

Just as she was about to head out the door to the market, the phone rang. This time Lucas sprang from the couch, and then just as quickly passed the phone to her. Lydia wasn't even sure if he knew who it was, other than it wasn't for him.

"Hi Lydia, this is Karen." she sounded tinny, so Lydia figured she was on her cell phone. "I'm in your neighborhood and wanted to bring by these things I found for you and grandma. My boss is sending me out of town again, this time to Miami, and I want you to have them before I leave. I'd give them to grandma but she is still not quite ready to head outside yet, so it would be a while before she could get them to you…is that a problem."

"No, not at all, come on over," Lydia replied. She was pleased it would be one less chore to do later on, plus there wasn't anything on her grocery list that couldn't wait a few more minutes.

"Give me ten minutes and I will be there."

❖

"So what do you think?" Lydia asked Faye as they sat in Lydia's back yard on the comfy patio chairs, with two big glasses of iced tea between them. It was a nice, warm day with a slight breeze blowing through the yard. With the younger kids playing at the neighbor's house down the street, it gave Lydia the opportunity to pick her best friends brain without interruption, and in a peaceful setting.

The information that Karen had brought back from Ohio had left Lydia with a funny feeling. She couldn't put her finger on it but there was something in the additional pieces of the inquiry report that disturbed her. So much so, she hadn't been able to fall asleep the night Karen had brought the papers by. Lydia kept reading over the inquiry file, looking for something—anything that would make the Captain appear less like the ass he had been.

As she had suspected the full inquiry file ended up presenting a different picture than the extracted version had. Some additional testimony had been left out that gave a whole new view of the Captain and his relationship to his family. The main thing that stood out in all the letters was that the Captain had serious control issues, possibly to the point of verbal or physical abuse. But even with all the "eyewitness" testimony submitted to the court (some of which seemed to be quite guarded), there wasn't anything specific to pin him on, just a lot of conjecture.

It had gotten to the point that the more she read, the more appalled she had become. Lydia knew that there had been, and still were men, that treated their wives deplorably. It was simply a sad state of reality. And the Captain had been no different.

What Karen had brought back in the complete file were letters written by those same friends and family members, attesting to certain situations that they had encountered both, at the Bower home on Peach and the mercantile. From what Lydia could tell those letters had initially been submitted to the court and then sorted according to relevance. For some reason though, the few that looked to have been deemed worthy for further consideration, had been cast aside. There had been a note, "submit to panel" placed in the upper right hand corner of each of those envelopes. Of those marked, Lydia found three that stood out from the group. Those three in particular, seemed more factual, and a lot less gossipy.

Lydia assumed the reason they had not been copied the first time was because there had been no reason to. From the notes taken during the inquiry by the clerk of the court, not one of those letters had been presented during the actual hearing. But Lydia realized that didn't mean they hadn't been read behind closed doors.

She knew that people who lived 'in town' tended to know a lot more about their neighbors, than say the people who lived on farms. Distance made all the difference in the world. That rule certainly seemed to apply to the Bower family. It was apparent from the letters the court had received, that the Bowers' had been scrutinized by almost everyone. Lydia took all those detailed letters, with all their insinuations, and made brief notes on those that showed common themes.

Lydia noted that there were two main concerns expressed by those neighbors that kept rearing their ugly heads. The first was that neither Amelia nor Katherine ever ventured out on their own unless they were going somewhere specific. "From the witnesses' observations, those times either involved shopping, at the mercantile; going to work, at the mercantile; or out with the Captain, probably to the mercantile."

The other theme that appeared frequently dealt with the children. It was implied that they were always out running wild all over the Bower property, as well as through the neighborhood at all hours. Lydia assumed the repeated references to the "wild children" was a not-so-subtle hint at the lack of discipline at the Bower household, namely the lack of a male figure to rein the children in.

Lydia decided to focus on three letters she had chosen from the "approved" stack. She found that the same themes repeated themselves once again but with additional information supplied that put a spin on the accusations against the Captain. The first letter that Lydia perused had been written by one of the Bowers' neighbors, a man named Mr. Joseph Crawford. Lydia was surprised at Mr. Crawford's candor regarding his encounter with the Captain.

Dear Panel,

My name is Joseph Crawford, and I am a neighbor who lives behind the Bower home. I was asked to state any concerns I've had with Mr. Bower, and am doing so here. When Mr. Bower was married to Miss Amelia, my wife and I observed the two older children simply ran her into the ground. She would do all the work in the house and gardens and they would continue to play and not help her at all. The oldest two were big enough to help. My wife and I were never sure whether the children simply couldn't or wouldn't help. We would overhear her ask and then plead with them. Eventually the poor girl gave up entirely. One day, I actually took the Captain aside to suggest that he hire a cook, or housekeeper to help. At the suggestion Mr. Bower just laughed and said there was absolutely no way he would pay someone to do something his wife could do for free. I decided it was wise not to bring it up again even when I saw the condition Miss Katherine was in. I realized there was no point. Nor did I speak with Mr. Bower again after that incident...

Lydia got the distinct feeling there was probably more to the conversation than what Mr. Crawford had expressed in his letter. Much of which might have helped Lydia form an even clearer picture of what the Captain was truly like. But Lydia pondered, if that was the sanitized version, she hated to think about what had really happened.

An Old Fashioned Murder

The next letter was from the Bowers' next-door neighbor, Blanche Robseon. Her description of the Bower household was far from flattering and a little disconcerting too.

Dear Inquiry Panel,

My name is Blanche Robseon and I am the next-door neighbor to the Bower family. I was asked to write and share my concerns, so here they are. I was shocked that when Mr. Bower married Amelia, the older children gave her absolutely no respect. They would run all over like wild animals ignoring her orders. The babies listened better to her than they did. I noticed this pattern repeated when he married Kate. The older children pulled the same thing on her, although I must admit the little ones listened pretty well. I could hear Kate begging Mr. Bower on more than once occasion to discipline the children, and he would refuse. In a motherly way, I would comment to her occasionally on how tired she seemed. One day she told me flat out that she had just given up trying any discipline with the children. She also mentioned to me, when we would talk over the fence, that she was tired a lot, and that Mr. Bower demanded a great deal of her, especially that everything be tidy. Kate also told me she spent so much time trying to corral the older children and take care of the babies that she didn't have time for anything else. She confirmed my prior suspicions, that her husband didn't feel it was his place to discipline the children. Her explanation was that since he was busy during the day, and Kate had care of the children, he felt she should be the one in charge...

Poor thing Lydia thought, she couldn't even use the threat 'wait until your father gets home' to evoke any behavior change. Even though Mrs. Robeson's letter was the longest of the three, it was the most informative.

Lydia continued to read:

...I asked Kate if she had seen the doctor, and she told me that her husband didn't want to spend the money for her to make a visit. She confided to me she had been saving up her egg money for an appointment. It was only a week later that she died. I was terribly saddened by her death, for I felt I had made a friend. But I was even more concerned about why she had died. Even though Kate hadn't been feeling well, she hadn't looked really horrible, just unkempt and exhausted most of the time. Her death just seemed so sudden. And if I may express it here, in this written statement, I found it odd that Kate was the second of Mr. Bower's wives to die so suddenly. It is not my place to make any judgments. That is in your hands, and the good Lord's...

Lydia was impressed with Mrs. Robeson's honesty. Lydia had clued in right away to the statement that the Captain didn't want to send her to the doctor, and the fact that Katherine was saving money to go on her own, whereas in the Captain's testimony to the inquiry panel, he stated that he was the one who suggested she go. Somewhere along the way he had seen the light and Katherine hadn't been forced to spend her little bit of savings. Or it was possible that he changed his story after talking with Mrs. Robeson, who from the sounds of it would have *made* him see the light.

The third letter had caught Lydia's eye because it dealt with the running of the mercantile. Mrs. Sarah Sullivan was, according to her testimony, the postmistress for Saylesville. Lydia found her description of the working conditions at the mercantile very enlightening.

To Whom It May Concern,

My name is Mrs. Sarah Sullivan, and as you know I am the postmistress for our fine community here in Saylesville. I felt the need to express my encounters with the Bower family, particularly Katherine Bower, in the hopes it will help shed some light into your inquiry process. I stop and do my shopping at the mercantile on my way home at the end of each day. I knew Mrs. Melissa Bower only as an acquaintance. She never socialized much. I met Mrs. Amelia Bower, when she too worked the counter at the mercantile. She was a bit friendlier. But the nicest of them all was Mrs. Katherine Bower. I knew from talking with her at church that she had the children, the house to take care of, and the business to work at. At times, I know she was simply overwhelmed. On days when Katherine worked, and I stopped in, the babies would be playing in a sort of pen right behind the counter, while she helped the customers. From what I could tell she was there for most of the afternoon, from around noon to three, sometimes four. I asked her one-day where everyone else was, because I knew that there was a man and woman who lived behind the mercantile. I assumed they not only managed the store, but worked there as well. She told me that she was giving the clerks an afternoon break. I was appalled that they would abandon her with the children, and then expect Katherine to be able to wait on the customers at the same time...

The letter continued:

...Since I go in at different times of the day, depending on my schedule, I couldn't help but notice she was always alone. So one day I asked her again where everyone was. She told me that Mr. Charles was out ill and his sister was working on the books. When I

An Old Fashioned Murder

asked if Katherine could ask for help if she got busy, the poor thing replied—'Oh no. I am not allowed to'..."

Lydia got the feeling that Mrs. Sullivan considered it an injustice (and rightly so) for the Captain to make his wife work at the store, and take care of babies at the same time. With two apparently capable employees to cover the store, there was no reason for it. On top of that, someone else to be there, and not willing to help Katherine if she'd needed it was more than Mrs. Sullivan could fathom. Lydia agreed with Mrs. Sullivan's observations.

Lydia noted that at the end of her letter, Mrs. Sullivan's final statement was:

...To be honest your honor, I truly think that both of the Captain's wives were overworked. I also feel that Mr. Bower didn't have a clue as to what was going on either in his home or at his store. Please bring out the truth for his children...

Sadly, those three individuals were not invited to testify later during the inquiry. The only thing Lydia could think of was that the Captain, being a prominent businessman, and influential in the community, made the panel wary. Testimony like that would make him look even worse than the accusations Katherine's parents had brought forth.

Thinking on his testimony, and that of his neighbors, Lydia wondered if the Captain had been that bull headed and overbearing with his first wife, or had she been just as cold, stubborn and driven as he was? Was that the reason why he had placed her on such a pedestal? Were they two peas in a pod?

Lydia had to remind herself that just because the man was domineering and insensitive it did not necessarily make him a killer, did it?

Next Lydia decided to see if there was a complete report included for the doctor. Something, anything that was more specific than what had been included in the first copy request. She couldn't imagine a final determination of death being omitted from the inquiry report. But after a thorough search Lydia could find nothing. She decided that either Dr. MacKay hadn't been able determine a cause of death, or if he had, it had been stricken from the file, like those letters had been omitted from being read during the inquiry itself. Lydia hoped she would be able to verify the cause of death with the vital records Karen had brought back from the courthouse.

Lydia did find one other physical testimony given during the inquiry but not included in the original copy, that being the testimony of the Captain's clerk at the mercantile, Silla. She also caught that unlike the other testimonies, the court clerk didn't record a last name for Silla—she was listed only as "Clerk Silla." Lydia wondered if that had been deliberate, or simply a slip on the clerk's part. The omission wasn't important, Lydia thought, just strange coming out of a court of law."

As Lydia recalled from the previous reading, Lissa, the oldest child, had taken the younger children to Silla, when Katherine's mother had found her on the floor of the kitchen. Lydia found Silla's portrait of the deceased young woman to be replete with pity. She almost stopped reading once she had started, it had bothered her so, but she knew she needed to see the whole picture.

She also realized that there was something about Silla that was nagging at the back of her mind. For some reason, that woman's name sounded familiar in another way. Lydia knew she would have to go back and double check the genealogy that Julia had provided.

First she tackled Silla's testimony:

"...Lissa came running down the street with a passel of children following her. They were screaming and crying. Lissa was holding the smallest one, who I believe is two. She told me that she thought Mrs. Bower had died, and she needed a place to leave the children before the doctor came, and then the black wagon. She started crying even more and kept saying that she didn't understand why she had lost so many mothers. I asked her how she knew that Mrs. Bower was dead, and Lissa told me she knew by how she had looked. Lissa told me she had decided not to wait around and see. I will be honest and tell this court that I felt sorry for the later Mrs. Bower. I had talked with her several times before she married Mr. Bower and tried talking her out of the marriage. But she was very stubborn and insisted that Mr. Bower could make her life easier. She told me she wanted to relieve herself as a burden on her parents, since their farm was struggling..."

Lydia would have liked to see the looks on Katherine's parent's faces when that had been said. Were they still there

An Old Fashioned Murder

when Silla spoke or had they left by then? Since it didn't say what order the testimony had been given in, they could have sat there and listened while their dirty laundry was exposed to the community.

Silla continued by stating that,

"...I noticed the child was not doing well right after the marriage. I explained to her after they were married, when she would come in for training at the mercantile, that being married to Mr. Bower was a challenge. I also explained to her that he was quite demanding but you earned his respect if you towed the line. I thought that Katherine was a spinster looking for an easy life and felt she got a big shock when she married the Captain against my advice. Melissa, his first wife was such a strong and enterprising woman. The other two girls, simply speaking, were not a testament to her memory."

WHOA! Warning lights popped on in Lydia's brain. How dare that woman make such judgments about someone else? From that little bit of information, Lydia *knew* that Silla admired the way the Captain had treated his family. And to some extent she had even helped it along.

At that point Lydia sat the file aside (hurling it across the floor had been an option) and started to look at the other information Karen had brought back. She decided to try and make an attempt to read more of it later. But Lydia was finding it too emotionally draining to see someone's life being reduced to gossip and innuendo in that way. It also appeared that all the Captain and Silla had done in their testimony was try to justify what he had done to those poor women. The inquiry hadn't been assembled to determine Katherine's cause of death—it was to establish whether he had been at fault. Deep down, Lydia knew that neither question would be answered directly from that file.

On the list Lydia had given Karen were the death entries for the first four wives. She knew they would all be in the same place and it would have taken the clerk a few minutes to copy all of them at once.

The first one she found in the pile was for Melissa and her child. They were listed side by side on the page, with the cause of death being diphtheria, just as family lore had said.

The next was Katherine's, which was out of order date wise. On her death entry the cause of death remained blank. So the doctor had made a statement albeit not a direct one. The omission showed he had been puzzled by Katherine's death, and if he was the only physician in town, he'd probably been there for the death of Amelia as well.

A wave of relief washed over her when she finally found Amelia's entry. The pages had just gotten shuffled around a bit. The cause of death had been left blank like Katherine's, except for a tiny note in the margin saying "possible concussion." Lydia assumed that note was most likely related to her fall when she collapsed. Once again, not a formal cause of death but something that may have contributed to it.

Number two on Karen's list had been a visit to the local cemetery, and number three was a peek at the mortuary records, which she hadn't been able to get to.

All of these thoughts and feelings had been running through her mind while she waited for Faye to finish reading the inquiry papers.

"Well, it sounds like he was very controlling. Almost like what we see now in the jail more and more, men who are verbally, physically, and even sexually abusive," Faye stated in her no nonsense fashion. "But you're right, there really isn't anything that spells it out. But you know back then no one talked about stuff like that, and the men who physically abused their women, hit where long sleeves and skirts would hide the bruises. Actually it's not that much different than today, where long sleeves and pants do the same covering." Faye shook her head and looked away. Lydia knew that Faye was experiencing more unpleasantness on the beat than she shared with Lydia. She supposed that there wasn't anything that could truly prepare a person for what existed out there beyond their safe little world.

"That's what I got, too. It had to be pretty bad for a male neighbor, and most likely a peer, to approach him in a man-to-man fashion, and be put off that way. Even if the poor man's wife put him up to it, it must have disturbed him so much, he consciously never spoke with the Captain again, even when he saw the same thing happening to Katherine." Lydia pulled out the letter from Mr. Crawford. "The tone was almost like he was surprised that the Captain felt that way, which reinforces the thought, that although they were neighbors, they certainly weren't friends." Lydia then pulled out the submission from Mrs. Robeson again. "Here in Mrs. Robeson's written testimony, she mentions how the Captain refused to take the time to discipline his own children. Those poor women had no back up whatsoever. If Lance ever did that to me, he would be sooooooo sorry. What's funny is the man was so controlling regarding his wives' day to day activities but he couldn't even control his own children."

"Remember, spare the rod and spoil the child and all that. He obviously didn't follow the advice of the times. Wonder what they would think about children in this day and age?" Faye contemplated. "I was impressed with Mrs. Robeson. She truly sounded like she wanted to befriend both of them but made that connection with Katherine. Maybe she hoped to be something of a mother figure to them, and help guide them along."

"I wonder if either Amelia or Katherine truly knew what they were getting into when they married him?" Lydia remarked. "According to Silla, she tried to warn them. She was the one that stated they were farm people, right? Maybe they really didn't know the Captain that well. It would be interesting to see how they were introduced."

"Why do you think her parents didn't come and help sooner?" Faye asked.

"People didn't talk about unpleasantness. Plus I suppose with them being farmers, and even though they weren't that far away, it was still a chore to just get up and leave on the spur of the moment. Unlike today, where we get in our car and go, they had wagons and horses to deal with. Nothing was easy, everything required pre-planning," Lydia responded, thinking about her own family. They had been farming people too, and the world back then revolved around the seasons and the work that was generated from planting and harvesting. There was no vacation time like present day descendants enjoyed.

"Now here, the doctor says she came to him complaining of being tired and thirsty… diabetes maybe?" Faye threw out the suggestion. It had crossed Lydia's mind too, but the pictures that she had of Katherine didn't show someone obese, but then that would not necessarily have ruled out juvenile diabetes either. "What about a poison? Could he have poisoned her?"

"That's a thought but wouldn't that cause terrible things to happen, like convulsions and stuff? I mean these two women, three if you count Mildred, all died suddenly, without what society calls the violence of death. At least they don't mention anything like that in these papers anyway."

"That should have come from the doctor or even the mortician. They should have noticed trauma when they attended her, and in the mortician's case, when they prepared her for the funeral." Faye shook her head and tapped the pile of papers. "There is nothing like that mentioned here, unless it was stricken from the record or removed before filing."

Lydia nodded. "My thoughts exactly. If the Captain were of influence in the town, it is possible that he could have had enough clout with the judge who presided, the sheriff, or even the town clerk to have something like that removed. I mean, back then people named their kid one thing and later changed it to something else, never thinking to notify the courthouse because they felt there was no reason too. They didn't consider the court to be what we do now—God."

"That's true. Deaths that never got entered because the person didn't hold land anymore. No land no law. No need for a trip to town." Faye nodded. "There was respect for the court if you wanted something from someone, a lawsuit or such but not with reporting things that you felt weren't important. Yeah, there were rules but not everyone had scruples." Faye laughed. "What the hell am I saying, there are people now who don't have any either. Bribery isn't a new thing in this world, is it?"

"I guess not. I don't know, maybe we're taking too much of a leap here," Lydia said as she leaned over and grabbed another handful of Chex-mix.

"Just because he was a hard ass doesn't mean that he was abusive to his wives. Right?" Faye took the last swallow of iced tea in her glass, and sat it down with a tiny thud. "Can I have another one? I'd like to think on this for a while."

Chapter Seven

Lydia cleaned up after Faye left and then started dinner. She was making a pork roast with rose potatoes and green beans. It was another dish that she had been practicing, that so far hadn't killed anyone. Such an odd thought while she was standing in front of a stove.

As she stood in front of the stove, stirring the green beans, she began to mull over the information they had collected so far. She realized that there were too many open-ended things. How did the Captain and Katherine meet, Amelia and Mildred too for that matter? Were they all farm girls like Katherine? Did they all look to the Captain to save them from hard work? Did he save Katherine from the life of a doomed spinster (as Silla suggested) who would eventually have the task of taking care of elderly parents? Reflecting on the women's ages at marriage, they were considered spinsters, was this their final chance at marriage? Maybe they were so desperate to marry they accepted his proposal without thinking it through first. Or was he so debonair he swept them off their feet? Did they attend the same church? Did their fathers attend the same lodge? Lodge membership was big back then, a place for men to socialize without the stigma of being in a bar or saloon.

Lydia knew Katherine was out of the town boundaries, because of the reference to her living on a farm, so the three to five mile rule for dating was out the window at least for her. It had to be connections. Land records, or a plat map showing the owners of the local farms in the area, might help with that one. Also it wouldn't hurt to see if there was a county history with the Captain in it. It might prove interesting reading.

After thinking everything through, Silla kept popping out to the forefront, and Lydia wanted to know why. After dinner she was going to start putting the papers Karen dropped off in order and look up that woman's name. It was hard keeping track of the wives, clerks, children, and neighbors.

It was amazing how something she thought would be so simple, ended up being so complicated. Even though, once you looked past all the work ahead, it was actually a very interesting project. So far no one in her family could quite compete with the Captain.

Lydia checked on the roast and pulled it from the oven, thoughts still churning in her head. She knew the films needed to be looked at, so before Faye left they made definite plans for Saturday afternoon. Lydia would then call Julia to see if she felt up to meeting at the library on Sunday during her two-hour volunteer stint. It was half-way for both of them, and maybe some of the things Lydia had gleaned out might jog Julia's memory some. She also wanted to ask if there were any other living relatives, an elderly aunt or uncle that might remember something. If the Captain's younger children were still living, they would be in their late nineties. Maybe even their children might remember something. It was worth a try.

Her own brood was out-and-about now that school was out. Lucas was playing ball down the street, Sarah was playing inside with her friend from next door, and Beth was out shopping with some friends. Overall the evening was running smoothly, and dinner might even be ready before Lance got home.

Then after dinner—organize, organize, and organize—no matter what.

❖

"Here you go." Lance leaned over and passed her the cup of coffee. He had taken Sarah to get her nightly ice cream treat and the coffee bar was right next-door. Lydia had passed on the ice cream but took him up on the decaf latte. There was enough caffeine in the decaf and sugar in the flavoring that she would be fine for at least another hour. She didn't want to stay up too late since she had work the next day but she wanted to get through the information as soon as possible.

Lydia had her laptop set up at the dinning-room table with the papers spread around her. She had created a computer spreadsheet to help organize the data as she found it. She also created a time frame so she could visualize a pattern of events, before and after.

"Thanks." Lydia kissed him quick. His hands were cold as he passed the coffee to her. Lydia wasn't surprised considering he had been out in shorts and a t-shirt. She had to remind herself it was June and the start of the summer months, therefore getting progressively warmer. But unlike her spouse, she was perpetually cold, and until the temperatures hit eighty, there was no way she would be in shorts and a t-shirt. The only thing that Lydia could figure was the imperviousness to cold must be a throw back to his Pacific Islander heritage, because it certainly wasn't from his New England side. All the kids took after him with the darker complexion and tolerance to cold, but their bone structure and hair composition was all Lydia. They had gotten the best of both of them.

"You wanna' help? It would make it go faster?" She knew what his answer would be but she threw it out there anyway.

"I don't think I would know what I am looking at. You would have a better chance. Plus I need to do some work anyway for tomorrow. I'll be a sounding board if you want though," he said as he started to walk away. Running away was actually more like it.

Lydia shifted her attention to the papers in front of her. In addition to the spread sheet, she had made a mini family file on her laptop using her genealogy program. As she sorted through the information Julia provided, she came across the formal family group sheet that Julia's Uncle had put together. On the screen she entered Captain Andrew Bower as head of house and then his first wife Melissa Stewart as the primary wife. She had the option of switching wives into the main position as needed. But for time line purposes Lydia wanted to keep the family in order according to event.

Next she put in the three children by that marriage; Melissa (Lissa) Junior who was born in 1885, Elias 1887, and Clarkson 1889. She had the birth and death for Melissa Senior, and added that information in; born 1860 and died 1893. She then added in the Captain's vital information; born 1851 and died 1920. Lydia finally entered in the only other death date she had for this branch of the Andrew Bower family, which was Clarkson's death in 1893, two days after his mother.

Next Lydia added Amelia Brown, wife number two, her birth being 1870 and marriage in 1895. She died in 1900 leaving two children; Emma born in 1897 and Mollie who was born in 1899 and barely two when her mother died.

Wife three was Katherine—Kate. She was born a year after Amelia and died in 1904. She then entered in Julia's mother, Amy, and her then her Uncle Cyrus. Amy was born in 1901 and died in 1999; Cyrus was born in 1903 and died in 1993. Both children too young at the time Katherine died even to remember her.

Next was wife number four, Mildred Wells, the only one to have the luxury of dying in bed, and not of childbirth, which was the most common cause for that place of death. She was born in 1880 and married the Captain when she was also twenty-five, in 1905. She died in July of 1907, giving birth to one child, a boy, Daniel, who was born in May of 1906.

Lydia thought it ironic that the mothers died at such a young age, whereas several of those children had lived to very ripe old ages of over ninety, and one close to a hundred. She caught that Daniel didn't have a death date. She made a mental note to ask Julia about him. If he died after Julia's mother that might have been why it was left off, or by some chance he might still be alive.

Finally Lydia entered the last, but not least wife, number five Priscilla Drake. The Captain married her in December of 1907. She was born in 1855 and died several years after him in the summer of 1932. So Silla was the one to outlive him, by ten years. Lucky her.

Priscilla – Silla? One in the same? Was that what had been bothering her? Was the Silla of the inquiry, the one who watched the children while Katherine laid dying, or already dead, wife number five?

"Lance, can you come here for a minute?"

❖

"Do you have anything in the pile here that lists employees at his business?" Lance asked as he helped Lydia sort through the stack.

"There should be a journal somewhere. I know it was in the pile when Julia gave me the box of information. It's not fat, just thin and large, almost like a day planner with a worn, brown leather cover as I recall. Could one of the kids have moved it some place? I have had this stuff here for almost two weeks, and I know I didn't do a thing with it." Lydia was exasperated and she was starting to lose it. No one would take it, and it certainly didn't have legs.

"Could something have been laid on it, and then picked up with it?" Lance asked. "Maybe Beth or Lucas had a book on top and then accidentally took it upstairs. Just because they know this stuff's off limits doesn't mean that they weren't over here." He started up the stairs. "Let me check their rooms. Nothing gets too far from their floors so it may just be laying there."

Lydia sat waiting for Lance to return, trying her hardest not to panic. The journal was too big to be thrown away and not noticed but just the right size to be moved accidentally as Lance suggested.

"Found it!" Came a yell from upstairs. Lance then ran down holding the book above his head. It was just as she described it.

"Okay, where was it?" Lydia asked. If she bet money on it she might win. "Lucas?"

"Yep. On the floor under his math book. He must have taken a textbook out of his backpack, and then picked it all up, and put it back inside without checking to see what he had. He said he couldn't remember when it was."

"I'm not surprised. No actually I am, he knows what a math book is." Lydia laughed. She wasn't being mean. She truly loved her son, but he was not a self-starter. Initiative was not his middle name. They both knew one day the door would open and he would "get it." Until then they just had to be patient.

"One mystery solved, now let's look at the second one." Lydia carefully took the fragile journal and opened it. The opening date was 1882, so according to the information he opened his shop a year before his first marriage. The monthly accounts were well organized and recorded in ink. If it was his handwriting it was very neat and clear, which would make life a little easier. They sat together and looked at each page. Two pairs of eyes were better than one, especially when it dealt with finances and employees. If Lydia was in a hurry, she tended to be the impatient one and would skim while looking for the information she wanted, missing vital information. Lance on the other hand was a lot calmer and would help slow her down.

They progressed through each year. It contained mostly dollar figures, with initials attached to some of the dollar amounts. They didn't look like personnel records at all, but purchases and sales entries. So where did he keep the names of who worked for him?

The ledger stopped in 1915, five years before his death, which meant there was either a second book floating around or he stopped working in 1915. Possibly retired? Lydia flipped to the back and found nothing of help, until a slip of paper fell from one of the blank pages. It was neatly folded into fourths and the paper so yellowed it had made an imprint on the opposite page of the book. Very gently she un-folded it and looked at what appeared to be a woman's cursive handwriting. After reading a couple paragraphs she realized it was a mini history of the store, written down for posterity, but not shared as such. Who knew how long it had been in there. Lydia read the document to herself with Lance leaning over her shoulder.

"It says here," Lydia read out loud. "The building was bought by Andrew's father in June of 1882. He wanted something for his son to do to keep him occupied, since he had finished business school. He wanted to marry Melissa, his school sweetheart but her parents would not approve the engagement until he was situated in some kind of trade or business venture.

The store was an immediate success. Since Andrew was able to have their living quarters built behind the store—Melissa, when she wasn't taking care of the children—worked the counter and helped the ladies of the township with their needs and purchases. This worked well until their third child was born and things became rougher. Andrew then decided they needed a place of their own to live in. At her suggestion he had a wonderful Victorian style home built not too far from the edge of the main road in town. It was the first such house of its kind in town. They both worked on the design and helped make it a show place.

A little while later Melissa and their son became ill, and they both died soon after. If it hadn't been for his very loyal staff at the mercantile the place would have folded immediately, since he was so grief stricken he wouldn't leave the house for several weeks. His clerks, Priscilla and her brother Charles Drake, watched the store and carried on the business until he was recovered and able to return to where he belonged."

Lydia smiled. There it was—what had been nagging at her—although not how she thought she would find it. The big question was: who wrote the mercantile history down, and why did they stop at that point?

The possessive tone of the missive made Lydia wonder if it could it have been one of the later wives, or maybe another relative? The composition gave an early peek into the Captain's life, and the enormous love he had for his first wife. Lydia found the description of his grief heart wrenching.

With the circumstances being what they were at home—small children and no mother—it forced him into remarrying. Whether he liked it or not, there would be no real replacement for his loss. His relationship with Melissa would also set the tone for every other relationship he had. No one could or would ever replace her.

She re-read the piece of paper she held in front of her. It had been the name, Priscilla Drake that had been bugging her.

"This is great!" Lydia exclaimed as she hugged the piece of paper to her. "In the testimony for some reason Silla's surname was never given, not even at the end of her testimony."

"It could have been left off in haste?" Lance added.

"Possibly...But I made the mistake of not following through like I should have," Lydia admitted. "When Mrs. Sullivan asked Katherine who was in the store to help her, she said Mr. Charles was out ill and his sister was working on the books." Lydia wanted to kick herself thinking about it now. "I just assumed his last name was Charles, not that she was referring to his first name!"

Lance patted her on the back. "We'll that's one problem solved. Glad I could be of help." He winked at her. "I am going back to guy TV." He said as he left her to her task.

Lydia knew now for sure that Priscilla was the clerk at the mercantile; it was the name–Silla/Priscilla and the Drake was simply the icing on the cake. Even though she was ninety-nine percent sure about the relationship, she wanted to confirm it just to be sure.

She knew of at least two ways to nail this one down. The first was getting a copy of the marriage license, which was on one of the two films she had ordered.

The second was to examine the plat map and town directory that were on the second roll of film. The directory started about the time the Captain opened the mercantile and ran continuously until 1935. Since Saylesville was a little larger than most towns in rural Ohio and close to both Columbus and Chillicothe she had lucked out finding the directory.

Using those tools Lydia planned to look for Miss Priscilla/Silla, and see where she lived, double-checking her occupation and residence. This was on the assumption she was alone and on her own. If it matched, Lydia would have wife number five as a not only a neighbor but also an employee.

What a coincidence.

Chapter Eight

"Film day," Faye called as Lydia did the last minute rush around the house trying to get ready to leave. There was feeding the cats, feeding Sarah, and running that last load of laundry before she made the mad dash out the door, leaving Lance with the rest.

"Almost done, and boy, do I have an interesting one for you."

Lydia grabbed her purse and followed Faye out the door dragging her laptop bag behind her. "How's that?" Faye asked as she loaded Lydia's bag in the back of her truck cab.

"It looks very possible that wife number five was the Captain's store clerk. The same one that Lissa, the older girl took the little ones to the day Katherine died."

"What a tangled web we weave." Faye got into the car and started the engine. "You don't think she was involved do you?" Faye asked as she backed the car out of the driveway.

"Nah, I just think it interesting that she worked for him, lived so close to him, and obviously had such a good relationship with his children, that Lissa felt comfortable taking her siblings to the woman during a crisis." Lydia buckled her belt and sat back. All she needed now was a helmet and a roll bar and she would feel safe.

"I guess he decided at some point she made a good wife in addition to employee," Faye commented.

"Apparently so. It took him three wives in between though."

" So what are you going to look at today?" Faye asked as she sped down the freeway past the airport.

"Well I'm going to try and find as many of the marriage records as I possibly can today. I ordered the films starting from 1880 to 1910, as well as the town directory. What's nice is the first part of the town directory roll includes the township map, so I can place these people where they lived. And if all goes well I want to search the 1880, 1900, 1910 and 1920 censuses. Julia's Uncle Cyrus seemed to worry more about collecting information that he thought might help, than documenting what he already knew." Lydia closed her eyes as Faye changed lanes. She tended to move over, not looking before she merged. "To be honest, I don't really think that he took the accusations all that seriously, unlike Julia's mother. He seemed to work on other branches, leaving this one to molder. If he did know more it isn't there."

"Are you going to look into Amelia and Mildred's families, too?" Faye asked. Now they were zipping past the interchange, almost there.

"Maybe just a little bit. I want to see where they lived and see what kind of business their father's were in. I know that Katherine's was a farmer, but I know nothing about the other two. They could have lived in town or out in the country, who knows." Lydia could see the library looming in the distance. It would take another ten minutes to travel the three miles to the gates. The street was being worked on which didn't help any.

"So, Madame Detective, how are you going to prove whether he killed them or not?" Faye asked as she zigzagged in and out of traffic.

"I think once I have all the pieces to the puzzle and can see the Captain's life from all angles, it might make more sense. There is so much left to do. It's kind of like being on jury duty where all the evidence isn't in yet. We now have some idea of his personal character. We know he probably married spinsters and that he had a hard hand but that doesn't mean he killed them. There are so many heart diseases we know of now that can kill someone in their teens, it could be the same sort of thing. This could simply be a terrible coincidence and a lot of pain for naught," Lydia said as Faye pulled into the parking space and they started to get out of the car. "But in answer to your question, I am not sure if we will ever prove he did or didn't do it, we'll just have to see what comes up and what the day holds."

An Old Fashioned Murder

"Want to know what I think?" Faye asked as she opened the back of the cab.

"What?"

"Something's off, I can't tell you what, but something is. And when you find it, I'll know it."

"Little sure of ourselves, are we?" Lydia teased.

"Always," Faye responded.

❖

Lydia found sitting at a microfilm reader was less stressful than sitting at work in front of her computer all day. Sometimes though her neck and wrist would hurt from turning the microfilm on the reader, and occasionally some tension would build, when confronted with a problem to solve and no solution in sight. Since it wasn't her family and there wasn't a personal relationship involved, she decided that she would take it easy and see where the chips would fall. Faye was a row over at one of the zoom readers so she had the end to herself where she could mumble and fuss under her breath and no one would care.

The first roll of film she loaded on the microfilm reader was the town directory. Since she was looking for specific people that task would go quickly. The roll included the directories from 1888 through 1921, and the plat map (showing the residents of the surrounding farming communities) made in 1898 of the township. The second roll took the directories up to the thirties.

Lydia took the film to the reader/printer and copied the sections of the township. She planned on going over that later at home, once she had the locations of the people and places she needed to document. When she was done with that chore she headed back to her reader, and with the list of names at her right she started to scroll through from the beginning.

She knew she was looking for Andrew Bower himself but his wife Melissa might be listed with him. Then there was Amelia Brown's family. Brown could be a problem depending on how many there were in the area since it was such a common name. But with the help of the census' she could then narrow that down, too. There was Katherine Stowe and her parents, Jack and Carrie, Mildred Wells and her parents, and finally Lydia located Priscilla "Silla" Drake.

The first year yielded a Frederick Bower on 12 South Street. Lydia surmised that Frederick may have been Andrew's father if he lived in town, as Lydia suspected. The tone of the mini history hinted at such. Above Frederick in the listing was a David Bower at the same residence and then Andrew Bower with his main residence and his business at 22 Main. His wife Melissa was not mentioned.

She found Stewart Hay and Feed also listed on Main Street with a Stephen Stewart as proprietor. Then below it was an additional entry for Stephen Stewart on Peach Street. Since that was the only Stewart Family, Lydia guessed it was probably Melissa's fathers business and home addresses.

There were four Brown's in the directory—Daniel, Richard, Fenton and Carson. She noted Daniel on Smith Street, Richard at 10 Main, Fenton on RR 42 and Carson on CR12. Lydia thought Richard might be a possibility, although his house was on the other side of the street and down. It was likely that they could have attended the same church since there was no such thing as parish or congregational boundaries back then, at least in small towns. The rural route was off a bigger road, and the county road was a smaller vein of road off of the rural route. Rural routes tended to be big dirt roads, sometimes paved, and usually considered a "major" road into town. Interstates and major highways were an invention of the 20th century automobile.

Katherine's father was listed as on RR 42 and he was the only Stowe listed. At least that was easy. Next there were two Wells families, a Thomas Wells on CR14 and a Benjamin on Clark Street. Finally there was only one Drake listed, and that was Charles Drake of 14 Main. Lydia looked closely but she could not find a Silla or Priscilla listed. So Charles was a Drake for sure. She needed that one piece of information to connect Silla to Charles. Lydia figured that would come in a later directory.

Lydia skimmed the next ten years. She copied the pages in the 1886 directory and then didn't copy anything again, although she made notations, until one of the addresses changed. That event happened in 1891 when the home address for Andrew changed to 4 Peach Street, which then reminded Lydia that Melissa's father had also lived on Peach. That must have been at the time that the Captain and Melissa's house was completed. Melissa didn't die until 1893, so at least she got to enjoy the fruit of their labor for a couple years.

And then Lydia hit pay dirt. Finally in the 1893 edition of the town directory Charles was still listed with a woman named Priscilla just below him. The address given for them was 22 Main. So from what Lydia could tell it looked like they moved into the little place attached to the back of the mercantile.

To Lydia, it seemed like a smart business move for the Captain, since he had Charles as an employee from at least 1888 if not earlier. Charles would have been trusted to take care of the business day and night as well as weekends. The curious part was Priscilla suddenly appearing on her own. Lydia pondered why Silla hadn't been mentioned previously. The easiest explanation was that she had been under age, and as Charles' dependent, hadn't been eligible to be listed on her own. Lydia noted that in parenthesis beside both their names was "Mercantile." So from this bit of evidence it looked like she was one in the same woman.

In 1899 Charles was still guarding the store but the major change Lydia found was that Priscilla had moved out and listed at 10 Peach Street. There it was. That reference made Lydia's heart leap. She surmised from the separation of residence that there had to have been some kind of a rift between them for Silla to move out on her own. If anything, it cemented what Lydia knew about Silla at the time of Katherine's death.

Did Silla buy the house? Rent it? Lydia knew it was very unusual for a single woman to be on her own, even with a steady income. The exception would have been if the woman had been a proprietor, such as a milliner.

Lydia now knew she had concrete proof that Silla Drake, the clerk, was Priscilla Drake, wife number five. The first piece of evidence had come from the inquiry, where she had been named as an employee both through the postmistress's testimony as well as Silla's own. Mrs. Sullivan had solidified it by actually naming Charles as Silla's brother, even though her name wasn't mentioned specifically.

The next link came with the note found in the journal that listed both Silla and Charles Drake, her brother, as being the primary clerks for the mercantile. Taking those items, plus the pedigree chart, as well as their listing in the town directory convinced her. But being the thorough genealogist she was, Lydia needed that one last piece of documentation to put the icing on the cake, and the Bower-Drake marriage record was it.

For now Lydia set that train of thought aside and went back to extracting information from the directories. She noticed that starting with 1899, the wife's name was being listed in parenthesis next to the husband's. Under Bower she found Amelia listed as the wife of Andrew.

After a little more scanning Lydia decided she didn't want to do too much more on the wives' families until she could look at the 1880 census and see if the girl's names were recorded with any of the prospective parents. Other than Jack and Carrie Stowe, Lydia had no choice but to narrow down the families through the census. Then she could focus on one name per directory and see if they moved. There was that off chance though, that either Amelia or Mildred weren't even from the township. If that were the case the marriage records, assuming they were married in the county, would be vital to finding where they came from. If they weren't located in that county by some odd chance, it would make solving the mystery of how the Captain found and married them a little more difficult.

Lydia rose and checked the clock. Not too bad, she had been working for about an hour. A few more years to go and she could move on to the census.

But it was time to stretch first.

❖

An Old Fashioned Murder

Taking change from her bag she headed out of the microfilm room and into the main book area. In the back corner, near the emergency exit was the snack area. The vending machines provided cookies, chips, sodas, water and some of the best home-made sandwiches ever. Lydia and Faye had learned that one of the Missionaries, a former caterer, prepared the fresh sandwiches every few days. If Lydia and Faye were unable to grab a snack on the way, or didn't have time to drive down Santa Monica Boulevard looking for food, this was the next best thing.

Lydia didn't feel like a sandwich today though, just a soda. After pulling the chilled drink out of the hand trap in the machine she opened it and sat at the long table, her back to the vending machines. The bulletin board was filled with pictures of historic leaders as well as newspaper clippings about the pursuit of genealogy as a hobby. It also occasionally featured blurbs on the volunteers who worked in the library.

A chair was pulled out beside her and Faye sat down.

"Break time huh?" she asked.

Lydia nodded. "There are like a billion of those directories, and they just seem to keep multiplying, I decided I needed a bit of caffeine to see me through the last batch."

One of the Missionaries, Brother Brady walked in and dropped some coins into the snack machine.

"How's it going ladies," he asked. "Any luck today?" His smile always made Lydia glad that she made the long trip up. He had been a long time volunteer worker and she always appreciated his kindness and help.

"Yeah, a little. I'm working on a project for someone else. How about you?" Lydia asked.

"Not too bad. I miss the crowd though. You two are the last of our handful of regulars now. So many are using the Internet exclusively. Saturday is the best day for keeping busy but the week nights...boy, am I glad to leave at nine."

"How's the book going?" Faye asked Brother Brady. He had been working on writing a western for some time and during each visit he shared his progress. He had even asked

Lydia, knowing she worked in a library, what resource he could use to find a publisher or agent.

"I am up to chapter twelve. I just finished writing a rousing gunfight between my hero and a Black Bart type. The love interest is off looking for her father's killer, and my hero is trying to get there before she does."

He folded up his bag of peanuts, which he'd only munched a few of, apologized for his brief visit, and then made his exit. Lydia looked at Faye and they both agreed it was time to get back to work.

"Directories huh. Sounds like fun." Faye commented. "I'll stick with death records. Even if they are in Italian."

"To each his own." Lydia said tossing her trash. "I prefer English myself."

❖

Lydia finished with the directories and then spent the following two hours tied up with census research. She used one of the online census indexes to narrow down her search for the names she had gleaned from the town directory and had also picked up two additional names in 1880 for the Brown family. She extracted all the names she could from within the county and then headed back to the microfilm reader. The best part was that there was only one reel for that county so she didn't have to worry about what roll she needed since the library allowed one roll at a time.

It wasn't until the fourth Brown family, Carson, that Lydia hit pay dirt. The household included a little girl, age ten, named Amelia. From the census it appeared that they were in Sutton Township, which was the next one over from Saylesville. Lydia made a quick note on her legal pad to remind her that they had moved from Sutton to Saylesville Townhip sometime between the 1880 and 1888 directory. Pin pointing their location could be taken care of later. A look at the plat map she had copied would help solve that problem.

An Old Fashioned Murder

It seemed odd that they would have included everyone in the county in such a small directory like that but then if it was based on a paid subscription—which most publishers of that time required, they may have decided to include anyone willing to pay. Lydia also realized that it could mean the Brown farm was a successful one. Most farmers' who made just enough money to survive, tended not to be included because they could not afford to pay the fee. For others it was a status symbol, as she was sure it had been for the Bower and Stewart families.

The other problem had been the with Wells line. Lydia had found two possibilities—Thomas or Benjamin. No other Wells' names had come up in the index search for that county, so she figured she had the field narrowed. Lydia rolled to the section she needed on the film, and found both names where they belonged. Looking at the ages Thomas looked to possibly be an uncle. He was too young to be Mildred's father but the perfect age to be her father's younger brother. Next she rolled to the citation for Benjamin and found the family at the edge of town. His occupation was listed as blacksmith, and in the household was an infant just three months old named Millie.

Finally Lydia located Priscilla and Charles in a boarding house at 14 Main Street. It confirmed for Lydia that they had lived together before the 1893 move into the house behind the mercantile. In 1880, they were both single, and born in the same state, West Virginia. Lydia also noted that their parents had also been born in Virginia, so that confirmed that they were brother and sister. He was twenty-five and she was twenty-three.

To be on the safe side Lydia checked the index and found that there were only two other Drake names listed in the county. One was a single male and the other was a widow age fifty-five with three children all under fifteen living at home. Lydia wondered if this woman might be Silla and Charles' mother but upon closer look the woman had been born in Indiana.

After contemplating the census citation for Charles and Silla, Lydia began to think that they had been alone in the world and had come into the county together. Her first thought was that maybe their parents had died and they were starting a new life. If so they would not have been the first to do so.

Looking at the demographics in relationship to the Captain's marriages was very interesting—two of his wives were farm girls and two were town girls. She knew it would have been more difficult for the Captain to meet the first two unless they came into town regularly. Mildred had been on Clark Street, and with her father being the blacksmith, more than likely had business dealings with Captain Bower. A match made in heaven so they say. Melissa's parents had owned the Hay and Feed on Main Street and lived on Peach. The "sweethearts" term fit well since they had probably known each other for years. Meeting Silla was just as obvious, since she worked for him. Her employment being a case of who you know, her brother being the link between her and the Captain.

As for the farm girls, the church had to be the answer or a relative or friend to both girls who lived in town. For some reason though, Lydia really felt a pull to the Sunday meeting place. Sadly, that was one of the items that Karen had been unable to get to. Still, wasn't too late to contact them in writing if she still felt the need later.

Faye came over and stood beside her. "Lunch?" she asked, stretching left and right.

"Am I ready!" Lydia said, stretching herself. "I have a good start. When I get back I'm going to move on to marriage records before I hit the rest of the censuses. Any luck for you?"

"Kind of. Nothing I really needed but it helps to verify my great-grandfather's brothers and sisters. I really should work on my dad's side for a while…maybe when we get back."

"Pizza or sandwich?" Lydia asked. It was her day to treat, when Faye let her.

"Pizza. Maybe some sort of Italian osmosis will come out and help me when we get back."

After lunch Faye moved her stuff over by Lydia, since she had finished using the smaller films which required a zoom reader. Time was running short and Lydia still needed to look at the marriage records and then hop to the 1900, 1910 and 1920 census.

An Old Fashioned Murder

The marriage record reel ran from 1860 through to 1909. That was about the time that most vital records films ended. Since they contained original records anything later tended to infringe on privacy laws. Anything needed after that usually had to be requested from the county courthouse in writing, or through the historical society, and with even later records, the state archives. Lydia only needed the records through 1907 when the Captain married Priscilla.

Lydia scrolled through the marriage index slowly. Under B for Bower Lydia found the Captain's marriage to Melissa Stewart. Below that she found his marriages to Amelia, Katherine, Mildred and finally Priscilla, who in the index was listed as Silla.

By the time the Captain had married, most of the marriage records included the license and return. These records included the residence of the bride and groom. The return portion included where the marriage was performed, and if a member of the couple had been underage there was a place for a parent or guardian to sign, to give permission to marry. Why couldn't all her family's records be so revealing?

According to the marriage entry, the Captain and Melissa were wed in her home, with a justice of the peace presiding. Lydia found that curious. It wasn't like they were on the prairie with absolutely nothing nearby. Lydia figured that it was possible that either one, or both of them, lacked a church affiliation. From the dates of birth for the Captain and Melissa's children, Lydia concluded that an impending birth was not the reason either. Since they had both been close to, or at age thirty, they may have just wanted to get married and get it over with. In some cases, with the right pull, the preacher from the family church would come and marry them at their home if there was a need.

Oh well, Lydia shrugged, it really didn't matter since Melissa wasn't the focus of this whole study anyway.

She walked over to the reader/printers and copied the page, then after a quick walk around the room she sat back down and continued. According to the chronology the marriage for Amelia was next. The marriage record stated that it took place at the Saylesville Methodist Church, officiated by the Reverend Foster.

That reference helped with Lydia's theory about the couple meeting at church. If Amelia's parents were Methodist and the Saylesville Methodist church was the only Methodist church in town that would explain quite a few things. Lydia continued on and discovered that Katherine's nuptials followed suit with the same church and same minister. In addition to Amelia and Katherine, he also married Mildred there but Reverend. Johnson was the officiator.

Finally it came to the marriage record for the Captain and Silla. Everything fit, ages, places of birth, place of residence but what didn't click right away for Lydia was the place of the marriage. They had been married on Christmas Day, 1907, and once again not in church but at the home of the bride, by the Justice of the Peace.

Lydia sat back in her seat and thought, Christmas Day at Silla's home by a Justice of the Peace. Why? The Captain had a home of his own with tons of family. And the previous marriages gave the impression that he had a church he attended as well. Why change the pattern again?

"Faye, what do you make of this?" Lydia asked, as she explained the perplexing pattern to Faye. She then sat back in her chair while the wheels turned in their heads.

"Being an older couple maybe they didn't want the hoopla of a big marriage. Since he had been married so many times to younger women, and probably had big affairs, he just wanted something quiet at home," Faye volunteered. "Or, maybe his church wasn't her church?"

"That's a possibility but why Christmas Day? Wouldn't you want to wait until after the holiday? I mean I know it wasn't as big of a deal then as it is now but why not wait?"

"I don't know. Unless one of them was ill and didn't think they might live past Christmas? Your mother-in-law does that to you every year—what going on five now?"

"Very funny, it's only been four, this Christmas will be five." Lydia laughed. Her mother-in-law really was in poor health but considering everything, she was actually doing rather well. So every year had been her last since her illness had begun. "I won't dismiss that actually. It could very well have been possible that one of them thought their time was short and wanted to speed it along but which one? Remember too, he did have a one year old at home; maybe it was more just to get a body in the house to take care of the child. Can you imagine a woman in her fifties having to raise a one year old? That alone gives credence to the idea that she must really have loved the Captain."

"Or she was whacked," Faye said matter-of-factly. "What's it called, unrequited love?"

"Yeah, maybe that was it. If she *really* wanted him, she didn't have much of a choice did she? I guess her raising such a young child wasn't that out of the ordinary back then. It happens quite often now," Lydia remarked, reflecting on the trend of grandparents raising grandchildren due to custody battles, children with drug problems, in prison, or rehab. Back then the child could have been left for very different reasons, a widowed male who just couldn't raise his child due to grief. Lydia had discovered, while doing her own research, that there were some widowers that even abandoned their children with relatives because they were reminders of the deceased spouse.

"Now that I think of it the tone of that history on the business seemed, well, possessive. You don't think Silla could have written that do you? If she did, it fits our scenario about the unrequited love thing," Lydia proposed.

"It's highly possible. It was all about the Captain and his staff. If she did how do we find out?" Faye asked.

"I don't know but I bet if we hunt hard enough we'll find something. She certainly didn't wait all those years for nothing," Lydia added.

❖

When Lydia got home that evening she called Julia to set up a meeting for the next day. Church was at nine, and since she didn't have to be at the library to open the doors until noon, she would be able to have a nice breakfast before heading down. Julia said she would be there at one, since she was driving herself. Her granddaughter was out of town still and wouldn't return until Tuesday.

So the next morning the family piled into the Suburban and headed off to church. The sermon was on trying to understand the motives of people in your daily life and not judging them too harshly. Lydia wanted to know if that applied to dead people too. If that were the case, she had a long list of her own to think twice about.

Afterwards, they hit the little diner on the corner by home and had breakfast. It was a small luxury for them to all eat together anymore, especially with Beth in college and working; Lucas who seemed to be chained to his computer most all the time now (except when Lydia threw him out of the house to play, or he had homework), tended to eat quickly and then run back upstairs to continue whatever game he was playing with; and Sarah was simply growing up way too quickly. Lydia knew that her family was changing and savoring the moments, including their Sunday breakfast, was precious at best.

As they sat and waited for their food, conversation slowly turned to the day's activities. Beth wanted to get home to do laundry, and then she had to go into work for a couple hours. Lance needed to mow the lawn, Lucas had homework to finish, as well as his own laundry to do, and Lydia wanted to go home to regroup before she headed to the library to meet with Julia. There was still a lot to cover on Julia's family, and Lydia knew she had to stay focused or she would lose it. That seemed to be happening a lot lately. Most of it was from being spread too thin—but wasn't that the norm now for most people?

When they arrived home, Beth ran up to throw her clothes in the washing machine before her brother could, and Sarah went to the back yard to play with her kitchen before her father got there with the lawnmower. Lydia, as planned, locked herself in her room with Julia's family, looking over her list *again*—Church records, mortuary records, cemetery records. There was still so much stuff to find and explore.

Lydia plopped down on their bed with the pictures Karen had taken at the Methodist cemetery and started to look at the placement of the headstones. Karen, bless her, had taken pictures of the position of the stones together, separately, and within the cemetery.

She observed that they were arranged in an interesting pattern; Captain Bower in the middle, Silla to his right, and

An Old Fashioned Murder

Melissa to his left. In front of those, was his son, Clarkson, and wives Amelia and Katherine. Lydia noticed that there wasn't a stone for Mildred, so she made a note to look into that issue later on.

The stones for the Captain, Melissa and Silla were big and made of polished granite, with both the Captain and Silla's being identical. Melissa's looked a little more worn, attesting to the fact that she had been buried first. The cemetery wasn't entirely in the picture so she wasn't sure where their plots were located in relationship to the road or any other landmarks.

She flipped through three more before she realized what was amiss.

Lydia had expected the other wives to be in the same row, buried according to the order in which they had died, therefore closer to him. She hadn't expected Silla to be right beside him since she had been last.

The last three photos in the stack solved the mystery.

How did it happen that the other wives and his infant child were buried in front of and not along side of him? The son Lydia could kind of understand but it was almost like Amelia and Katherine had been dismissed, put aside like they had been in life.

Lydia couldn't decide whether to call the mortuary or to write them. She had always been much better expressing what she needed in the written form, and waiting a week really wouldn't hurt anything since she wanted to take a better look at the mercantile journal. Lydia also wanted to start mapping out residences on the plat map, which she had copied from the microfilm before they were kicked out of the library.

Julia wouldn't learn much during their meeting, but maybe Lydia would be able to jog from her memory some from the information she had found.

She packed up what she had and headed out the door. Lydia hoped that when she went to bed later that night that she would sleep. Lately, she was finding that when she did fall asleep, all she dreamed about was Julia's family.

They were getting to her more than she wanted.

Chapter Nine

Julia arrived at the library promptly at one that afternoon. Once again they settled at the big oak table. Lydia placed the information in front of Julia. She had everything in family order starting with the family group sheets for each marriage and then the corresponding pages of source information.

While Julia scanned through the pages, Lydia went inside the kitchen to make them some tea. Normally liquids were discouraged when working with the books, or any original documentation, but since this session would not include books, and only copies of documents, it was safe. She prepared an herbal tea for Julia and a cup of Earl Gray for herself, in order to give her a boost of energy.

Muriel wasn't due in, so if any patrons happened along it was all Lydia. She didn't think Julia would mind the interruptions too much but had warned her ahead of time anyway.

"Let's go over what I've gathered for each marriage, and then we can discuss it. I'm hoping this will trigger a memory of something you know but don't realize, or something you overheard and forgot." Lydia took a sip of the tea then slid the cup and saucer aside. She then pulled out the first group of papers, that of the Captain, his wife Melissa, and their family.

At Lydia's insistence Julia had gone through her family pictures and sorted them by family before she came. Lydia found that putting a face to a name, made the person more than just a name with a date.

"This is the only picture I have of Melissa. She was a pretty one, although she was a big girl. I think she was German and Scotch by descent. My mother remembered her half-siblings well. She was allowed, when she got older, to associate with her half-brothers and sisters. Even though some of them were considerably older, she still had a bond with them, maybe from mutual tragedies. All of the children from Melissa and the Captain are gone now." Julia laid the picture down and picked up the family group sheet.

"Did you spend any time with your cousins in Ohio as a young girl?" Lydia inquired, thinking this would be a good time to start asking about living relatives.

"Off and on through the years. The older ones would pick on my brother and I practically the whole time we were there, so we tried to avoid them when we could. I did make friends with one of Aunt Lissa's children, Corey I think. He was very cute and very polite...quite different from his siblings, and the other cousins." Julia thought for a moment.

"Did you ever talk with them about the family at all?" Lydia asked.

"No. My brother and I were advised not to ask questions when we visited. Just to play and have a good time," Julia sighed. "The cousins back there seemed to have this bond that we just never could break through. Maybe it was because they remained in Ohio and lived near each other. We didn't have that. My mother moved away and married young, so until I was about three or four, I didn't even meet my grandparents, or know I had tons of other cousins from my grandfather's other marriages."

Scattered families were fairly common Lydia thought especially with the advent of modern transportation. The mobility after World War II and Korea, aided in the separation of families. Many soldiers, and the women who worked in the factories, left their homes looking for better lives in a booming economy, the west coast being one of those destinations.

Lydia's parents had met and married in California during World War II and after a number of moves finally settled there. Her summers were spent with her mother's family in Iowa. It wasn't until she turned eight that she even knew her father had siblings in Maine, and a whole other batch of cousins too.

"That I can relate to." Lydia nodded. "Can you list your aunts and uncles who are still living. If we get into rough patches where we need additional information, they might be helpful."

"There's Uncle Daniel. I still correspond with two of his daughters. He also moved to California as a young man, but lived farther south from us. He was very good about keeping in touch with my parents at Christmas. My mother told me once he didn't really associate too much with Melissa's children either. She did remember hearing somewhere that he had been close to his stepmother Priscilla since she raised him. He's in his late nineties and still pretty spry from what I have heard. I'll contact one of the girls, if he can't help, maybe she can. I think too, there are some cousins still living from the earlier marriages but I'll have to check on that and then make the list."

"Perfect. Now let's get back to the information." Lydia showed Julia the births for Melissa's children, including Clarkson's death. She then showed her the marriage record and census entries for that marriage. She had hurriedly squeezed out those last items before they'd been thrown out of the library. It had almost become tradition with them: either Faye waiting for Lydia to finish, or Lydia waiting for Faye.

They didn't worry too much about the staff being angry at them since the volunteers knew both of them and their habits quite well after so many years. It had gotten to the point they would ask Faye what case she was working on, or patrol she was assigned to, or ask Lydia what the kids were doing, and where her husband was traveling to next. No matter what though, they tried their best not to take advantage of the situation, if they could help it. There were just some days they simply couldn't.

Lydia then showed Julia a copy of the mercantile history that had fallen from the journal. She had made a copy since the original was brittle and starting to disintegrate. Lydia waited quietly as Julia silently read it. It was the statement that came from Julia's mouth after she finished reading that threw Lydia for a loop.

"Priscilla wrote this, didn't she?"

Lydia blinked and then looked at Julia curiously. "That was my first thought too actually. Why do you think so?" Lydia asked.

"Well, you talked about triggering a memory, and this certainly did it." Julia looked into Lydia's eyes. There was a pain there that Lydia couldn't quite put her finger on. Once again she refrained from interrupting and waited for Julia to continue. "I was born in 1926, and I remember being about six and we took a trip to Ohio. We rode all the way in a really old, used Model-T Ford that my father had scrimped and saved for. He was a baker and made the best bread in the world but it didn't pay well. We had saved enough money to travel by car and afford it. My older brother was eight, and my sister was two...Rough trip back then with small children." She shook her head at the thought and then continued. "Priscilla was dying, so it was like 1932 and my mother felt she should go since she was an elder, even though she wasn't really close to the family. My mother had grown-up on her grandparent's farm, as you already know, which was just outside of town. They stayed away from Saylesville after Katherine's death. I think my grandparents thought it would be too hard on the kids to be stared at, and whispered about. They were doing all their business in Lancaster or Chillicothe by then...basically my mother had not associated with any of them because of that." Julia rubbed her forehead in an effort to bring back a memory buried in her mind for close to seventy-two years.

"Take your time," Lydia encouraged.

"It took several days, but we got there. Priscilla was on her deathbed when my mother entered the room. As far as I know they had only met once or twice before, when the Captain died and when her grandmother Carrie died I think," Julia took a sip of tea and then continued. "My mother was in there for what seemed like forever, and my father kept walking us around the block to keep us entertained. Finally he walked us into town and showed us the store my grandfather had owned, and the church where my mother had been christened, and then took us for ice cream near the park. I knew something was up because it was rare for my father to spend money on something so frivolous since we didn't really have much to begin with."

"That must have been hard on you little ones. Waiting around for someone to pass," Lydia sympathized.

"Yes, it was...after a while we headed back to the house. Finally my mother came out with tears in her eyes. I faintly remember my grandfather Stowe being there and hugging her...he seemed so old. My grandmother had died just a year or two before. All my mother could say was...how dare she?"

"How dare who? Priscilla?"

"Yes. Since I was so little, I thought maybe I had dreamed it. But then I talked with my brother about it before mother died and he told me no, it really did happen, and he remembered it too..." Julia looked at Lydia, this time the sadness was gone, and there was a fire in her eye. "My mother was sobbing in my grandfather Stowe's arms, and told him that Priscilla said that her father never loved her mother, and that he only married her to take care of the children. That he really loved her, Silla that is, and he had waited all those years to marry her."

"Remember, the fact he married for convenience wasn't that uncommon Julia. I know it sounds awful but it was done all the time. The couple eventually ended up either loving, hating, or having mutual respect for each other," Lydia was trying to soften what Priscilla had said. She knew it would be no use, because Priscilla had wounded Julia's mother with such a callous statement and in turn wounded Julia. "They really weren't married long enough to know what that path would be."

"That's true, but to tell my mother he loved Priscilla all along...could that have been true?" Julia asked with a pleading tone. "This note you found..." Julia waved the letter in the air, "had to have been from her. It is so self-centered, so...so... her."

"Simply because she said that to your mother, doesn't mean she wrote this." Lydia said. Taking the letter she glanced at the writing one more time. Lydia didn't know what to say. The sheet of paper wasn't signed, and even though Silla, and her brother were prominently mentioned, there was no concrete way to prove who the author was. And Lydia hated to admit that her gut feeling, and Julia's far away memory didn't make the author Priscilla.

"No, it's because of the last thing my mother told my grandfather Stowe. She told him that Priscilla said that if it hadn't been for her and her brother Charlie, the mercantile wouldn't have survived because the Captain had been a poor businessman, and only married women who he thought could run the house *and* work the store. She also told my mother that other than herself, Melissa was the only other woman who had been strong enough to do it, and that my grandmother had been a weak, stupid girl who would never have been able to do it even if she had lived." Julia slammed her tiny fist onto the table. Lydia was amazed that such anger could come from someone so small.

"She said that? Are you sure?"

"Yes. Like I said, I thought I dreamed it until I talked to my brother and then mother brought it up to me again when she handed me the box of papers. She told me that she never hated anyone in her life except for Priscilla Drake Bower, and she hoped that she rotted in Hell."

Lydia sat speechless. What direction was this on-the-side research project heading in? Lydia knew genealogy wasn't just about dates, and places and names, that it included the whole thing a family was but for someone to be so mean on their deathbed. Almost like a vengeance. That was just cold and cruel. If this verbal venting from poor Julia was coming out from just a mini history written on a piece of paper, what else was coming down the road?

She had to admit there was a lot of spit and fire in that little lady, much of which had been bottled up for many years. Lydia just had to channel it in a positive way or they would be bogged down in mire, and lose sight of the goal. Did he, or didn't he do it?

"She was cruel wasn't she?" Lydia sympathized. Lydia could relate. An aunt by marriage had been exactly like that, cruel, and spiteful. She had done some seriously underhanded things to people in her father's family, even destroyed some relationships, and Lydia's parents had never forgiven the woman.

"Yes, she was," Julia said as she took a sip of tea trying to compose herself. "I'm sorry. I didn't mean to get so angry but those things she said hurt my mother so badly. I mean...she never knew her mother, and to have someone say such awful things about her...it just killed her."

"I imagine it did." Lydia agreed. "I guess if I heard that and then read this I might think exactly the same."

"To be honest, I hadn't even thought about that encounter until I read this," she patted the paper in front of her on the table. "The reference to..." Julia read from the note. "'...If it hadn't been for his very *loyal* staff at the store the place would have folded immediately, since he was so grief stricken he wouldn't leave the house for several weeks. His clerks Priscilla and Charles watched the store and *carried on the business* until he was fully recovered and returned to *where he belonged.*' How does that sound other than, than...'"

"No, I see what you are getting at. And I suppose finding it in the mercantile journal might make more of a case for it as well," Lydia dug into the papers and pulled out the photos that Karen had taken, handing two to Julia. "It was when I saw this photograph, the thought crossed my mind. Look where Priscilla is in relationship to the others..." Lydia pointed at each stone. "See where she is, right next to him. They should have been buried as they died. Even if the plots had been purchased at one time, Amelia and Katherine should have been buried by him but look who is...Priscilla and Melissa. If they were buried as they died, Priscilla should be the last one. She's not, she's front and center."

"He died first." Julia commented absently.

"Yes, he did." Lydia nodded. She knew exactly what they were both thinking.

"Is that why you wanted pictures of the cemetery and stones?" Julia was calming down, and thinking a bit more clearly.

"One of the reasons... yes. I figured it was worth a shot, just to see. Burial is more than people think it is... It tells relationship, and sometimes it can even tell how other family members felt when the deceased was buried. For instance, I had an ancestor who married twice. The first wife is buried with *her* family; the second is right beside him for all eternity. Either he didn't have the money to bury her, which I doubt, since he was a successful wharf builder or her parents didn't care too much for him and wanted her buried with them." Lydia pointed at the photograph. "I think there was a big power play going on here, and it would be interesting to know why."

Quickly they perused the other family groups since it was starting to get late. Right away Julia caught the absence of a cause of death for both Amelia and Katherine on their death entries. Even Mildred's cause of death had been listed simply as "unknown" hinting that there had been no apparent illness or disease found.

Lydia told Julia that she had shot off a letter to the mortuary in Saylesville asking if they had any records from the turn of the century, and if so, how far back they went. .

As they wrapped it up, Lydia reminded Julia that she still had the newspaper articles to search, which should arrive at work within the next week.

The only other thing Lydia wanted to do was to sit down and attempt to decipher the mercantile journal with the faint hope that it might help somehow. From what she could make out, there were monetary transactions listed in some kind of code. Her goal was to see if she could make heads or tales of it.

The plan then would be for her and Julia to re-group, just to make sure that there wasn't anything still missing. Once again she reminded Julia that even after everything was said and done, there may not be a way to conclusively prove that Captain Andrew Bower killed anyone.

Julia smiled and took Lydia's hand in her frail one. "Thank you for everything. We can only prove what is there, and hope that we are right. I'll keep looking through my mothers things and see if there is anything that will help. And I promise I will call my cousin this week, and see if Uncle Daniel is well enough to visit. As I recall he lives in a resident care facility near his daughter down towards San Diego. If he is up to it, maybe we can visit him."

"That would be fine." Lydia assured her. "Just let me know when. I'll let you know when I hear from the Mortuary."

Lydia walked Julia to her car, just as Muriel pulled into the lot. It was her day off and she just couldn't stay away. Lydia gave Julia a hug and waved her off down the driveway.

Muriel walked over and stood beside Lydia. Muriel had started to shrink over the last couple years, and Lydia was beginning to feel like a giant at her five-foot six inch frame. Before Lydia's mother had died she had shrunk to five feet, losing four inches. It had gotten to the point where Lydia had to bend over to hug her goodbye. Quickly she shrugged off the image.

"So how's it going?" Muriel asked as she tossed her canvas bag with the logo "Genealogists never die, they just lose their census" inside the door. Muriel had enough binders and papers in there, that if she were ever assaulted, the perpetrator would be seriously sorry.

"Okay I guess. I wish I could give Julia more but it just isn't coming smoothly. There's something lying underneath it all and for the life of me I can't figure out what it is." Lydia shook her head. So much for easy answers.

"Show me what you have and maybe I can help. Sometimes it takes another eye to see what's right in front of you."

"Would you mind?" Lydia asked. She hated asking for help, it was one of her major character flaws. And as Lydia reminded herself, she usually ended up sorry when she didn't.

"Not at all. May I take it home and look this evening? Since I'm all alone, I don't have the competition for time like you do, with the hubby and kids."

"It's all yours." Lydia said as she handed it over to her

Chapter Ten

    A few days later Muriel called Lydia asking for additional time with Julia's papers. Her sister had taken ill, and she was going to Arizona to spend a couple days with her while she recuperated. Muriel promised that once she was home, the file would receive her undivided attention and she would have it back to Lydia's house before the end of the week. That was perfectly fine with Lydia, since she'd needed a break from it anyway.

    With the brief break Lydia actually got some long overdue housework done. She even recruited the kids (after a bit of arm twisting), who were now off for the summer. With everyone pitching in, she was able to catch up on things she had been putting off—like calling her aunt back east, and writing some long overdue letters.

    Lydia couldn't resist running out to the mailbox each day to check and see if either the church or mortuary responses had arrived. Since it had been almost two weeks since she sent for them, she felt one of them should be arriving any moment. She had hoped to receive them before the films at the Family History Center were returned to Salt Lake City, just in case there was something she may have missed.

    On the bright side, the Saylesville Gazette films had arrived at work via interlibrary loan. She had ordered the films that included issues printed after each of the deaths—Amelia's, Katherine's and Mildred's. A surge of excitement went through her as she took the first roll out of the box and loaded it onto the microfilm reader.

    By using the dates on the front page of each newspaper, Lydia went straight to the issue she needed, scanning it to get familiar with the layout. The first page contained national and world news; the second page was mostly business announcements and ads; and the third section was local news. Lydia found it tedious reading each page but after a while she hit pay dirt and found a blurb referring to Amelia Bower's death.

It was written that, "...She grew up in the Saylesville area, attending the local school. Later as a young woman, she helped her parents on their farm before meeting Capt. Andrew Bower at the Methodist Church. The Captain and Mrs. Bower were married for only a few years before the Lord decided it was her time to join him. The town stands by the Captain in his time of grief. Services will be Monday, at the Saylesville Methodist Church at two p.m. Family only is requested."

Since there were no additional articles about Amelia's death for at least three weeks following that initial one, Lydia jumped ahead to the Katherine period. The editor of the paper had changed, and so had the layout. He had gone to a gossip column type format, and on page three under Saylesville proper, was the announcement of Katherine Stowe Bower's death.

It was reported that, "...She had died tragically working in her kitchen. Although fire had not consumed her it was heard that her heart had tragically given out on her instead. Her husband Captain Andrew Bower, could not say if she had been ill or not but the clerk at the mercantile, Silla Drake did mention that she never seemed to have the energy to carry out the duties required of her. The funeral will be at the Saylesville Methodist Church on Sunday at noon. Please send food donations and sympathy cards to the Bower family at 4 Peach Street."

Lydia tried to ignore the dig regarding Katherine and her lack of stamina. Sadly she was getting used to seeing Silla's catty opinions in print, and that cutting comment was just another example. Lydia wondered if anyone in the Bower or Stowe household had been offended by those comments? Lydia certainly would have been, and if given the chance would have called the woman on it too.

After a bit more winding, Lydia found an additional article printed two weeks later. The Sheriff had posted a notice stating, "...A hearing regarding the death of Mrs. Katherine Bower will be held the following Wednesday, in the

An Old Fashioned Murder

Courthouse in Saylesville, at two o'clock in the afternoon. Anyone wishing to express their opinion may do so in writing within the next week. The letters can be left at the Sheriff's office on Main Street between ten and two. They will be forwarded to the panel investigating Mrs. Bower's death. No gossip please. Only facts presented will be considered."

The newspaper announcement answered one big question Lydia had had. It explained why Mr. Crawford, Mrs. Robeson and Sarah Sullivan had not been asked to testify in person. Whoever had screened the initial letters deemed those three to be gossips, their opinions scandalous. Simply put, they would have made the Captain look bad.

Even though Lydia was running late, she really wanted to finish Katherine's portion before she left. She left her stuff at the reader/printer and dashed over to the periodicals desk, which was quiet for the moment, to call Beth. After a bit of cajoling, Beth agreed to pick Sarah up from daycare.

Fifteen more minutes was all she needed.

She hoped.

❖

Eventually her perseverance paid off. The last article Lydia found on Katherine provided the information she was searching for. It was the final decree of the inquiry panel, and located under the heading "Court Minutes."

"It was the consensus of the inquiry panel that Mrs. Katherine Bower's death was caused by some sort of heart trouble possibly brought on by exhaustion due to the running of the Bower household, as well as her work at the mercantile. Although no direct negligence could be attributed to any member of the Bower family in her death, there was no proof that an indirect cause was not the case either. Therefore it was the decision of the court, that her two children Amy and Cyrus be put into the custody of their grandparent's Mr. and Mrs. Jackson Stowe."

The implications made by printing that final report in the newspaper spoke volumes. The court, given very little direct evidence, had no choice but to weigh the indirect. And indirectly the Captain looked like an insensitive ogre (which he supported by his own testimony), who drove his wife to collapse. If her heart had been bad, as suspected, the stress of keeping up with all the things expected of her simply pushed her heart over the edge.

It was then Lydia realized that neither the notes taken during the inquiry, nor the official decision made by panel, had been included in either the extract Uncle Cyrus had requested, or in the copies Karen had brought home. Lydia wondered if they had been misplaced, or deliberately removed from the file. Sadly she realized that they would probably never know what the final catalyst had been in the panel's decision.

Since it was getting late, and Lydia's eyes were getting tired, she decided to save Mildred's death for another day. She had the films for at least another two weeks, which was plenty of time to come back later.

❖

Slowly over the next few days Lydia worked down her list. She found the next big item was the deciphering of the mercantile journal. In order to focus on it without interruption, Lydia found a corner study carrel at work in the student area, where she spent breaks and occasionally lunch trying to crack the code. She tried working on it before bed each night but it was so "exciting" it simply put her to sleep. Then she had tried working on it after dinner but by the time she cleaned the kitchen, and put Sarah in the tub, her enthusiasm had waned. So Lydia found there was no other choice than to do it during the day.

She started on page one, and tried to figure out what each of the codes meant. After a while of staring at the page, Lydia recognized it to be some sort of short hand. The names were not spelled out, just abbreviated, and each one referred to what appeared to be different suppliers. Lydia knew it would be hard to tell where the items had originated without complete spellings and since there wasn't any kind of cheat sheet to help decipher them she was at a stand-still. On a saved the townspeople time, and saved the mercantile from selling merchandise that might spoil since refrigeration wasn't a viable option yet. Eggs could be kept anywhere, and if a woman living in town was in the middle of baking a cake and ran out, it was either the neighbor, or the store.

The Captain probably obtained most of his food items from local farmers as well, which insured freshness. Also many women would sell their extra canned goods, and eggs to the mercantile, taking the money and tucking it away for a rainy day.

The knowledge that the Captain's own wife had to sell her eggs to the neighbors so she could save up to visit the doctor seemed so sad to Lydia. Katherine probably felt it easier to accept pity from her neighbors than to be humiliated by her husband.

As Lydia continued on through the journal she found a separate accounting sheet for the purchase of some roots and herbs. The root list included sweet potatoes, beetroots, parsnips, and turnips. The herbs included things like dandelion root, horseradish root, and some plants that she figured might be used as medicinal home remedies: hyssop, lavender, wormwood, foxglove, chamomile, elderberry, licorice, bayberry bark, sage, basil, and thyme. Overall most of the plants on the list seemed perfectly reasonable to be sold through the mercantile, except for maybe the foxglove. Lydia had heard somewhere it was a poisonous plant, but who knew, maybe for some purposes it was all right.

Just when she thought she was done, Lydia found one more sheet following the roots and herbs page. That page was a nice long list of dry goods: candles, utensils, farm tools, horse equipment, lighting supplies, irons, and skillets; all kinds of day-to-day items a household could use. And finally, there were some clothing items: nightgowns, shirts, underwear, overalls, and bonnets, primarily things to wear.

With all that merchandise to keep track of, how would two clerks be enough? But then Lydia reminded herself, if your wife and later your kids helped out in the store, the overhead would stay low, and a profit would certainly be made.

whim she had even felt inside the leather cover but found nothing.

After several attempts, Lydia got to the point where she could actually figure out quite a bit of what had been ordered. The supplies were in groups and listed by supplier, with each similar type of product lumped together but on separate pages. There were leather goods such as shoes, belts, hats, jackets, and gloves in one group. The next set looked to be woolen materials that included bolts of fabric, blankets, jackets, socks and flannel shirts. Another entry looked to be dry goods; flour, sugar, starch, rice, baking powder, so on. There was even a supplier for medicinal products – two actually from what Lydia could tell. One supplier sold things like rubbing alcohol and hydrogen peroxide, things that were known to clean and treat wounds. The other supplier provided items like patent medicines (Uncle Bob's Elixir and something called Mother's Helper), in addition to Castor oil, peppermint extract, and laudanum.

Lydia also found entries for distilled spirits: whiskey, rum, and so on. She figured they had probably been sold to customers for all sorts of ailments, such as pulled ligaments, as well as normal body aches. Lydia was pretty sure that any other usage would have been frowned upon if suspected.

The Captain apparently did not deal with true medicinal items, since that would be taken care of by the doctor or a pharmacy, assuming there was one, and controlled closely by both entities. There would be no reason to have anything like that distributed by a mercantile.

The final column that Lydia worked on appeared to be actual food items. The list wasn't very long, but what was there included things like: canned goods (fruits and vegetables), some fresh foods such as corn, carrots, onions, eggs, and cheese and bread.

Lydia wasn't surprised by the short list, since many city dwellers grew their own produce in their gardens, as well as keeping a few practical animals — chickens for fresh eggs and maybe a cow for milk.

Dairies were also starting to become more common around that time. The milkman would make his rounds every day with his cart selling milk, cheese, cream and butter; it

An Old Fashioned Murder

Now if she could only track who he purchased the supplies from, and how much in quantity. It probably wouldn't help solve any great mystery but it might tell Lydia where he did his business, and where he traveled to in order to do business.

Before she closed the book, Lydia contemplated what kind of weapon the Captain might have used if he really had murdered any of his wives. Since there had been no apparent trauma, poison was the only thing Lydia could think of. But from what she could tell there wasn't anything that he sold in the store that could do too much harm.

She would keep looking.

❖

The next day, Lydia unlocked her front door as she balanced two grocery bags, her purse, and a tote bag containing Julia's family files. Close on her heels was Sarah, pulling her rolling backpack. As the door opened they were met by two cats, both determined to escape to freedom. Simultaneously, both Lydia and Sarah stuck their feet out to keep them inside, as they pulled their parcels and bags into the entranceway.

Slowly they worked their way to the kitchen, setting their bags down just as the phone rang. Glancing over to where the phone should have been, Lydia noticed that as usual it was not in its cradle. Just after the ringing stopped Lucas came running down the stairs, the cordless phone in his hand. If he had been any faster Lydia was sure it would have hit her in the face.

"There's a guy on the phone from some mortuary. He wants to talk to you." For a moment Lydia thought she had spotted a glimpse of concern in her sons face. If so, it disappeared as quickly as it had appeared. "You're not planning your funeral or anything, are you?" Lucas asked, taking one of the bags, and placing it on the counter. His concern was almost touching. Lydia knew it would be short lived.

"Very cute...No, I plan on doing that sometime before I retire, which won't be for another twenty years at this rate, thank you," Lydia said as she sat the last bag on the counter.

She snatched the phone from her son's hand. Lucas gave her a shrug and then ran back up the stairs. Sarah crept up behind her and pulled on her arm. "Go watch Noggin while Mommy talks, Ok?" Lydia gently asked Sarah. The little girl nodded, as she ran over to the remote to change the channel.

"Hello," Lydia said into the receiver as she opened the fridge door with her right hand, cradling a bottle of juice in the left, and the phone between her ear and her shoulder. That particular balancing act had taken years of practice.

"Hi, this is Brad Cummings, from Cummings and Sons mortuary in Saylesville. You sent a letter with some questions, and I thought since you included your phone number, it might be best to call and answer them in person."

Lydia noted that he sounded very friendly, and very young. "Yes, I did. I hope the letter wasn't too long." Lydia apologized.

"Not at all. My Dad officially took over the business a couple years ago, and I have been working summers to help him out. He gave me your letter for something challenging to do, and I figured what I found out would probably take way too long to put in writing." Brad explained eagerly. Lydia smiled to herself. His eagerness was infectious.

"Great..." Lydia began. Brad, excited, cut her off at the pass.

"First off, I was lucky. My family has owned this place for four generations, and they were really anal about keeping records, which worked out great for you. But to be honest I've learned more about death in the last week than I ever wanted to know." He gave a deep sigh. Lydia knew mortuary's were a vital part of being buried but she would not have liked to live, or work in one either.

"So what do you have for me?" Lydia didn't want to dampen his enthusiasm but she figured this call was going to cost the mortuary a pretty penny and she didn't want to get Brad in trouble by spending too much time on the phone.

"Oh sorry, these entries were just real interesting." He cleared his throat. "Your people were in two different books, some before 1900 and the others after. My dad was pretty impressed too, mainly that my great-grandfather and grandfather were so thorough." He took another breath and finally jumped into it. "Okay, let me start with Amelia...She was taken care of by my great-grandfather personally. He recorded her date of death, spouse, and other living relatives, all of which you noted in your letter. The cool thing was that he made this note in the margin...'No apparent cause of death...Doctor asked me to double check. No apparent trauma. Some saliva around the mouth. Consistent with heart failure...no other signs. No bruising from falling or hitting head in the barn can be noted.'"

"Interesting," Lydia said into the phone. She recalled the doctor had listed a 'possible concussion' as a cause of death. With the additional information from Brad, Lydia now knew that the doctor's diagnosis had been a guess. It had been just something to enter so the death certificate could be filed. With their standing in the community it was possible too that the doctor had been pressured to name something as a cause by the family.

"Yeah, it is. Okay, now the entry for Katherine...My great-grandfather had her listed as Katy. In going through the books, I noticed the only regular notes he made tended to be about the condition of the corpse; and that was if he had to do a lot of work to make them presentable for viewing. I think he did that so he wouldn't get blamed if they looked bad." Brad explained slowly. "What I am getting at it is—the comments I am finding he wrote in regards to the people you asked about, are really unusual. It seemed the more detailed the notes in the book, the closer he was to the deceased. In other words, he seemed to like Katherine because he made some detailed notes about how he worked on her to make her look nice but the interesting thing he wrote was: 'Knot on top back of head from striking floor. Doctor said...still alive when he got there but went fast. Doctor stated heart went wild during move to couch. Died by the time he got her there...Doctor asked if I would look for trauma, or possible heart trouble signs. None found. Second death. Strange. Follow-up with parents.'"

"Oh so, he's the one who tipped off Katherine's parents to the odd circumstances. It wasn't the doctor, or her husband, it was your great-grandfather. That makes a lot more sense," Lydia said happily. Since the doctor's description of her death had not been included in the inquiry report, Lydia was pleased she had taken a chance with writing the letter. Sometimes you just never knew what would happen.

"After Katherine, I moved into the next book. Mildred was next. My great-grandfather wrote her name as Millie. Another one he knew fairly well I guess. She is noted as 'Found in bed, could not be aroused. No signs of suffocation or saliva around mouth. Doctor could not find trauma. Three. Something wrong. Need to talk with Capt. Bower regarding this.'"

"So your great-grandfather started to clue in. I suppose when you see so much death things start to stand out when you least expect it huh? Millie must have triggered his memory. Does it say whether he ever talked to the Captain?"

"No and I looked too. I did find the death notes for Captain Bower and his wife Silla though if you're interested."

Would she be interested? Heck yeah!

"Oh yes, am I interested!" Lydia had started taking notes as soon as she had put the juice in the fridge. She dug up a permanent marker, and the back of a garage sale flier to write her notes on. She never could find a decent pen, or piece of paper when she needed it.

"Well Captain Bower died of a heart attack. That was confirmed by his bluish coloring, and my grandfather, he had started working here at the time, was having a hard time making him look natural. Doesn't that sound awful?" Brad said sounding slightly troubled. Lydia got the feeling that the mortuary business might not be his cup of tea. "My grandfather also noted that Silla his wife, didn't want him to be handled any more than necessary, and that she wanted to be in the room during the preparation. My grandfather made an additional note that he'd discouraged her but she insisted."

"Wow that took guts didn't it?" Lydia said finishing her statement with a whoosh.

"Sure did. My dad was impressed too. He told me he had met only one other person who wanted to be there during the preparation. He said today wasn't like the old days, where the family did everything from cleaning to preparing the body for burial. Back then the burial was swift because there was no embalming, and if there was a viewing it was immediate. That all changed with the advent of mortuaries. To be honest I can't

An Old Fashioned Murder

see why anyone would want to be there for something like that anyway, unless they had a morbid curiosity or something."

"Was there anything specific about Silla when she died?" Lydia asked crossing her fingers.

"Not about how she died, but what she requested. To me this was kind of nasty but my dad said it was done occasionally. She stipulated that when she died, Mildred was to be moved to a family plot her parents had in the Saylesville town cemetery. It was then requested that Amelia be moved from beside the Captain, and placed in that empty plot that Mildred would vacate, which was next to Katherine. She was then to take Amelia's place, and her stone, being Silla that is, was to match identically to his. They were all buried in the Methodist cemetery which is across the road from the church."

"Damn. Why am I surprised?" Lydia said into the phone. She immediately apologized. "I'm sorry, that was rude of me."

"Nah, I've said worse. I could say worse about her but then that wouldn't be very Christian like now would it. My dad said I need to watch my language especially if I am going to be a minister. The congregation wouldn't care for my expletives." Brad laughed.

"Not going into the mortuary business?" Lydia asked not surprised.

"Nah, my older brother Todd is. I'm outta' here. Methodism here I come. That's if I graduate and all. Two more years of college and then my dad said I could make my final decision."

"Good for you," Lydia meant it too. It was nice to talk to someone focused on his or her goals. Beth was like that, and she counted her blessings each and every day. Lydia saw so many kids at the community college that weren't even remotely sure what they wanted and basically wandered aimlessly through life.

"Well thank you Brad for your time. Can we send you anything in reimbursement for your efforts, and the phone call?"

"No, I enjoyed this. And don't worry about the phone call it's all a part of the business. It was kind of fun and way more interesting than taking messages and quoting prices over the phone. I copied all the pages for you. My dad said that was all right since you were inquiring on behalf of a relative. I'll get those pages in the mail for you tonight." Brad said. She could hear him shuffling papers. Lydia figured he was probably getting ready to go home, since it was three hours ahead there. "I hope I was able to help. If you need anything else, please call me. I'll include my dad's business card inside. I'm here from ten to six normally. Since there was a viewing tonight, I had to stay to lock up, so I thought I would call."

"Oh Brad…thanks so much. You have no idea how much this helps!"

Chapter Eleven

Muriel, who was back in town called Lydia to see if she could drop the files by the house later that evening. Lydia couldn't wait to hear what Muriel's impressions were of the Bower household. She also couldn't wait to share the conversation she'd had with Brad, hoping it might prompt some more ideas.

When the doorbell rang Lydia ran to the front door before the kids, or cats could get there first. She took Muriel into the living room and shut the French doors so they could talk in quiet.

Muriel handed Lydia the photocopies.

"Tell me what you were so excited about when I called?" Muriel asked. She had just come from the gym, and was still in her sweats. The gym had a senior's yoga class on Thursday nights that Muriel enjoyed going to. It was less impact on her joints and she liked the instructor, who was in his thirties and blond. When Lydia had feigned shock, Muriel reminded her that aging didn't mean you were dead.

Muriel sat and listened, nodding as Lydia relayed the information that Brad, the future minister, had imparted on her. Lydia also filled her in briefly on the information she had found so far in the newspapers as well.

"You have been busy." Muriel commented. "Let me throw out some of my ideas and see whether it matches yours." Muriel had made a list so she wouldn't forget anything. She sat tapping her head with the pen. "Senior moments, have to make notes now so I don't forget stuff."

"What's my excuse?" Lydia asked laughing.

"Three children, full time job, and the eccentrics at the society…do it to anyone. Okay, let me lay out what I came up with, this is my own interpretation mind you," Muriel said as she settled in. From what Lydia could tell by her relaxed posture, her interpretation was going to take a while. "As noted, Melissa's life, and death was pretty straightforward. She died of a disease that was just about everywhere back then."

"Right…" Lydia agreed. She knew Muriel liked to tackle items in order but Lydia felt she could leave out the "known stuff," simply to save time. But then for Muriel leaving out the extraneous stuff would simply ruin her tale. So Lydia let her continue without interruption, no matter how painful the experience might end up being.

"She was his sweetheart." Lydia nodded. "And from the information in Julia's family files, his father set up the business for him so he could take care of his future family. But her age when they married made me think he really just strung her along for a while, business or not. According to the mercantile history you found, he wasn't that great of a businessman but with his wife and clerks doing most of the work." Muriel checked off the first note.

"Sounds right so far," Lydia agreed.

"Now then…Melissa dies leaving two children. So the Captain needs a wife and starts the he-man hunt. Now I couldn't tell if he actually attended the local Methodist church, or just the wives did…" Lydia went to interject but Muriel held up her hand. "You never know…it could have been that he didn't even go there right? He did marry at home the first time; maybe not his religion, or he converted after his wife's death."

Lydia looked at Muriel with pleading eyes. It was getting late and re-hashing the family history wasn't helping her keep her eyelids open. It had been a long day and getting longer by the minute.

Muriel took the hint and continued. "So back to topic at hand…he marries wife number two, Amelia, who as we know was single…never married before. She's young by today's standards but back then just the right age to take care of children, work the store, and then bear a few more children…okay so far?"

"Right as rain." Lydia wasn't seeing anything new in the story so far but then Muriel wasn't done yet either.

"Onward. Wife number two produces more children as expected...she's found dead in the barn. No trauma that anyone can find, just flat out on the ground," Muriel clicked her tongue. "That feels off to me. It sounds like some kind of heart condition...maybe a stroke, or an aneurysm; things which we only know about now; but then I'm not a doctor either. Too bad you can't get the doctor's records on her before she died. The symptoms might be the same as Katherine's."

"Good point. Hadn't thought of it but would they even be around anymore?" Lydia asked.

"Check the phone book, or talk to that young man at the mortuary's dad. Sometimes records went to the new physician, sometimes they were destroyed, and sometimes they went to the mortuary if there wasn't anyone else interested."

"Made a note..." Lydia said, although she decided she would only pursue that avenue if she had to.

"Now as for Katherine...we know her parents were farmers, and just like Amelia the child was older at marriage. I wonder if she was homely or shy?" Muriel asked to no one in particular. "Personally I think I might have been wary of him, even though it was only one seemingly odd death. But then if she didn't want to be viewed as a spinster, and he was her only offer, she probably jumped at the chance. As for the Captain, repeat performance. He's looking for someone to take care of children, and give him more — not too old not too young. And he isn't looking to get too attached since he's been a widower twice. Maybe the circumstances harden his perspective and expectations; especially if he was forced to settle down by necessity. For some reason, I see him more as a 'former" romantic. He felt he did what he needed to marry the woman of his dreams, and then she died, and so did his dreams. I mean whoever wrote that history, or whatever you call it, said he wouldn't come out of the house for days."

"A valid point. That description doesn't sound like a killer does it? But how he reacted to the others deaths and mourning is unclear."

"Very true dear." Muriel soothed. "I was devastated when Larry died, just about killed me. Then I met Joe, and everything changed. I still had a hole in my heart, but the rest of it was filled again for twenty wonderful years. But when Joe died, I had been down that terrible road, and my adjustment...the mourning was different. People probably thought I was cold. I was just resigned to the fact I was not meant to be with anyone, and I adjusted to it. I will not marry again because I can't, and won't be in that position again. I have two wonderful children, and three terrific grandchildren. There is no reason for me to marry again but there was for the Captain whether he wanted to or not."

At that moment Lydia knew why she admired Muriel so much. It was because she was honest, and loving, and understanding, for the people in the present, as well as the past. There were a lot of people who could take lessons from this lady.

"So you think maybe the Captain, having been burned twice, just decided to shut down emotionally instead of getting hurt again?" Lydia reiterated. "And since he married again only because he had to, he didn't care who it was, as long as they fit his criteria. He seemed so cold and worked them so hard. Didn't he care how he appeared to the whole town?"

"Who knows? The way the neighbors told it, the Captain was already hard hearted before he married Katherine. It is quite possible Melissa's death ruined him for anything that might be remotely good. Maybe he didn't care what the town thought, nor did he care what his wives thought." Muriel adjusted herself on the couch and put her foot on the ottoman near the window.

"Talk about dysfunctional." Lydia remarked.

"Dysfunctional is relative." Muriel assured her in all seriousness. "Now it seemed like he worked a lot, at least early on. It isn't too clear what he did after Melissa died but it sounds like he must have made himself scarce to both business and home. I think that was so he wouldn't be in the home he built for the wife who was gone, with another woman taking her place..." Muriel held up her hand as Lydia opened her mouth. "...Whether he put that woman in the

An Old Fashioned Murder

house or not. That of course wasn't going to stop him from his husbandly duties. Obviously."

"Obviously. What do you think about the notes the mortician made. The doctor and the mortician thought the deaths were odd but couldn't explain why. Do you think the Captain, assuming he didn't do it, thought it was odd too?"

"Hard to say. He may not have thought about it until Katherine's parents brought it to the attention of the sheriff, and if what you said is correct, they may not have even thought about it, except for the fact the mortician brought it to their attention." Muriel mused. "Here's one for you. Why didn't the issue get brought up again when Mildred died?" Muriel asked as she checked off two more lines on her list.

"As for that, we don't know it didn't. Not all the facts are in yet." Lydia reminded her.

"One other tact for you to take, see if you can find the court record that *shows* the children being transferred to the grandparents. That will tell you if he fought for custody of his children, or if he just let them go. That might show how much compassion he had left inside of him."

"I can't believe I hadn't thought of that one! I could kick myself! Especially after reading the announcement of their removal in the paper."

"That's what genealogy is all about. You never finish putting the pieces together."

"That's what I am afraid of..."

"Eh, you'll solve this one," Muriel assured her. "Now finally we get to Mildred who we know died in her sleep. She was another replacement, same age range, possibly same circle of friends. Why would anyone advise this girl to marry him, especially with his track record, God only knows. With small town talk, I am positive that she knew what had been up. She was a town girl too, right?" Lydia nodded. "...It was another silent death, another question mark. And what gets me is the man marries again after her. But he breaks his pattern on the last one, and marries his loyal clerk who is considerably older than the others, closer to his deceased first wife's age, and therefore not of child bearing age. Did he give up on younger women dying on him, or maybe he figured an old one might actually outlive him?" Muriel crossed off another line. She looked at Lydia. "Did he really love her...or, did she wait and finally nail him? She wasn't so old she couldn't take care of a child."

"I thought about that. Faye and I discussed that whole issue the other day in fact. We wondered if she was waiting in the wings the whole time ourselves. But the big question is — what did she do to convince a man, who married younger women, to even look at her—to even consider someone who had *worked* for him for all those years?" Lydia asked.

"Blackmail?"

❖

Lydia thought about that final statement of Muriel's for several days after. It was possible the Captain just never saw Priscilla in that light — as a wife. He saw her as an employee certainly, someone he could trust with the store. Lydia thought looking at the Captain's pattern, that he would have married someone younger; not only because of the children but because he was looking for someone energetic enough to help at the store. But then Silla had already proved herself there, hadn't she?

But as Lydia and Muriel speculated, with his track record and the undeniable gossip regarding the deaths of his former wives, no one in their right mind would want to take a chance and marry him. Priscilla may have been the only one left. And the ironic thing was, of all of them, she was the one to outlive him by a good twelve years.

Lydia realized that she never revisited the cause of death notation for Priscilla with Brad. He'd just said there wasn't anything unusual notated, and that the Captain had died of a heart attack.

So when Lydia got the package in the mail from Brad that morning, she sorted through the photocopies looking for Silla's entry. Lydia found it with the notation Brad had mentioned about the moving of the stones but nothing about the cause of her death. The death records Lydia had ordered ended with 1909. Lydia knew that neither the Captain nor

Silla's death records would be on that film. There hadn't been a cause of death listed in either of their obituaries that Julia had provided her either. When the time came she would have to go through the historical society for that one since they held the death records from December 1908 to December 1944.

Muriel's suggestion of blackmail still bothered Lydia. The only thing that Lydia could come up with was that possibly Silla may have figured out that the Captain had something to do with the deaths. Maybe something tipped her off, she confronted him, and he confessed. But then that would be too much like the movies. Or did Silla find some evidence in the store to make her suspicious? There was nothing in the journals that really stood out so it would have had to come from somewhere else. He wasn't home when Amelia and Katherine died, and it wasn't clear whether he was there during the death of the third wife.

So Lydia decided it was time to look at obituaries, ones other than the Captain's and Silla's. Lydia figured it best to check through the stack of information once more for any additional clippings before she ordered any more film from the Ohio Historical Society's Newspaper Archive. She wanted to check for Amelia, Katherine and Mildred's obituaries in the stack one more time as well since she hadn't located them when she was searching for the articles on their deaths. None of the death announcements had been written as "official" obituaries, so there was always the chance that when she had rushed through the papers looking for a mysterious cause of death, she had simply missed them. At this juncture though, Lydia really wanted to double check the obituary for Priscilla.

In hindsight, she may have written her own.

❖

Lydia made the trek to the Tri-Cities library the following Sunday. At least one Sunday every month Lydia got the whole day off, and Muriel came in instead. But the night before Muriel called in a panic. Her sister had taken ill again and Muriel needed to head back to Arizona. Lydia had no trouble saying yes, especially since Muriel had bailed her out on more than one occasion in the past. So Lydia called Faye right after to ask if she could meet her at the library instead of home. Lydia had wanted Faye to go over the mercantile journal independently of her, just to see if there were any clues she might have missed.

In the meantime, Julia called to report that she had called her cousin to see if Uncle Daniel was still cognizant enough to meet and talk with them. Her cousin assured her that although he was somewhat wheelchair bound, his mind was as sharp as a tack and she thought the visit would do him a world of good. Lydia told Julia she would check with Lance to make sure he was free to watch Sarah. Julia then volunteered that Karen would drive them, and then hang out at a local coffee shop until they were finished. Since Karen had been working weekends and traveling so much she just wanted to get away for a few hours without any commitments, and a nice drive was what she had in mind.

Lydia thought that was very kind of Karen. She was pleased to know that Karen was still supporting her grandmother; and offering to drive them was a nice way of doing so, without having to do research or run errands.

Lydia followed her usual routine when she arrived at the library. She opened the doors and windows, turned on the copy machine and coffee pot, and then fed the stray cat that hung around. They called her Scooter. She was a gray striped ball of fluff, and as sweet as could be. They figured she had been a house cat and abandoned in the park about the time the house was moved to its location. Scooter was scared of most people, except for Lydia, Muriel and another volunteer Barb, who wasn't there except maybe once or twice a month.

After a while, two people came in. One was Mr. Parsons a former policeman, who worked as a security guard for extra income to help supplement his retirement, and a young girl. Lydia approached her to ask if she needed help. They didn't have a big library but if you weren't sure what you were looking for it could be intimidating.

"May I help you?" Lydia asked. The girl looked to be about seventeen, with bright blue eyes and long brown hair, which was pulled back into a ponytail. She held a notebook and pencil in one hand, and was carrying a bright orange backpack. Lydia figured she was probably there for the genealogy project required of the life skills class taught at the high school. They'd had a number of the students in the library over the years, and Lydia could usually spot them when they walked in. In Lydia's day the project was done in a home economics class, and it was called family life. That was how Lydia had gotten started doing her own genealogy but back then she had nowhere to go nearby to do research. This generation was much more fortunate when doing such assignments. There were so many places to go to find the information both physically and online.

"Yeah, my teacher told me to come here for help. We're doing a project for class and I have to come up with three to four generations of family. I need to work on both sides but I'm having problems with my dad's, and need some direction," she seemed shy and spoke hesitantly. "My parents are divorced and my dad lives up in Oregon and my mom won't talk to me about his family. I really don't want to turn in just one side of the page Mr. Thompson gave me...you know...half a report. So I wondered if you could help me?"

"First off, you need some kind of base to start working. Things like names and places and so on. So for that you will need to contact your dad or his parents if they are living." Lydia knew this might be a touchy subject but if she did want to work her dad's side that basic information was a necessity. "Have you tried calling and talking to your dad?" Lydia prodded. Divorced families were hard especially when relations between the parents were still touchy.

"I tried but his girlfriend kept answering the phone and I felt awkward. She's why my dad left and I didn't want my mom to know. That's when I asked mom, hoping I could avoid calling my dad again, but she wouldn't talk to me about it, other than to say my grandparents were dead and to just tell the teacher I couldn't find out anything."

Oh boy, Lydia thought, this could require a counselor to mediate. After a moment of thought, Lydia had an idea, and walked the girl over to her desk.

"First off tell me your name. My name is Lydia," she said, trying to put the girl at ease. The poor thing almost looked like she was ready to cry.

"Amber...Amber Clark."

"Okay Amber, lets do this. Do you have your dad's phone number on you?"

"Yeah. It's right here," Amber opened her binder and pulled out a tiny sheet of torn paper. Lydia could tell it had been used often because it was all wrinkled.

"With your permission, let me try and get your dad. This way you don't have to talk to his girlfriend, and your mom won't be upset with you for calling. I know that sounds bad, and we're kind of fudging here, but this is really between you and your dad, not anyone else. If he chooses not to talk with you that will be his decision, okay?"

"Okay." Amber agreed. She seemed relieved to have someone take over the task. There was no tug of war with this scenario, and Amber ought to get what she needed without anyone pulling her in either direction.

Lydia dialed the phone. She made a mental note to reimburse the society for the long distance call. Usually Lydia had a calling card on her but it was at home on the dresser. Lance had used it on his last trip and Lydia hadn't put it away yet. After about four rings a woman answered the phone. Lydia tried to use her best professional voice.

"Hello, this is Lydia Proctor from the Tri-Cities Genealogical Society Library in California, and I am calling on behalf of Amber Clark. She's working on a school project, and would like to speak with her father on some issues she needs clarified for her assignment."

There was dead silence on the other end of the phone. Lydia was wondering what was the woman thinking? Hang up? Answer? Pretend she didn't mean to pick up the phone?

Lydia patiently waited for a response. Finally a choked answer came out. "He's at work. Why didn't Amber call herself?" She asked hesitantly. Lydia felt like she was reliving her call from the Historical Society, the day Julia had contacted her. Except this time she was on the other end. The whole scenario didn't seem so strange anymore.

"Amber found it uncomfortable to call because of the situation between her parents', and to be honest, she didn't want her mother to overhear her talking with you," Lydia decided to be straight with the woman, she had nothing to

An Old Fashioned Murder

lose. "With the assignment being due, she came to the society looking for help on the recommendation of her teacher. Unfortunately without basic information I can't guide her in the right direction. So I'm trying to help her by being the middle person." Lydia looked at Amber and she nodded.

"I wish I had known. I thought they were hang-ups. Let me give you his number and Amber can call him directly. Tell her I'm so sorry. We truly didn't mean to put her in the middle like this." The woman sounded honestly apologetic, but there was nothing for Lydia to say. That was for Amber to hear directly from her father and mother.

Lydia wrote the number down, and passed the piece of scratch paper across to Amber. "I'll pass this number along. Thank you for your help." Lydia said as she hung up.

"Mom wouldn't even give me his work number. She said it was only for emergencies. I think she just didn't want me talking to him," Amber started to twirl her long brown hair around her finger. "I'll call him, get the information, and turn the assignment in. Mom never checks my homework so she'll never know. I tried to tell her it was my family too, not just her and grandpa but she wouldn't listen. She's so mad at him."

"Divorce can be a bad situation." Lydia consoled. Even though she hadn't personally experienced it, she knew of someone who had, and how hard it had been on her. "My girlfriend went through something similar when she was your age, and her parents were at odds until the day her father died. She was allowed to talk with him but it took a long time, so don't give up." Lydia smiled and stood up. "What I would recommend though is that you be honest and tell your Mom you talked with him. You don't want it coming out in the wash later and have her angry with you too. Just tell her you came to me, and we called around till we got his work number so you could speak directly to him. It's not a total lie. She may not be happy you did it but she'll be relieved that you didn't talk directly with his girlfriend." Lydia knew deep down what they had done was wrong but she didn't want to turn the poor girl away either. Amber was more in the middle than Lydia could ever be. She just hoped that the mother didn't go gunning for her later. Nasty divorces like this certainly brought out the worst in people. Especially the woman scorned.

"I'll go home and call him now. Mom's at work and my sister's at camp so I can talk without interruption. I'll use the calling card in my dresser from camp last year. I promise I will tell her. I just want to do this part first, and then tackle her last…One parent at a time."

Chapter Twelve

Before Amber left, Lydia showed her some places to search on the Internet to help her on her way. She also told her that once she had some basic information that she should come back and either Lydia or Muriel would help her. She figured with the challenge Amber had facing her, she trusted Muriel the most beside herself to guide Amber and understand her needs. Not that the other volunteers couldn't, she just wanted someone that she knew for sure would be compassionate, in case another crisis arose later.

Just as Amber left, Faye came in and dropped her bag on the table. One bad habit that Faye had was that she took her original documents with her—everywhere. Lydia had tried talking her out of it for ages, even promising to show her how to cite her documentation in her computer program, that way she would still have the basic information but be able to leave the kitchen sink home. So far she was having little success.

Mr. Parsons looked up from the book he was buried in and smiled at Faye. He was a good-looking man. Distinguished is how Muriel described him, on more than one occasion Lydia noticed, for being in his late sixties. Tall and lean with gray hair, he always neatly dressed in Dockers pants, and a variety of golfing shirts. He was good-natured and polite but you could feel the cop in him when he talked genealogy. He looked at genealogy like a case that would never end, which didn't bother him much since he enjoyed the chase as much as the capture of the suspect.

Mr. Parsons had been one of Faye's strongest supporters when she decided to apply for the police academy. He was also the one that recommended she meet the son of a former partner as well, who was also on the force. It ended up being not only a career change for Faye but also a match made in heaven. So whenever he was there, and Faye came in, they would catch up on who was working on what and where.

Lydia gave them a few moments to talk, heading over to her desk to wait. A few minutes later Faye politely excused herself, and then headed over to where she had unceremoniously dropped her bag.

"So what's up girlfriend," Faye asked, drawling out the girlfriend part.

"Very street, where did you get that one?"

"Actually MTV or VH1 I think. It's always good to see what the teens are up to; especially when you are spending more time arresting them, than home with your spouse," Faye sounded a little glum.

"You're not getting discouraged are you?" Lydia asked concerned.

"Not really. Scott's just on a different schedule than I am, and we only see each other for a couple hours. I've been working longer shifts in juvie because some of the guys are on vacation, so that couple of hours has been more like fifteen minutes. The shifts switch again this week, so that should change. I hope I go back to adult offenders, they're easier to accept in a way than the kids," she brushed the hair from her face as she leaned over to pull out her laptop and binder. "I knew this wasn't a nine to five when I took it on, it just hits home when you have another person in the house. Glad I don't want kids, they would have to raise themselves, and then I would end up arresting *them* for loitering or theft."

"I still think you would have made an okay mom but I understand how you feel. And don't beat yourself up about how they would've turned out. I would have gone over at least once a day to let them out and feed them, you know that." Both Lydia and Faye laughed at the unlikely scenario.

Faye had come from a divorced home where her father was gone more than he was around. Essentially she had been raised by her step-dad who had died a few years ago, about the time Lydia's mom had passed. Just as Faye was figuring out her father and some fences were being mended he died.

Faye had never gotten resolution, and after a long period of introspection, decided that the relationship with her father would cloud anything she ever had with a child of her own. She was forty now, and knew if she was going to make a decision it had to be soon. But with the recent change in career, and the demanding schedule that was part of being a police person, it gave her the ultimate reason not to have any. Scott, who had been married previously and the father of two teenage boys wasn't as concerned about having anymore children, especially since those two were heading off to college in just a few short years. So the decision had worked out well for them both. Faye's mother on the other hand was not at all pleased with the situation, and made sure to mention that displeasure on a regular basis. Lydia knew it was ultimately her friend's decision and wasn't her place to try and change her mind. Faye was a great stepmother, as well as a great aunt to her brother's children, and that was just as important.

"Well look at the bright side you have a challenging job, great spouse, cool stepsons and me for a best friend, you just can't go wrong."

"Yeah, yeah, yeah...so show me this journal so I can finish and then work on my own problems." She sat herself down pulling her chair closer to the desk. The expression on Faye's face was like a lion waiting for the kill. Lydia wasn't so sure if she wanted her to work on the journal after all; she might rip it to shreds.

"Thanks a heap. No more positive reinforcement for you. You can just wallow in your own misery for all I care!" Lydia pulled out the leather journal and gingerly passed it over to Faye.

"I just might do that miss high and mighty. Show me what you need."

❖

A few moments later after Lydia had everything out and arranged, the two of them huddled over the journal.

"It just looks like codes, or a really weird shorthand to me but then what do I know." Lydia threw her hands into the air. "I called the main branch library and asked for the microfiche for Chillicothe on temporary loan. I even paid extra for twenty-four hour delivery."

Since Lydia knew the librarian through networking, there wasn't a problem as long as all the pieces were returned. Otherwise there was a charge of ten dollars per lost fiche.

"Okay, so what do I do with the fiche?"

"Didn't you take code breaking 101 in the police academy?" The look on Faye's face pretty much shut that joke down. "Fine...First look over the journal and see if you come up with the same information I have." Lydia passed Faye the legal pad she had written her notes on. "Then use the city business directory, and check the listings to see if any of these abbreviations match names of businesses in the city. Knowing how frugal the Captain was, he probably wouldn't send too far for supplies because the cost would be prohibitive. It would have to travel by train, or rented wagon, which would cost money. If it wasn't too far, he could easily take a wagon of his own and visit the suppliers himself, load up the wagon and bring it home saving a ton of money and time."

"So how does this help?" Faye asked. The look on her face suggested that she had better things to do with her time than chase down mercantile suppliers for the hell of it. The angry lion look was returning.

"You don't have to do all of them," Lydia said exasperated. "I just want you to concentrate on the time frame around each death, from maybe the year before, and then right after. I am looking for something he could have used to kill his wives. Something used medicinally, like an herb, or a root...whatever."

"Oh, I get where you're going with this. It's hard to tell what he bought, so by searching the supplier and matching it to the supplies noted you could make sure that he wasn't hiding anything lethal. Making sure he was on the up and up right?"

"Pretty much, and all I needed was someone with a truly suspicious mind. That's you." Lydia smiled as sweetly as she could.

"Fine. I take it clothiers and barrel makers aren't a concern?"

"Not unless there is something coming in the barrel that looks suspicious."

"I hate to say it but most everything they used back then was suspicious, and would probably be on a poisonous or environmentally unfriendly list now."

"Yes, I know. But there were roots and extracts that in mass quantities could make someone very sick and kill them. I have been searching the Internet a little..." Lydia smiled and patting herself on the shoulder. "...I just hope the FBI doesn't come after me for planning a murder..." Lydia shuddered and continued on.

"Searching for bomb parts maybe, poisonous plants...doubtful," Faye shook her head in exasperation.

"As for those items...on the surface it would look like they were being purchased for some back home, cure all type, remedies, which was done all the time. And like I said they would probably be made into tea or poultices, which from the searching I've done, somewhat supports that thought. But some, if ingested in large or frequent doses were fatal. He's a merchant, right. Who better to carry, and or use such products and not be suspected?"

"My God, you're getting like me. Want to join the force?"

"Which side? Empire or the Rebel Alliance?"

❖

They worked steadily for about an hour. Faye was seated at the table by the south wall with the fiche reader, journal and a note pad. Lydia became even busier when two more visitors came in both of which were new to the library, so she never got around to working on her own family at all. It was just about closing when Faye finally pushed her chair back, looked around and stretched her neck. Lydia hadn't heard a peep from her all afternoon which worried her. Maybe her theory was off base or Faye was *really* ticked at her.

Lydia let the last person out and then locked the door behind them. She turned the open sign to closed and pulled the rolling shade down in the window. They had planned to stay after closing and work for a bit longer. Staying later wasn't a problem since Lance was home with the kids. Lydia also figured she owed Faye some uninterrupted research time for helping her with this fairly frustrating project.

She decided to kill some time, so she went back to re-shelve some books. A little while later she heard Faye's raised voice.

"The patent medicines were bought in Chillicothe as you thought. A company called Potters Friendly Medicines sold him two crates before each death. Since the inventory isn't with this I cannot say how much came in a crate, how much was *used* or, how much he sold. I can't even tell if he picked it up, or it was delivered." Faye pointed at the item on the journal page she was referring to. "Now I did notice that there was no supplier in the directory for any of the herbal items that were purchased. I thought maybe those might be from a local farmer. Since he was money conscious, that would be a low overhead, no middleman and would save him money."

"Any hints as to who it was?" Lydia asked.

"Only one. There are initials, three letters and the same each time, so I would check the Saylesville directory for someone with those initials in a rural setting. That's assuming they could afford to be in the directory."

Faye rolled her head and a pop came from the back of her neck. "Fresh roots would probably be more appealing, especially if people were using them for home remedies."

Lydia nodded in agreement.

"Anything in the barrels that looks suspicious?"

"Other than whisky, rum, and some medicinal alcohol? Nope. You were right on with that one. I didn't see anything that looked out of the ordinary. Unless he was smuggling in something like opium, or some other illegal substance, which I doubt, everything looks fine," Faye stood. "I did do one thing though. I made a list of all the roots and herbs that were noted in the journal, for the time period you asked about. I figured you could take those, along with the list you made, and use your Internet skills to search each one to see how lethal they can be."

"That's exactly what I had planned. I'll want to see what they were used for normally first and then head to the covert after." Lydia explained. Thinking more to herself but expressing it out loud she asked, "Could he have done it over a long period of time, making them sick but not killing them. Like Munchausen's syndrome?"

"That is a possibility. But how would he know what the adverse uses could be. He would have to be a skilled, or at least knowledgeable herbalist to administer it, otherwise they would have died immediately." Faye tapped her pencil on the table. Something that always told Lydia she was thinking productively. "Sounds to me more like a woman's method for murder, if you ask me."

"But there weren't any women around, just children— unless the Captain found someone willing to show him what to do."

"Doubtful, that would have been risky. Unless they were accessories to the crime, I can't imagine someone not thinking it odd, that he was inquiring about ingredients for home remedies. No, I hate to say it but that was a female's domain. Other than his figuring out how to subtly feed poison into their systems, there is no evidence pointing to his doing it." Faye shook her head. "Notice I said *his* doing it. Once again, could there have been someone else?"

"I just don't know. So I'll keep on looking."

❖

Lydia kept that tidbit Faye had thrown out in the back of her mind. She had to admit it went along with her earlier thoughts that the weapon might be poison. She then thought about the family structure and the dynamics. If it was someone, other than Andrew himself, who could it possibly be?

She started with the oldest child first. Lydia pulled out the family group sheet for the Captain and Melissa with the pictures attached. There was a sepia print of Lissa, which showed a sweet young girl; slightly chubby with braids and a white three-quarters length dress. Looking at the innocence of the picture, Lydia just couldn't see her as a murderer. But then Lizzie Borden had looked normal too.

What did a murderer look like?

Lydia supposed that Lissa could be a suspect but she was really just a teenager at the time of both Amelia and Katherine's deaths. Lydia wondered if there was an age when Lissa would have been considered old enough to be trained in the art of preparing herbal remedies; and if not formally trained, would she have known what the different herbs and roots were used for, and the consequences for using too much. Of course the big question was—if it was Lissa, why only three stepmothers and not all four. What was so special about Priscilla, other than being her father's employee? But then Lydia reminded herself that Priscilla was the one Lissa took the children to when Katherine was dying. Some sort of bond maybe?

Before putting aside the picture and family group sheet on Lissa, she double-checked that Lissa was twenty-two by the time Mildred died. That put her as a possible suspect. Lydia knew that usually by that age, most young women were married and out of the house. Sometimes there was a daughter that stayed to take care of the folks but that wouldn't have been an issue for Lissa since there were still young children at home, and a new stepmother in the wings to take over the care of the household.

As a point of reference, Lydia dug around and found a loose picture of Silla and the Captain together. It looked to have been taken when they were a much older couple. Silla seemed to be fairly short in comparison to the Captain. Physically lean, her face was narrow with pinched eyes, a large nose and puckered mouth; her hair bun almost as big as her head. The Captain on the other hand was tall and lank with a mustache. His hair was salt and pepper and he sported a pair of pincer nose glasses.

Lydia stared at the picture in wonderment. Even as a young woman Silla would not have been considered a beauty, as an old woman, she was almost troll-like in her features. Lydia wondered what the Captain—who by all standards would have been considered somewhat dashing, even as an old man—saw in her.

Hopefully Lissa hadn't followed in her stepmothers' footsteps, marrying later in life. If she had, then Lissa would be on the "list" for sure. To solve the issue Lydia need a good look at the census. The family group sheets Julia's mother and uncle had written out had not included the children's information past their births.

If Lissa was out of the house on the 1910 enumeration, then she might have married sometime between Katherine's death in 1904, and then. Lydia hadn't gotten to the 1910, or 1920 censuses, so that would be a top priority on her next trip to the Family History Center. If Lissa was out of the house at the time Mildred died, then she was a less likely subject for motive and opportunity. Plus, if Lissa was out of the house, would she have even cared who her next stepmother would be?

The only other children living at home when Mildred died would have been Emma ten, and her sister Mollie eight. To Lydia those two as killers was highly unlikely. Amy and Cyrus were living with their grandparents and according to Julia had little to no contact with the family until they were adults.

The only other possibility, which Lydia felt was a major stretch, was that they were making themselves ill to get the Captains attention. But for all three to do that was highly improbable.

Lydia was back to square one.

Chapter Thirteen

Early the next morning, Lydia called the Saylesville Historical Society. After being on hold for five minutes (and no elevator music to keep her mind entertained with trying to guess the song), she was finally assisted by a gentleman who seemed somewhat distracted. She had to repeat herself several times before he finally zeroed in on what she was looking for. The key to his "getting it" seemed to happen when Lydia had begun shouting into the receiver. She realized then that he was hard of hearing. What a start to the day.

She asked him if there was a town or county history that might contain information on Captain Andrew Bower, and would he be willing to copy it and send it to her. She promised to pay postage as well as copying costs, and then added that she would be sending her business card from the genealogical society, just in case someone ever needed something from sunny California. After some serious prodding she got him to repeat back exactly what she wanted. As she hung up she crossed her fingers and toes for good luck.

Lydia sifted once more through the information that Julia had given her, and low and behold found the obituaries for Amelia, Katherine and Mildred. The reason why Lydia hadn't found them in the Gazette was because they had been published in the Saylesville Monitor. She hadn't been aware of the newspaper's existence because the Ohio Historical Society had not microfilmed it. Lydia figured it was probably one of those one or two page papers that were always trying to compete with their bigger counterparts, and usually didn't succeed.

Finding those clippings had saved her a ton of time and trouble. Now she just needed to stay late at work one more time, go back to the newspaper, and look for a death

An Old Fashioned Murder

announcement for Mildred. She hoped the details would be similar in content to Amelia and Katherine's. On a whim (Lydia liked to call it her little voice talking to her), she had decided to extend the loan on the microfilms. Once again her instincts had been right on target.

Muriel was back from Arizona and decided to stop over at Lydia's on her way back from the gym. This time she was wearing a burgundy satin sweat set that looked very stylish on her. Lydia wondered if there was someone at the gym she might be interested in, even though she would never admit it. Lydia had always figured Muriel to be a tease when she was a young woman. It was highly possible nothing had changed.

Muriel arrived at the house around eight that evening. Lydia ushered her into the living room where Muriel began spreading out her notes. Lydia quickly made a pot of decaf coffee, and then scrounged up some left over tollhouse cookies—left over meaning the kids hadn't eaten them all. Finally they decided to get down to some serious business, and make another list (why did genealogists have so many lists?) of all the people who might be suspects. Lydia thought that was a pretty funny description of a bunch of dead people but then it wasn't turning out to be the typical family history she was helping to put together either.

Before Muriel had arrived Lydia called Julia and asked if she wanted to join them. She was the main reason for the meeting, and Lydia felt she should be there to listen or even give input. Julia was absolutely thrilled at the prospect, and decided to come whether her granddaughter was home to take her or not. Since night driving wasn't one of Julia's greater talents, she promised Lydia she would take it slow getting there.

Lydia was positive between the three of them they would be able to make a good suspect list from the information they already had.

Julia got there just a few minutes after Muriel. She declined the last cookie but did take Lydia up on the offer of coffee. Lance had already gone to bed since he had been up at five and home just before the girls arrived at eight. He announced wearily as he walked in the door that another business trip might be in the works. Lydia had said nothing.

The kids were scattered about the house: Beth was watching a movie, Lucas was on the computer upstairs (as always), and Sarah was passed out on the couch, a DVD still playing on the television, and two cats asleep on either side of her. She would have to ask Lucas to help get Sarah upstairs when they finished.

With little distraction, she was sure they could sit and talk, and debate character flaws until they were too tired, or it was too late to continue.

Lydia brought out a yellow legal pad and a pencil. Pen was fine for permanence but she had a feeling that their list of suspects would be moving up and down the list. They decided to do a round robin first. Each one would name a suspect, a motive, and a means, kind of like the game Clue, until they ran out of people. Lydia figured the list would be short since it was limited to a small town, with an even smaller social circle that revolved around the family.

Lydia began the discussion. "Well let's go with the man who started all of this, Captain Andrew Bower."

"Fine." Muriel said as she took a bite of cookie.

Just then the doorbell rang, and they all looked at each other. Lydia hadn't been expecting anyone else. Standing up she walked to the window and looked out. It was then she saw Faye's car in the driveway and Faye at the door dressed in her uniform.

"Well look what the cat drug in," Lydia said as she opened the door. "I assume off duty?"

"Just got off, and decided to stop on the way home. I have some thoughts about who might have done it, and wanted it off my chest before I went home and to bed."

"Come on in and join the club." Extending her arm out, Lydia used a sweeping motion to guide Faye into the house. "Welcome to Nancy Drew and company." She joked as the ladies chuckled.

"Hi," Faye responded a bit stunned. Lydia knew Faye wasn't expecting anyone else to be there.

"Hello," they chorused back. Julia stood, and Muriel waved. Muriel had known Faye for a long time so no introduction was necessary, but Julia and Faye had never met before.

"Faye, this is Julia. She's the lucky person who inherited the unique family I've been working on."

Julia extended her hand to shake, "Nice to meet you. Lydia told me how helpful you have been."

"Let's get to work, I'm an old lady and need my beauty rest," Muriel said, re-directing everyone back to the topic at hand. It was getting late, and although none of them lived too far, it was still best to get a move on.

"We were just starting a Clue like pattern, with a suspect, a motive, and a means. I had just thrown the Captain on the table," Lydia explained briefly.

"Can't I just toss mine out so I can go home and sleep? I have two days off before I go back on mid-shift, and I plan to sleep the entire time, unless Scott makes it home before I pass out." The ladies smiled knowingly. Lydia attempted to turn the topic back to less risqué things.

"Fine. You can go first. Just hurry up!" Lydia teased. She knew her friend was sleep deprived amongst other things. It was only fair to let her say her peace, and have her move along. They could debate her suggestion after she left.

"I think it's either Lissa, or Priscilla," she stated. Muriel leaned forward and nodded her head. Julia smiled knowingly, and Lydia looked dumb founded; so much for sharing her idea.

"Motive?" Muriel asked. She looked like a kid in a candy store.

"So Lissa would have her father all to herself of course, and for Priscilla same basic motive. I mean had she *really* waited patiently all those years? Or did she just act like it? The means next, right?" Faye asked as she loosened her belt, sat down on the edge of the couch, and ate the last cookie.

"Coffee with that?" Lydia asked sarcastically.

"Not if it's leaded."

"Spare me the cop talk, just ask if its decaf...and yes, it is," Lydia said, as she poured a big mug for Faye and added sugar.

For some reason Faye had taken to drinking it without cream or milk. Lydia figured it must be some kind of identity thing; all the guys at work probably drank it like that too.

"Once again, means." Faye repeated. "Either food or drink. Since the mercantile supplied the dry goods, and some of the herbs and roots for home use. It would probably be pretty easy to simply crush it up and then mix it in."

So Faye had jumped on Lydia's band wagon after all.

"If it was Lissa, her main opportunity would have been during food preparation."

"But wouldn't that make the whole family sick?" Lydia asked.

"She could have doctored just one dish couldn't she?" Muriel asked.

"And as for Priscilla she didn't live there. If she did it, there really wasn't anything that was sent to the house that would have been used solely by one person, right? She would have been risking everyone's life not just the intended victim. Everything was shared," Lydia protested.

"It was just a thought. It could also have been something that the women took only for themselves, a Tea, some coffee, a cough syrup..." Faye defended. Muriel looked at her cup and gently set it down. That gesture did not go unnoticed by Lydia. She was pretty sure it was simply because of the suggestion. She knew she shouldn't be insulted, or should she?

"Okay, I get the point. It's actually a pretty good idea, if we could only find a mention of something that was sent to the house that they specifically ingested. Not the Captain, not the children. So something like castor oil would be out."

Julia who was quietly absorbing the whole discussion finally spoke. "I agree with Faye, I think it was Priscilla too, I don't know why but I just do. Let's face it she was obviously obsessed with my grandfather, and she did get him in the end," Julia took her time trying to get her thoughts together. "Yes...she would have had access to the house, or as Faye suggested it could have come over from the store. Whatever it was made the poor things sick but not so sick it would be noticed right away...not till it was too late. If it had been blatant, that would have set Silla up to get caught, or put suspicion on the Captain...which it eventually did."

Lydia wasn't sure what to do. Agree, disagree? Was it too soon to make a decision when all the facts weren't in yet?

"Keep in mind, there are some things I'm still waiting on," Lydia said as she counted the items off on her fingers. "One is the information from the church, which we may not need now that we have the mortuary information. Two, I need to look at the census to track Lissa's movements. Three, I still need to look at the last roll of newspaper film, and lastly will be our visit with Uncle Daniel. Maybe something will come of those." Lydia took another bite of her cookie. "I still think it could be the Captain. I can't imagine a woman being so cold as to kill three people."

"Remember Lizzie Borden?" Muriel asked.

❖

They eventually did get around to making a list. The Captain was placed at number one, Priscilla two, and Lissa three, nobody four. There wasn't another soul they could think of to put on the list, at least not at that point in time. Muriel, Julia and Faye all voted Priscilla as number one, but acquiesced to Lydia for the fact that the original rumor, and start to this whole venture was the premise that it was the Captain.

As Faye was leaving she stopped and looked Lydia in the eye. "...remember don't discount anyone because of preconceived notions of innocence or frailty because of their sex. That was why Lizzie got off to begin with."

Before Julia left she confirmed with Lydia that the trip to her uncle's was on for Saturday. The goal was to arrive just after lunch when his brain cells had been refueled, and before his nap.

Lydia ran up the stairs to the bookcase, and pulled down the small book she had gotten at a seminar on interviewing. It covered everything from videotaping, to tape recording, to interviewing relatives; especially the elderly. Lydia thought it might help Julia form the questions she needed to ask Uncle Daniel. Lydia couldn't wait to get some additional perspective on the cast of characters, especially from one who remembered Andrew and Silla.

After Muriel and Julia left, Lydia straightened up the downstairs. She had started the dishwasher and then picked-up scattered clothes around the rooms. There were sweatshirts and shoes all over, and a backpack at almost every turn. She scooped up what she could carry, and then laid it by the stairs in the hope the offenders would see their stuff, and make at least an effort to put it away. One could always dream, couldn't they?

Even though Lydia agreed with the premise of poison being the murder weapon (if there was one), it was the thought that Lissa or Silla might be the prime suspect that bothered her. She wanted to think that women were above murder, except under extreme circumstances, like physical abuse, or self-defense. But she knew from the news, and true-life crime books through the last twenty years she had worked at the library, that there were plenty of cold and calculating women out there who had committed murder.

But in this instance, what would someone have to gain from the murder of an innocent woman? Maybe even three innocent women?

If it was the Captain did he want to save face for making poor marital choices, sort of like Henry VIII? Keep killing them off until you marry the right one? If it was the Captain didn't he think of the children, and their loss of a parent? Did he really want to put his reputation on the line by being associated with a string of unusual deaths? Of the three women, not one of them had died of anything considered normal. No typhoid, diphtheria, scarlet fever, TB, childbirth, small pox, snakebite, diagnosed heart trouble, or a plethora of other diseases and conditions that killed.

The Captain could have slipped whatever substance he used into their food when they weren't looking. In some households, depending on social station, the children ate first and the couple ate later, alone. She could have run out to take care of a sibling dispute, or get something missing from the table (since they apparently didn't have household help) and he could have easily slipped it into her drink, or quickly mixed it into her food.

An Old Fashioned Murder

If it was Priscilla, as the other girls thought, what was her motive? Like the others, Lydia could only think of one...getting the Captain. And she would've accomplished that by eliminating her competition. Unlike the Captain though, Priscilla didn't have the same opportunity to slip something into their food or drink—did she?

An opportunity could have arisen during the time when the women worked together in the store but only if all they had eaten lunch together. Otherwise the likelihood of Silla being able to do it was almost non-existent. Lydia recalled the suggestion that Priscilla could have put something into an item that was sent home for use. Once again, maybe something in the mercantile journal would give them a lead in that direction.

Lissa was the third and last option. So what she had a stepmother? Lots of young girls and boys did back then. It wasn't that uncommon. Could it have been the fact each successive mother was getting closer in age to herself? She may have seen them more of a sister figure than parental one? But then, that would be a really poor reason to kill someone. Or, as Faye suggested, did she see them as competition for her father's attentions? Having your own mother is one thing, having to share your father with someone whom you consider a total stranger was another. People have killed over similar situations.

There was something else nagging back in the recesses of Lydia's mind. It was something she already knew but couldn't put her finger on. Lydia looked at the clock. It was very late and she was tired, maybe it would come to her after a good night's sleep.

Friday afternoon, before Lydia left work, she ran the newspaper roll to the time period of Mildred's death, scanning for anything that might mention the event. By the time Mildred had died, it seemed like the paper just wanted to ignore the Bower family altogether. The only thing Lydia actually found was a blurb on the bottom of page three, which stated that during the previous fortnight Captain Andrew Bower's fourth wife Mildred had passed in her sleep. It mentioned a brief service at the Methodist Church and that the funeral would be on Thursday—period. Oh, well Lydia thought, you can't win them all. They already knew she died in her sleep, and even though she was young it wasn't really that uncommon, nothing sensational about it at all. And since there had not been a fuss like after Katherine died, it didn't even warrant the gossip section of the paper.

Her eyes were burning and her back ached. Lydia rewound the roll, placing it back into its box. She grabbed her purse from the floor, pad of paper from the table and then unlocked the periodicals storage cabinet to put the roll of film away. It was only then Lydia realized she was starving.

When Lydia got home, she was surprised to find dinner leftovers sitting on the table; Lance and the kids on the couch watching television.

"Give me the remote," Lucas shouted as he grabbed the remote from Sarah's hand. Lance's head bobbed back and forth, a sure sign he was sound asleep.

"Sarah, how long have you had the TV?" Lydia asked, trying to defuse the situation diplomatically, unlike her son.

"Not long…" She started. Lucas promptly cut her off.

"Since she got home from school. Dad told me I could have it at seven. Stargate is on."

"Sarah, if Dad promised it to Lucas, you need to let it go. He'll give it back after. If you want, why don't you go read for a while?" Lydia offered. Sarah sat on the floor tears streaming from her eyes. Lance's head was still bobbing back and forth.

"I'll come up with you. I need to get stuff ready for tomorrow. You can read and I'll work next to you. How does that sound?" Lydia encouraged.

Sarah nodded briefly and then ran up the stairs toward Lydia's bedroom.

Lydia ate the last of her dinner in a flash and then put her dishes, and everyone else's into the dishwasher. She flipped the switch on the washer and then started up the stairs to join Sarah, whacking Lance in the head as she passed. His head stopped bobbing.

Once she got upstairs she packed up her tape recorder, note pad and pencils, putting all the items into her "Scrappers have more fun" bag. That was something she hadn't done for a while—scrapbooking. After this was all over she would sit down and just crank some pages out.

Sarah was on the bed intently reading one of her chapter books. She hadn't even acknowledged Lydia's presence. Grabbing the file Lydia sat on the bed and flipped through it one more time.

A wave of sadness washed over her for a second. She was beginning to feel that even with all the research they had already done, they weren't getting anywhere. She closed her eyes for only a moment.

For the first time in over a month, Lydia was asleep before eleven o'clock.

❖

A bright and cheery Saturday morning dawned as Lydia rolled herself out of bed. Since she had prepared the night before, all she had to do was grab was her wallet, house key, and jacket once her ride arrived. The doorbell was an alarm for Sarah who would wake knowing someone—Lydia—would be leaving. If Lydia made it out the door before the bell rang she wouldn't have to pry Sarah off in order to leave. She was getting better about the dramatics if she knew the person but when strangers took mommy away it was a whole different ball of wax.

Lance was in the bathroom doing his hour-long morning routine. Rain, shine, weekday, weekend, he never deviated from his ritual. Lydia was the antithesis of a woman. She wanted to get washed, brushed, dressed and out quickly (unless it was something really important or fancy). Her motto was "no fuss, no muss" and she had always been like that. She and Lance in a way were polar opposites but overall they got along extremely well and had similar interests; just not genealogy, sports, or the bathroom. Lydia threw on her beige pants and a blue shirt with wooden beads accenting the neckline. Casual and comfortable.

She made it down the stairs just as a silver BMW pulled up in the front of the house. Lydia knew it wasn't Julia's car and as far as she knew, it wasn't Karen's either. At least not the car she was driving the day she came to the library.

"Nice wheels," Lydia remarked as she shut and locked the door behind her.

"It's my boss's. He's out of town and asked if I would drive it so it wouldn't just sit in his driveway while he was gone. Its not like I would say no, or anything," she admitted smiling.

Lydia was slightly envious because every time she saw Julia or Karen they were always the epitome of class and style. If Lydia had been in the driver's seat of that car, it would not have looked nearly as convincing. Case in point: Lydia noticed that Karen was dressed in a pair of khaki colored yoga pants, a tank top that coordinated with the pants, a light weight jacket and tennis shoes that Lydia could only afford if she sold her first born child. Julia was in a pair of beige tweed pants and a peach cashmere sweater. Her loafers were brown and contemporary, nothing like the shoes Lydia's grandmother used to wear that were clunky looking. Although her style was conservative it wasn't old fashioned.

Lydia would kill to be able to dress like either of them but on the other hand she liked being comfortable. She would never be able to pull off casual chic, nor could she handle tweed. It was a matter of fashion versus comfort. What a sacrifice.

Today at least Lydia knew she would be riding in style, no matter what she was wearing..

Julia leaned her head out of the car and yelled in her tiny voice. "He's a single male, hitting thirty-five...It takes a lot for a man to loan out his car like that. He likes her, and I like him."

"Yes grandma. You liked Ted and Mike too, as I recall," Karen retorted as she opened the trunk for Lydia to put her bag in.

"But neither Ted nor Mike let you drive such an expensive car!"

"Can we go now?" Karen asked as she slid into the driver's seat. It was like the car was almost made for her. Maybe her grandmother wasn't so wrong this time.

"Yes, we can." Julia said as she snuggled down into the seat. "Just don't let this one go without a test drive."

Lydia laughed with her hand over her mouth. She wasn't sure how Karen felt about her grandmother's helpful advice.

"I'll keep that in mind grandma."

Chapter Fourteen

Lydia's house to Uncle Daniel's nursing home was about an hour, to an hour and a half drive, down the packed 405 freeway. The greater Los Angeles area was known for its freeways—all of them notoriously bad. It didn't really matter what time of day; a ten minute drive would end up being a half hour or more depending on traffic, accidents and the simple stupidity of the other drivers zooming by.

Lydia took advantage of the snails pace to kick back in the back seat and watch the scenery roll by. She couldn't believe how many people were in Southern California and how many seemed to keep coming each year. Overall you couldn't beat the climate. Snow in the mountains in the winter; sand and sun at the beach; rain off and on from winter through spring, and mostly hot summers; which were not as bad as some places where severe humidity accompanied the heat.

The scenery and the stop and go had lulled her. Lydia had just started to doze off when they began pulling off the highway. They traveled another mile or two, down a tree lined side road, and then parked in a lot attached to the Mayfair Convalescent Hospital and Assisted Living facility.

Karen walked around and opened her grandmother's door. She then let Lydia into the trunk to get her bag, and walked with them up the stairs to the lobby area. An African-American gentleman sitting at the reception desk looked up from the paperwork he was processing, and greeted them. Julia explained that they were there to see Daniel Bower. After signing in as guests, he escorted them down two different corridors until they reached room thirty-five.

Just inside the door, sitting in a green faux leather recliner near the entrance to the bedroom, was someone who Lydia assumed to be Daniel Bower. The man looked old, with a small comb over, since there wasn't much hair left, and a wrinkly red blotchy face. He was wearing a worn green polo shirt, loose fitting khaki pants, and brown hush puppies shoes. His spry appearance surprised Lydia; but then she asked herself—how does someone who's almost one hundred look?

"Uncle Daniel?" Julia asked hesitantly. Lydia got the feeling from Julia's approach that she wasn't sure it was him or not. The old man looked up into her face and smiled. Lydia noticed that all of his wrinkles seemed to be curling up into that smile.

"No dear, I'm Walt, Danny's in the restroom. I walk him back from lunch and dinner each evening to make sure he settles himself down. I promised his wife Eleanor that I would watch over him while I was still able to. He isn't too steady anymore. He can still walk but he's really slow and falls sometimes, so I'm his guardian angel, I guess. I make sure he stays standing," he chuckled.

At that moment a terribly stooped man emerged from the restroom and glanced over to the company standing in his doorway. He was barely Julia's height and his clothes looked way too big on him, probably because of his stature. He was in a long sleeve plaid shirt, jeans and Rockport shoes.

"Julia?" He asked with a deep rumble in his throat. Julia walked over and took the frail hands into hers. She nodded as she hugged him, recognition on her face. In comparison to his gnarled ones, her hands looked like they were a twenty-year olds.

"Yes, Uncle Daniel." Julia replied. "Are you ready for a visit?"

"Sure am. Walt, you wanna' stay or leave? You're choice."

"I'll leave, just call if you need anything," Walt stood and headed to the door. "Nice to meet all of you." And with that he left them to their chore.

"I guess I should take my leave too," Karen said as she adjusted her purse on her shoulder. "You have your phone grandma, just call when you two are ready to leave. I'll find a coffee place nearby and do some reading while I'm waiting." She leaned over to the man who barely stood five feet and shook his hand. "Nice to meet you uncle, I'll be back later."

"Well have a seat," he gestured to the two chairs by the window, which was set up as a little seating area. The view out the window was a medium sized garden. One room in each corridor appeared to have a view of the gardens. In addition to the seating area, he had a couch and two soft ottomans. Behind the wall, which was really more of a partition, was his twin bed—a hospital issue, and the bathroom across from it. Lydia noticed that neither had doors, which was almost certainly for mobility, or easy access in case of emergency.

Even though he moved slowly, he made good speed. A moment later he plopped himself down in the recliner that Walt had been in originally. Lydia sat at the edge of the couch, and Julia pulled over one of the ottomans, taking a seat beside him.

"It has been a few years…" he said. It wasn't accusatory, just conversational.

"Yes it has. I haven't been doing much traveling since Pat died. Karen was the one who volunteered to drive us here. She has been such a blessing staying with me while she's finishing school, and working. She's off this summer from school and her company's been sending her all over the country on business. This is one of the first weeks she has been home consistently."

"She's a pretty thing, reminds me of you when you were younger," Uncle Daniel remarked, and Julia nodded in agreement. "Now other than seeing how I am, what is it that you need?" He smiled knowingly. For many elderly people visits other than immediate family members were rare unless you were on your deathbed. Even though he had been close to Julia, he could tell with Lydia's presence there that something was up.

"First, let me introduce you to my friend, Lydia Proctor. I should have done that before we sat down, old-timers disease I guess," Julia apologized. Uncle Daniel simply laughed at the irony; a seventy year old telling him about old-timers.

Lydia leaned over and shook Uncle Daniel's hand. It was warm, and from the grip, still pretty strong even with the gnarling. She could see this man lasting another few years if he was careful. He seemed very alert and very positive. "Nice to meet you Mr. Bower."

An Old Fashioned Murder

"Call me Daniel. Pretty girls get to do that," he laughed again. "Really...I'm not being fresh, I just don't see too many young ladies anymore unless they are grandchildren or great-grandchildren, and that doesn't count!" He adjusted himself more comfortably, which because of the softness of the chair, and the smallness of his size, practically swallowed him.

"Well Lydia is helping me with the family history," Julia explained. "And I wanted to know more about Grandpa Bowers' family, especially his last wife Silla. Since you were raised pretty much by both of them, I wanted to hear your experiences growing up."

Fantastic Lydia thought to herself. Julia had read the book that Lydia had loaned her on interviewing. From the sounds of her questions so far she had taken in every word. Julia had also avoided anything regarding the possibly murderous habits of his father. She was setting a positive tone so Uncle Daniel wouldn't shut down.

"Good, I'm glad someone is interested. But do you *really* want to know what they were truly like? You may not want to put some of this into your history."

"Well let's just see where it goes. We can stop whenever you get tired," Julia assured him. "Jennie said you have a lot of stamina but then so do I and I still get tired," she said as she settled herself more comfortably on the ottoman.

Their game plan was that Julia would ask the questions, and Lydia would write down the responses, making it easier on both of them. Since his voice was strong and clear they also asked if they could record him on audio-tape, and he said yes. It would be a good back-up in case they missed something. It would also be something to pass on to his children and grandchildren later on, if what was discussed wasn't too bad.

"Well I remember that they fought all the time. Not just once in a while but several times a day. She would tell him how to run the store and that was when I was old enough to work there. But then she'd turn around and make him a wonderful meal, or clean the house from top to bottom...although I usually got the floors to scrub, and the windows to wash. It was odd because he just wouldn't fight her. He would just get this sad look in his eyes and leave the room. She never verbally attacked me, thank God, but she

141

would go after him with a vengeance." He shook his head reliving the memories.

"When did you leave home for California?" Julia asked. Lydia wanted to know too, because other than Julia's parents he was the only other one to leave the nest in Ohio.

"I was sixteen...didn't even finish upper school. Elias had pretty much taken over the store and I just wanted out. I remember Poppa standing on the porch, looking so lost. He was getting up there in age at that time and I think he wanted me to stay and keep being a buffer between him and Silla but I just couldn't," he sat forward and looked right into Julia's eyes. "I may be sounding petty and mean but to be honest she wasn't my mother—as she told me repeatedly—and didn't act like one either. I think she would have been happy to see all of us off to our maternal relatives if she could."

"Why did your father marry her?" Julia gently asked.

"I think Poppa agreed to marry her for two reasons, although I never had the guts to ask him to confirm it. One was she was his last choice. I don't think anyone in town, or farm trusted him to marry one of their daughters, no matter what age. Secondly, she had proven herself to be loyal and efficient, and that was something he always admired and expected. If you disappointed him by not finishing a chore, or something happened and you were interrupted, he would get as angry as a bull."

"That goes along with what I have learned about him. Was he really that mean and cold?" Julia asked. Her tone was full of disappointment. Like Lydia, Julia was trying to find some sort of humanity in the Captain.

"Yes, but then he could also be as kind as anything. Hot and cold I guess you would say. Funny thing is...she was just like him but in a different way. She could be compassionate and caring to the customers, and then turn around and just rip you up after they left. For Pop...he was honest in that it was his true personality, he was never just mean to be mean, like she was. For Silla it was all show for the town. She wanted them to see how wonderful she was."

Lydia's mind went back to the history of the store, with the reference to the pat on the back for the loyal employees.

An Old Fashioned Murder

So maybe it had been Silla. If so when did she write it? After he died, or did she start it before and never finished it?

"May I ask about her brother Charles?" Lydia asked carefully. She didn't want to derail Julia but she was curious about the other loyal employee of the Bowers Mercantile.

"Him?" He scratched his head and then looked at both of them before he answered. "I was really young when he was around but I remember he was pretty much drunk most of the time. Barely made it to work each morning and he lived in the old house behind the store. I think he only got away with so much because he was her brother, half-brother as I understood it. She was younger by about three or four years but acted like the older sibling. She really babied him. Silla would tell people he was ill, or he had a hard time functioning, but you could smell the alcohol on his breath all the time, when he was standing that is. According to the gossips he had been like that for years. My brother's and sisters said he would sneak bottles of whisky and rum and when the stock got low he would hit the patent medicines, since they were over fifty percent alcohol as it was."

"What did Grandpa Andrew do about it?" Julia asked after she had closed her mouth. It had been hanging open most of the time he was talking. Lydia knew that Julia had no idea how dysfunctional this family really was, until now.

"Not a damn thing. I told poppa too, and I know Elias did as well. Poppa just continued to ignore him, like he did the store. Silla did it all. Pop would make trips into Chillicothe twice a month with his wagon for the big stuff. Later he bought a model-T to pick up the smaller items. I think he did it to get away from her but then Elias and I would get stuck being her lackey's. One good thing I can say about her, she sure could delegate!" He stretched his hands out and wiggled his fingers, probably to keep the circulation moving.

"Do you ever remember either of them, ever saying anything about my mother or the other wives that died?" Julia asked hesitantly. Lydia knew she wanted to get to the subject before she lost him. He seemed like he was getting a little tired, so it seemed best to get to the heart of the matter. They had certainly established that both, Andrew and Silla, had been no angels to deal with.

"When I was about fourteen, Amy and Cyrus came to the house to visit, they were starting to be allowed to come to town on occasion and they would sneak over to the house to visit. I remember one time the three of us tried to call a family meeting amongst us kids. Melissa and Elias were both married with families of their own. Elias was still working at the store and had plans to take it over when pop died. I knew from asking questions of Elias that we probably wouldn't get any answers from either of them. They'd had too much trauma from losing their mother, and then three-step mothers, who just as they were getting used to them, up and died. It was like being thrown back into the sharks and not knowing what you would end up with. Amy did know though years later from talking to Melissa that she liked all three women, she just didn't have the inclination to get close to them. She didn't want to be hurt. And I think with each death it got a little worse," he shifted in his chair. He was getting restless and maybe to some extent he was sorry he was dredging up the past.

"What about Emma and Mollie?" Lydia asked.

"Well right after your mother and Cyrus were taken by your great-grandparents, Amelia's parents came and took them too," he said to Julia, even though Lydia had asked the question. He had no reason to answer to her since it was their family.

Julia went slack, her hand drooped and her face went totally blank. Lydia knew Julia didn't know about those children being removed from their home, because when they had talked about the children at the initial meeting, Julia was under the impression the Captain had raised them.

Daniel looked at the shocked expression on Julia's face. "You didn't know that did you? From what I was told by Elias, the parents, being Amelia's and your grandparents, got together and talked. Amelia's parents decided that what the Stowe's did was a good idea. I don't think they trusted Dad either to be honest." Uncle Daniel held up his hand and motioned to Julia to scoot in closer to his side. Lydia figured their time was running short and he was getting weary. "I know what the rumors were. And to some extent I could understand them. My father was hard nosed and expected a lot but he wasn't an abuser in what we see and hear about now on the news. No... he never physically hit them that I am aware of. None of the kids ever saw or heard anything, at least that they talked about anyway. I do know that at one of the family reunions Melissa said he could be a dictator; very demanding and gave very little leeway for errors. So I guess in that respect he could have been considered cruel. But then on the other hand not one of us kids was ever touched. I was told he had left that task to his wives, who being so young and inexperienced, raising children not of their own mind you, were reluctant to strike or discipline. According to Melissa and Elias they all ran wild. I guess I was the only one who didn't get to, because I had Silla." He shook his head. "I'm surprised I lived to be this age actually!"

"Back to the family meeting," Julia brought it back to the original question. "What did you ask him?"

"Well, we asked him why Emma, Mollie, Amy and Cyrus had been taken away. We were all there when we asked, including them. Eh...he didn't like being confronted but we figured he couldn't get all of us at once," he closed his eyes like Julia sometimes did focusing on that one memory. "Poppa told us that he loved each of our mothers when he married them and that he still had not gotten over losing any of them. He said that he was torn when the Stowes' were given custody and then later when the Wells' came to get the other two but he didn't know what to do to stop them. He told us there had been some court stuff and they...I think he was referring to the Stowe's...tried to make it look like he had overworked them. They had implied he'd made them so sick they died. But he told us that wasn't so, that he just wanted them to work as hard as he did and to be strong and good mothers with the children. To be honest I had never seen him sad, other than the day I left anyway. That was the first time."

"What about Silla? I remember my mother having an encounter with her when she died and Silla saying awful things about my grandmother." Since the topic of blame was being brought up, Julia had decided it was time to throw Silla into the mix.

"Silla. What a piece of work. She would tell all of us how pop hated our mothers, how they were weak and useless...how she had to train them to work efficiently in the store. How the kids had to walk them—being the wives—to work so they wouldn't turn around, run home and cry in their pillows," Daniel just shook his head in disgust. "Pop didn't want to do the clerk training because he thought it deserved a woman's touch and yet he gave it to one of the most demanding, spiteful people on the face of the earth." He took a deep breath. Lydia could tell he was trying to calm down. If he had been hooked up to one of those heart machines, Lydia was sure the bleeps would be all over the place. "She would tell me that my mother was too young for my father, that he never should have married "children.""

Julia sat back and sighed. If anything, it looked more and more in favor of her grandfather being innocent. Silla on the other hand, was beginning to look capable of doing just about anything she had so much anger in her. Lydia could tell Julia was regrouping herself. She took off her glasses, rubbed her eyes and then leaned forward again.

"This is too much for you isn't it? I am so sorry I brought this stuff up…but since you are aware of the situation, I want to be honest." Julia put her small hand on the stop of his and squeezed. "The rumor circulating through my maternal branch, as you just mentioned, was that the Captain killed his wife, my grandmother. Now whether that was through over work, or some other substance is unknown. That's why I asked Lydia here to help me uncover the truth, such as it is. I've had my suspicions about Silla too and I am not trying to talk ill of the dead but at this juncture I wonder if she didn't have anything to do with them dying so suddenly." Lydia could tell looking at Julia's features that she had just taken a major load off her shoulders.

Uncle Daniel looked directly in her face, sitting up as straight as he could he said, "To be honest Julia I always wondered about her too."

❖

They all took a breather while the nurse came in to take Uncle Daniel's blood pressure and give him his afternoon medication. The nurse told him it was time to relax and that they should all think about winding down. The look she gave made it seem as if it should be sooner, as opposed to later.

An Old Fashioned Murder

Lydia thought it was a good idea also since they had a bit of a drive home, and had been there almost two hours.

Julia quickly changed the subject to lighter topics, which seemed to calm him down—Julia too. Just as they were getting ready to call Karen to pick them up, Uncle Daniel took Julia's hand in his. They could tell he was getting weary but he still seemed to have some last items to cover before they headed back to the lobby.

"First off, I am glad I knew your mother and my other half siblings. We all shared similar tragedies. It took many years for us to come together and talk, get past the crap that was told us. As I said, I never trusted Silla. There was something about the woman that made me lock my door every night when I went to bed—when I was old enough to do so. Didn't think she could find a ladder she could carry, to get in my bedroom window." He laughed as he smiled at Julia. "I glad someone finally came to share this with me, and I am glad it was you. None of the others wanted to hear that either Pop or Silla even, could ever have done anything harmful to anyone else. Total denial. But I never could let it go. Still can't." Uncle Daniel pulled a pad of paper from the table beside his chair. He then took a pen, which he could barely hold due to the curling of his hand, wrote down an address and handed it to Julia.

"What's this uncle?"

"This is my storage unit address. I'll call Jennie and ask her to meet you there. It's just down the block a ways. There are two boxes inside marked Bower in red ink that I want you to go through. It has stuff from the mercantile and items that were left when Silla died. No one wanted them because they were hers but some of the stuff was Pop's too. Even though Elias inherited the business, he didn't want any of the old mercantile stuff either. So I took the items because I thought someday they might be helpful to someone. Take what you want and destroy the rest."

"Thank you Uncle."

"No thank you. It was time this ended...now."

❖

Uncle Daniel called Jennie, and Julia called Karen. The attendant at the desk, this time a chipper young blonde about twenty-five or so, gave them directions to the storage unit. The attendant told them it was a facility run by the nursing home for a nominal charge. She then explained that many of the elderly wanted their things near. The units also came in handy when the residents were moved from assisted living to twenty-four hour care, and their personal items needed to be stored quickly. She cheerfully added that it was convenient for everyone. Lydia figured it was more like, if the bill didn't get paid it was a convenient way for them to recover some losses as well.

After taking the directions and thanking the assistant, she and Julia slowly walked toward the exit. From the directions, it looked to be only about three long blocks down the street so hopefully they could get in and out quickly and be back on the road before the commuters hit the freeway.

Karen pulled up just as they exited the building. Julia passed her the directions to the storage unit and they climbed in. Julia then gave Jennie a quick call as they got into the car to confirm she was leaving her house. After Julia hung up she explained to Karen and Lydia that Jennie lived close by and should be arriving to meet them in about ten minutes. They were to look for a bright yellow mustang.

Once they found the address, Karen parked close to the large gated entrance and then they simply sat and waited. Just a few minutes later the roar of an engine could be heard coming from up the block. Sure enough, a bright, almost blinding yellow mustang convertible pulled up. Jennie parked in front of them; squeezed in front would be a better term. Lydia watched as Jennie pried herself from her low riding car. She looked to be about mid-sixties, slightly chubby, with very blonde hair and sporting make-up that would make Tammy Faye Baker blush. She was wearing a very low-cut shirt that said "I ain't no old lady," a black leather mini-skirt that was almost as short and a pair of black four inch spiked heels.

"I didn't know they even still make those shoes?" Lydia mumbled under her breath.

An Old Fashioned Murder

"From the looks of it Cousin Jennie isn't giving up her youth easily." Karen remarked. Fighting all the way might be more accurate Lydia thought.

"Is she for real?" Lydia asked stunned.

"She is. But I don't think the hair, or the appendages in front are." Karen whispered.

"She certainly is accentuating the positive, isn't she?" Lydia found herself almost as stunned as Karen.

If it hadn't been for the whole surreal "Jennie moment," neither Lydia nor Karen would have momentarily forgotten that Julia was sitting there listening to their comments. Julia quietly cleared her throat and spoke up.

"She's the baby of the family and as you can see, wild as a March hair. I loved Uncle Daniel and his wife Eleanor. The two older boys were fun too but when Jennie got going…God help all of us. She would throw hissy fits like you wouldn't believe. I think she's on her fourth or fifth husband by now."

After adjusting herself Jennie started heading toward Karen's car. Her blond hair, which Lydia just knew couldn't be real was as wild as her personality seemed. The only thing Lydia could compare it to was one of Dolly Parton's bigger wigs—but Dolly's by far had been nicer.

"Hey cuz…" She squealed. "…So glad you could visit the old man. He doesn't get too much company lately. I've been busy working and Stan and Jim are up north and don't get down here often. How are you?" Jennie asked as she helped (more like yanked) Julia from the car. She gave Julia a big bear hug which practically swallowed Julia up, not to mention the spike heels made her a good foot or so taller than poor Julia. It was almost like being swallowed by a big blond bear.

"Just fine, thanks for meeting us here. This is my friend Lydia and my granddaughter Karen." Lydia was thoroughly impressed with Julia's cool demeanor. It was taking Lydia every ounce of her being not to stare. The mini-skirt alone was worth wondering about. How did she get into it?

"Nice meeting all of you," Jennie said as walked ahead of them. At the main entrance she proceeded to unlock a smaller walk-in gate. "It's just a small storage unit. Don't need a big one yet, since he's still using his furniture in his room there and we sold everything else when he went in the place." She gestured up the street towards the nursing home.

As she pushed open the gate she waved them through and then once again sped up ahead of them. How she moved so fast in those heels Lydia didn't have a clue. She noticed though that Julia was having a hard time keeping up with her cousin and apparently so had Karen. Suddenly Karen took a bit of a dip, enough so Jennie backtracked to check on her, giving Julia time to catch up.

Lydia leaned over to Karen as they continued walking and whispered in her ear. "Smooth move," she said approvingly.

"Either that or my grandma would be having a stroke right now." She smiled knowingly. "Thanks for coming along. I would have been no use alone and at least with the two of us we can keep an eye on both of them."

As Jennie reached the third row of buildings she punched in a code that allowed them to enter the first building. About halfway down the hallway, Jennie stopped at a unit on the left, pulled out a key and unlocked the door. The building was lit better than Lydia had expected. The one that she and Lance had rented years ago was so dark you could barely see what you were looking at. Even though the room smelled just a bit musty and there were a few dead bugs on the floor, the room was in pretty good shape.

"Two boxes right?" Jennie asked, as she leaned over and started inspecting the neatly stacked set of boxes near the wall.

"Yes, he said it had Bower written on them in red ink," Julia responded as she started up the other side of the wall. Karen and Lydia looked at the odd sized boxes that sat on the floor closest to the door. Lydia was sure that Jennie would be doing very little lifting since her nails were so long, so she was prepared to do doing some hauling if needed. There was always the chance that in those heels Jennie might topple over too, especially if she lifted a heavy box. Lydia wasn't sure why they simply couldn't have just driven up to the doorway so the loading would be easier. But why question why.

"Here they are!" Jennie called from the back corner. Lydia found her bent over, hidden behind some larger moving

An Old Fashioned Murder

boxes. She was tugging on some smaller odd sized boxes with great effort. "They don't look too heavy. Think you young women could handle lifting these for me. My back is just awful." Lydia figured her back would hurt too if I wore shoes like that.

"No problem," Karen said much more cheerfully than Lydia expected. She figured Karen was just probably glad the boxes had been found and they were getting out of there.

"You want to look at them now?" Jennie asked expectantly.

"No, your dad said I could have them. So I think we will take them home and sort through them." Julia said as pleasantly as possible.

"Now darlin' if you find something valuable in there, I am sure that you will let us know, right? Like a map to a gold mine or something." Jennie chortled.

Meow Lydia thought. It was true that some people in the world were dishonest but in the short time Lydia had known Julia, that would have been the last thing she would have thought. Lydia figured it was more likely that Jennie was a bit greedy and wanted to make sure she wasn't getting cheated out of anything.

"I promise, if the Hope Diamond should be in the box, I will make sure to let you know," Julia said as sweet as could be.

"That's fine." Jennie shot back sounding a bit defensive. From the sounds of it, Julia had hit a soft spot. "Dad said you're working on the family tree. Are there any skeletons I should know about?" She teased, apparently recovering from the little jibe.

"You just never know what you'll find," Julia responded as she turned and started for the door.

Chapter Fifteen

They found the drive home was actually smooth compared to what it could have been. As they got closer to home, Lydia asked Julia where she wanted to house the boxes. She was hoping of course that Julia would want Lydia to keep them. As hoped for, Julia suggested Lydia's house and then Lydia suggested back (it reminded Lydia of playing tennis) that Julia and Karen stay when they got to Lydia's house, so they could look over all of it together.

To Lydia and Julia's disappointment, Karen had to decline because she had a date at six. Lydia figured it was probably Karen's boss coming to claim his car. Glancing in the passenger side mirror, she noticed that Julia looked supremely disappointed, so she tried tact number two.

Lydia then proposed that Julia could still stay and then Lydia would bring her home when they were finished. Julia seemed extremely pleased when Karen agreed and the deal was done. If it hadn't worked out, Lydia would have invited herself over to their house, because one way or the other those boxes needed to be opened tonight.

Karen and Lydia started to pull the boxes out of the back of the BMW, when Lance came out of the house to see if they needed help. He carried the two medium sized boxes, which were relatively heavy into the living room, which provided a ton of space to spread out the contents of the boxes. Karen headed home, Lance brought them two glasses of water as requested and then they shut the doors softly and opened the first box.

There were tons of things packed inside the boxes. Lydia equated it to opening a treasure chest. There were some more letters and what looked like two additional journals. Lydia couldn't wait to get her hands on those. In addition there were even some campaign buttons from the early years of the twentieth century. Lydia and Julia both agreed they were probably the Captains. They were both pleased to find more old photographs. One of them was of a large group of people posed on the steps of an old Victorian house. The others were pictures of the outside and inside of the mercantile. This really brought home what the place looked and felt like. In one of them there was a young woman, probably mid-thirties standing behind the counter. Lydia flipped it over to find some faded writing on the back of the picture. Lydia had to take her glasses of to see what the inscription was.

The writing said 'Silla at counter, 1890.' She looked friendly enough, not as troll like as the other picture Lydia had. Uncle Daniel had mentioned that she had one face for the public and another for the family. This must have been the public view.

"Silla," was all Lydia said out loud. The face was happy, pleasant, someone who was content with themselves, at least at work. Very different from the other picture Lydia had in the files. "She was pretty when she was young wasn't she?" Lydia asked.

Julia leaned over to look at the picture Lydia was holding in her hand. She had been reading some of the letters that had been tied together with cording.

"Too bad the outside didn't reflect the inside." Julia sniffed.

"In her element apparently..." Lydia replied. In a way Lydia felt sort of sorry for Silla, even though she probably shouldn't. Apparently running the mercantile and pining away for the Captain had been her entire life. "...Think how sad to waste such a short span of time without any other interests or goals. All she had was the mercantile and the Captain."

"But also think...for him to wait through three, no four wives before marrying her, there must have been something about her he didn't care for," Julia replied. Even though it was a curt statement, the tone was softer than Lydia expected, especially knowing how Julia felt. Maybe she had thought some about what Lydia had said. Potential murderer or not, the woman's life had sucked and maybe that was why she was so bitter later in life—too many roads not taken.

"Or, as we discussed the other night, he didn't see her as anything more than hired help." Lydia reminded her gently.

"Yes, I suppose that's true," Julia conceded. "With luck, we'll learn more about both of them through these letters." She sat back against the couch, grabbed one of the stacks tied together and then began reading one at a time.

Lydia grabbed the two journals. The first one was the missing employee payroll account book and the other was the monthly stock inventory. For Lydia, finding those in the box was like striking gold. If something was used to harm Amelia, Katherine or Mildred, it would most likely have been processed through the store, where the weapon of choice would have blended into the woodwork. Or at least she hoped that would be the case anyway.

"Listen to this..." Julia began. "Dear Andrew...just wanted to let you know that I will be in town for a visit next week if you are up to company. Would love to visit with you and the children and if possible would love to see Silla too...So sad that she lost her best friend when you lost your wife. She just never seemed the same afterwards. I really miss those carefree school days, don't you?"

"Who's it from?" Lydia asked looking over at Julia.

"A Grace Johnson. A classmate maybe? It does sound like they went to school together doesn't it? Interesting...the comment about Silla and her *best friend*. Could that be Melissa?" Julia asked as she turned the page over. "The rest is just about the births of her children and visiting her parents when she arrived."

"Is there a date on the letter?" Lydia asked setting the journal down and moving next to Julia on the couch.

"No, none that I can see," Julia said handing Lydia the letter. "She had to be referring to Melissa. She spoke so badly about the other women and she was so flattering toward Melissa. It couldn't be anyone else."

"If that's the case it might make for an interesting triangle don't you think? Did he originally choose between Melissa and Silla? If so, that could possibly explain her anger through the years as she was being overlooked. And then the Captain added insult to injury by marrying women we figure he hardly knew and considerably younger as well."

"I guess it would insult me too. That's assuming that there was any real interest on his part there to begin with. Silla could have simply thought he liked her…misread his intentions."

"Misread them for twenty years?" Lydia asked amazed.

"Well?" Julia asked, as she tossed the ball back to Lydia. "She did, didn't she?"

Lydia nodded. Julia had hit the nail right on the head.

"That unrequited love thing again," Lydia admitted sadly.

Lydia picked up the journal she had laid down and slipped back over to her spot. Julia just sat there softly shaking her head. Slowly she folded the letter back up and set it aside. Lydia couldn't help but wonder what she was thinking.

"A few of these are the Captain writing Melissa, telling her about his adventures in the city buying things for the store," Julia told Lydia. "He wrote how much he missed her and couldn't wait to get home. It is a very different tone from that of a dictator, don't you think. He must have changed…"

"Maybe they both changed," Lydia picked up her thought. "Let me take a few. I need to look at these journals later since they are more detailed. Plus I would like Faye to go over them with the notes she took, to compare and look for any matches. It would be fun to see how close she came to her guesses."

Before she started to read the letters she took from Julia, Lydia decided to finish sifting through her box. She found some old post cards from Niagara Falls, a stack of stereo cards for old stereoscope viewers and a small black leather New Testament. She flipped through it and spotted a small piece of aged newspaper that had been placed in the area of the 23rd Psalm. Lydia read over it briefly seeing if it related to the Bower family in any way.

It was a small article about two children orphaned in West Virginia. Lydia wondered who had saved it and why. She flipped back through the book looking for some kind of identifier, initials or a name. Since there wasn't a name written anywhere in the book, she couldn't determine whether it had belonged to the Captain or Silla. In the end, she decided it wasn't relevant to what they were working on anyway. She placed the clipping back in its original spot and put the book back into the box.

"Here are a few more," Julia said, as she passed Lydia an additional stack of about seven letters. Lydia put the top back on her box and settled into reading the ones Julia had given her. For a while they both sat in silence reading.

"Oh my..." Lydia started.

"What?" Julia asked as she rubbed her eyes. They had both been reading constantly for close to an hour.

"My Dearest Captain, I wanted to express my sorrow upon the death of your wife Amelia. I know that she was not your ideal as a replacement for our dear Melissa but you did your best with the choice provided you. Remember that I am always here for you to help whenever and wherever, not just at the store...In Sympathy, Priscilla."

"Well, well, well," Julia said shaking her head. "That was certainly a not-so-subtle way of making herself known, wasn't it? But we know he didn't bite, at least not then anyway. Was she not forward enough?"

"Or too forward maybe?" Lydia suggested.

"I mean if we figured out what she was hinting at, he certainly must have too. Don't you think?" Julia suggested as she borrowed the letter from Lydia to look at it closer.

"I don't know...men can be pretty dense." Lydia reminded Julia with a knowing look. "I think though for a woman, especially back then, being that forward about your availability, particularly during a time of sorrow, would have been frowned on. But then he only had a year's window to make a new choice with little ones at home. Her window of opportunity would start ticking right away."

"Interesting choice of words...'did your best with the choices provided to you.' It sounds like the ladies sure weren't beating his door down does it?" Julia said as she stood to stretch. "I can't imagine someone with money, no matter how he got it, unless it was illegal, in that day and age not being considered a catch." Julia rummaged through her box and pulled out the pictures. "Here is one of him mid life. Even

An Old Fashioned Murder

as an older man, he was a fairly handsome. Not repulsive from what I can see."

Lydia mentally compared the pictures: the one she had in the file and the new one. He was one of those handsomely rugged men, a Harrison Ford type of profile actually. Not repulsive at all. "Could that have just been her opinion? Silla being the one who felt his choices had been too limited?" Lydia asked.

"Oh I would bet money it was strictly her opinion. Since we have been given small doses of her ego, she probably thought she was an expert on everything," Julia concurred. "Comparing someone like Amelia or Katherine to herself and Melissa…I'm sure she had felt he'd settled."

Lydia nodded in agreement. Looking at the clock she realized they had worked longer than planned and she still had to drive Julia home.

"Let's take a break for tonight. I will finish reading my batch of the letters and make notes on anything that might help. Maybe in a few days we can call Muriel and Faye and get back together again, for some more brain storming." Lydia suggested.

"I like the sounds of the Nancy Drew Crew, can we keep that. I used to love reading their books, even as a young adult. And it kind of fits us," Julia laughed as she picked up her purse and her portion of the letters to take home.

"Sure." Lydia assured her. She had originally done it to irritate Faye but now that she thought of it, it was sort of appropriate. They were trying to solve a mystery after all.

"I will finish working on my stack as well. I try and do some light reading before bed each night. I'll just read these instead and make notes before I go to sleep."

"If you start dreaming about them, quit and pick another time of day to do it though. This doesn't have to consume your every waking moment you know," Lydia reminded her.

"I will. But you know, sometimes the subconscious sends you messages, that when you're awake you just don't tune into."

❖

Overall Lydia found the letters to be very telling. Silla had not only expressed her condolences to the Captain after Amelia's death but with each subsequent death as well. Each letter became much more detailed as to why Silla thought he had made a bad decision in his choice of marriage partner. It was for that reason Lydia was glad that she had gotten that stack of letters instead of Julia, since the one concerning Katherine had been pretty cold hearted. Lydia knew she would have to report on what she had read, but felt it best to prepare Julia for the scathing remarks Silla had expressed in writing to the Captain first. The predominant feeling Lydia got while reading them, was that Katherine was the one Silla liked the least and she pretty much seemed to disdain all of them.

Lance patiently sat on the bed before they went to sleep listening, as she read each of the letters out loud. Lydia wanted an unbiased, second opinion, to confirm that they sounded as callous as she thought they did. Lance agreed with her the woman had some serious issues, self-importance being the major one. He felt that Silla's ego was out there in those letters for everyone to see. Lance seemed quite surprised at how blatant Silla had been. But then as Lydia pointed out the letters probably weren't meant to be seen by anyone other than Silla and the Captain.

"When are you guys getting together again?" he asked as they started to settle down for the night. She had snuggled in the crook of his arm and started to yawn. Lydia found reading before bed, especially on a work night always did her in.

"Thursday, because that's the only night that Faye has off this week. I called Muriel and Julia and they said six would be perfect. That way we can finish early."

"Fine. I should be home by six. I'll take the kids to dinner, that way you can talk and not get interrupted every five seconds," Lance offered. "If I'm late I'll call and warn you. Last I heard they were finalizing the trip and I want to pin them down before I leave."

"No problem. You never said where to." Lydia reminded him. She was way too tired to get upset about him being gone again. It was pretty much futile anyway she decided. He would have to go whether she wanted him to or not.

"You never asked," Lance said sounding a tad hurt. "Virginia. There are some classes I need to attend as a brush-up for that new graphics program they're forcing on us. It's only for four days. I shouldn't leave until Tuesday I think."

"Anywhere near Lovettsville? I've got some great-grandparents from around there," she said as she closed her eyes.

"Maybe, we'll just have to discuss that won't we?" He rolled over and the lights were out.

❖

The next day Lydia ran down the pending list again. She added the reminder to check on who was living in the Bower household, especially the children, in order to confirm Uncle Daniel's recollections. She didn't doubt him, but verifying information was what a genealogist did.

The one thing she could definitely cross off her list was the letter she had received from the Saylesville Historical Society. The letter stated that the Captain did not have a bio put into the county history. The only thing the gentleman had been able to find was a mention of the family being one of the first settlers of the town of Saylesville. They owned a tobacco farm for many years and then later opened the hay and feed, as well as the mercantile in town. He wrote that since it was a small item, only one page, there was no charge. Although that had been a disappointment, it wasn't the end of the world.

On a whim, Lydia called her friend Maggie at their local historical society to ask what she thought the chances would be that the patient files of a physician in a small town might still be in existence. Maggie told Lydia what she already knew—probably not. The AMA might have something but on the doctor only. If the practice passed on, the files might have passed to whoever took over the practice. But if the patients were dead, the chance that they had been tossed was high. Lydia mentioned Muriel's suggestion about the mortuary.

Maggie proposed that if they had them, Brad's father would have suggested them as an additional place to look. Reluctantly, Lydia had to declare that lead a dead-end too.

So it was back to the things on the list she could do, which included a chance to pick apart the new mercantile journals. Since Faye had been unsure as to the provider of the roots and herbal items, Lydia wanted to see if a supplier might pop-up. Once she had narrowed the list to a few possibilities, Lydia planned to take the name of each root and herb and run it through Google one more time to try and find information on their symptoms and side effects.

The big question though was: could any of them have been lethal enough to kill?

Next she wanted to look at the composition of patent medicines from that time period. She thought about ordering some microfilm, maybe just one roll, to look at newspaper ads from the time period but then another Google search might just do the trick for that too. She decided to try the cheaper and faster route first.

In the back of Lydia's mind lurked Silla's brother Charles and his drinking problem. She wasn't sure why but that issue continued to bother her. Lydia decided it wouldn't hurt to look into his life a little more either. His cause of death could be interesting, only if it was related to something other than an alcohol related disease. With three questionable deaths already, she really hoped his would be something normal.

She still had one more small stack of letters to go through that had been tied with string and placed separately in a carved wooden box with the Captain's initials on the lid. The box gave a good indication that they were his personal letters, as opposed to the ones that Julia and Lydia had read previously, which were all Silla's.

Lydia had passed the letters she had already read on to Julia. She made sure to warn her of the contents in the hopes that she wouldn't get any more upset than she already was. Lydia knew Julia wouldn't necessarily be surprised by the contents; it was the oozing of hate toward Katherine that poured from them, that Lydia was afraid might make a bad situation worse.

An Old Fashioned Murder

Lydia also sent a follow up letter to the Saylesville Methodist Church. She was giving them just few more days for a reply, before she broke down and gave them a call. There was every indication, by their lack of response; that the church could very well end up like the county history—a total dead end. But it was worth a shot.

Eventually Lydia grew tired of the list and sat it aside. She decided a change of pace was required, so for the rest of the evening she went back to reading letters. Before she settled into comfort on the couch with the stack and her note pad, she decided to call Faye to see what was up for the weekend. She hoped that maybe they could go to the library for just a few hours on Saturday so Lydia could get a final look at those marriage, death and census records and then cross them off her list too.

❖

As foretold, Lance was upstairs packing for his next jaunt, which was to Denver for at least a week, much longer than the four days he had originally been told. The Virginia trip had been postponed at least for now, so Lydia figured those ancestors in Lovettsville would have to wait a little while longer. Sarah was helping him pack which gave Lydia time to quickly call Faye before he finished.

"Hey, long time no hear..." Faye started as Lydia adjusted the phone to her ear.

"Could say the same for you..." Lydia tossed back at her.

"Sorry. It has been a bear changing shifts and my body is still adjusting to getting up when the sun rises." Faye explained yawning. Lydia could tell she was getting ready for bed, so she tried to keep the conversation short.

"Are you off on Friday or Saturday? Or, I guess I should ask if you needed any thing at the library..."

"I feel so used. All you want from me is my skill at driving." Faye said sounding a bit put off. Lydia knew better and ignored the comment.

"I wouldn't go that far…" Lydia retorted. She had known Faye long enough that she could tease her about her driving, although in some cases it wasn't all teasing.

"I'm hanging up now…" Faye said sounding wounded. Then she started laughing. "I'm available Saturday morning but according to my spousal unit, I must be home before three so I can attend a surprise party for my sister-in-law. Is that okay?"

"More than okay. I just need a couple hours to tie up some loose ends. How do you feel about meeting one night after work for a group meeting? I figure we can go over the evidence and then see if we can pin point ourselves a murderer?" Lydia straightened her back. She was getting tired too but really wanted to get a start on those darn letters.

"Sounds good to both. See you Saturday at the usual time and then we can talk about a meeting date for the other. How much longer do you think it will take before you're ready to present the case?" Now she was starting to sound like a lawyer, the cop mode was bad enough.

"Oh, maybe another week or so. I still have a bunch of stuff in the box to go through. You can come and help me do some sorting if you want, or we can do some journal comparing instead if you like…" A groan emitted from the other end of the phone.

"That's almost as bad as filling out a traffic accident report…do I have to?"

"You're already familiar with it. And wouldn't it be fun to see how close you came in your deductions of the supplier and supplies?" Lydia added.

"I get the hint. We'll talk that over on Saturday too." Lydia could tell Faye was starting to get testy. She wondered if this was how Faye reacted to reviewing a couple of journals, how did she handle the tedium of routine police procedures, like filling out paperwork and writing traffic tickets?

But then Faye had always been one of those people, that if she liked something, she threw everything into it, like genealogy and police work. If Faye could just look at this project as a type of detective job, maybe she would have more enthusiasm for it. Hadn't she told Lydia on more than one occasion, that she wanted to be a detective someday? Talk about tedious and grindstone. Another yawn started on the other end of the phone line. Lydia knew her time was up.

"Okay crabby, you get some beauty sleep and I'll see you Saturday." Lydia teased as she hung up the phone.

Chapter Sixteen

Friday after work Lydia dropped Beth off at work, Lucas off at his friend David's house and then she and Sarah headed home. She made a quick dinner for the two of them, Mac and Cheese for Sarah and a hot dog for herself. Lance had safely arrived in Denver, so she was back to being a single parent again. Sarah had some alphabet practice work to finish for pre-school, so Lydia put her at one of the desks in the study and then seated herself across from her. She opened her laptop, booted it up and then started the great Internet search for a weapon.

Before heading up the stairs, she grabbed the first journal off of the dinning room table as well as the accompanying notes that she and Faye had made. She planned to concentrate on the herbs and roots that the mercantile had purchased right before the deaths of each of the wives. Faye had narrowed it down to about seven, so Lydia started at the top of their list performing an Internet search for each one.

After tweaking her search terms a bit, Lydia finally found one especially good website based in England. It provided a comprehensive list of medicinally used herbs and roots, as well as a detailed description of each. Unfortunately by the time she got to E, not one of them looked even remotely possible when matched against Katherine's symptoms. It was when she got to the description of foxglove she seemed to hit pay dirt.

The description Lydia had of Katherine's symptoms had been sketchy at best and had been taken from the inquiry testimony that the Captain and the doctor gave, as well as the notes provided in the mortuary records, as supplied by the doctor. Even so, Lydia had to admit that what she was reading sounded quite familiar.

An Old Fashioned Murder

Foxglove, according to the website, was used to regulate the heart but in larger doses it could be fatal. The extract could be taken from either the seeds, or the leaves of the flower. The use of the plant went back to the 1500's and it was recommended that only skilled physicians or herbalists use the plant for medicinal purposes. It was the base for Digitalis, which heart patients used when a heart attack seemed eminent, or was having heart circulation problems. Its primary purpose, according to what Lydia was reading, stated that it helped in the circulation of blood through the heart, to help keep it pumping. It could take twelve or more hours for the effects to be seen. It was a powerful diuretic and could be hard on the kidneys.

Lydia also learned that the action of Digitalis administered in all forms should be monitored closely, as it was liable to accumulate in the system and then manifest its presence all at once as a poisonous action. The increasing use of the plant could also cause the activity in the heart to increase so much that the muscle would hypertrophy.

She found one other plant had the same effects and could be substituted if foxglove stopped working. That was lily-of-the-valley. Lydia would have to check that one too, even though it wasn't on their "to be searched" list. Just because it wasn't on the list, didn't mean that it hadn't been used, it would just make the case a little harder to prove.

Lydia highlighted and double starred the foxglove and then penciled in the lily-of-the-valley beside it. Continuing on, she zeroed in on the next herb on the list which was wormwort. Lydia found that the primary function of wormwort was to aid in the relief of digestive difficulties. The chance of poisoning was possible but slight and the symptoms listed weren't anywhere close to the ones she remembered Katherine having right before she died.

Lydia then went back to the entry for foxglove and printed the page. Once again she compared Katherine's symptoms, to the descriptions of poisoning from the website.

Katherine had been thirsty, which was a sign of diabetes but it could also have been a product of the diuretic side effect of the kidney's not functioning properly due to the foxglove poison. Lydia also surmised that Katherine, being tired, could have been as Lydia originally suspected a product of the patent medicine she had been taking. Or, the foxglove poison could have put her heart into flux. The heart palpitations Katherine described to the doctor during her visit, as well as the irregular heartbeat he noted when he found her, certainly gave an indication of the presence of Digitalis being in her system. Her heart not knowing what it needed to do anymore, literally wore her out.

Unfortunately, in the end, it was simply conjecture since her symptoms were way too sketchy. Lydia simply didn't have enough proof, at least not yet. But it was a darn good start.

The next topic to be investigated was: what was the base ingredients found in patent medicines. She wanted to know exactly what they were, what they contained and how they were administered.

As Lydia stared at the screen, the strangeness of the whole project started to weigh on her. She found researching the motives of a possible murderer was such a strange thing to be doing. The mentality behind it was so foreign to her. It was one thing to be nasty, boorish and cruel to your family but it was entirely something else to go beyond those traits and kill another human being. Would the Captain have made the effort to poison his wives? Would he have even cared what he used if he did?

But then looking at someone like Silla with her obsessive nature, you just had to wonder if she wasn't just a little off the edge. Her letters exuded pure venom and she treated her stepchildren with total disdain. She was self-centered to the point where from what Lydia could tell, Silla felt she could do absolutely nothing wrong. And, once again, exactly why did the Captain wait through three additional marriages before finally marrying her? Had he only seen the personality she showed the customers, until after they were married? A Dr. Jekyll and Mr. Hyde kind of thing? What was the true attraction? Love? Power? Or as Muriel suggested blackmail?

Lydia realized there was no question, either of them could have done it. But if so, who was the more likely candidate. Her gut feeling was that the answer was somewhere in those letters, either the Captain's or Silla's but that would have to wait until after she finished the great Internet search.

Back to Google...

❖

Lydia spent another twenty minutes searching the Internet for more information on herbs and their side effects, just to make sure she had covered all her bases. It was always better to have too much information than not enough. Finally she began to explore patent medicines and what she gleaned turned out to be rather interesting.

Just as she had gotten settled in with her research, Lance called sharing with her the weather he had encountered when he landed in Denver, which had been nice and hot. They cut the conversation short when he was summoned to dinner, promising to call her back when he returned. Lydia was pleased with that compromise, since she wanted to finish what she was doing before she lost steam.

A second small detour though, derailed her again. Sarah, who had finished her homework, wanted her reward of apple juice and a snack. So Lydia spent the next few minutes running up and down the stairs in search of the requested items. Normally, she discouraged the kids from bringing food and drink upstairs. It was a rule she had tried to enforce when they moved into the new house three years ago. But slowly both Beth and Lucas had started sneaking up the drinks and food and Lydia just sort of gave up.

The library was all about *not* bringing in food or drink because of the computers and damaging the books, not to mention the carpets and furniture. At the genealogy library they had made a compromise, one that Lydia had initially balked at, but later gave in to. Many seniors (they were the majority of their patrons) could not go without something; either food or drink for too long, because of various illnesses. So it was decreed that the patrons had the option of not using the books and equipment while they were consuming, or they could take a break and go into the back kitchen area and eat. That mode was similar to the Family History Library and its centers, which had a snack room available for patrons. Many of Tri-Cities patrons chose to take advantage of the forced break and eat inside the kitchen area, since they couldn't do anything sitting where they were anyway. Except for that one time Lydia had met with Julia and the library board meetings, she had been a good girl, consuming her snacks in the back room.

But Lydia had to admit, her children were something else entirely. Lucas would bring in all kinds of snacks, which always left crumbs of food and sticky matter. Ants always seemed to work their way inside the room through cracks and places Lydia didn't even know existed. Beth was slightly better, only because she tended to take her dishes down when she was finished and brought up only water to drink. And unlike her brother, she did her eating while she was studying or writing a paper. That could never have been said for him. All of his time in the study revolved around online gaming. The area around the computer was where Lydia would find the old pieces of bread crust, smelly socks stuffed behind the computer tower and candy wrappers in between the chairs and legs of the desks. She did her monthly inspection with some yelling and screaming behind it (more from her than them) and then she would end up cleaning the mess anyway. If anything, it gave her a truly intimate look at the daily habits of her children, things that she would rather not know, nor would the dentist.

Once they got back to the office, Lydia placed Sarah and her snack at the big desk with her ABC pad and pens. Lydia plopped into the chair opposite, refusing to move again until she was finished with the assignment awaiting her.

From what she could discern there was a ton of information regarding patent medicines on the Internet, including references to some Chinese mixtures that were still being produced today.

Lydia actually found patent medicines to be rather interesting. She was surprised to learn that the use of patent medicines in the United States went back as early as 1790 and continued to be popular into the beginning of the twentieth century. Lydia always assumed that the medicine had come as a liquid only but she learned that they were also sold in pill form as well. There were medicines for just about every ailment known to man at that time. Mother's Helper was just one of the many products geared to women. The most famous brand during the 1800s being, "Lydia Pinkham's Vegetable Compound" a cure all for "female complaints." According to the description provided in newspaper advertising, it was designed to help with the change of life, amongst other things, as well as faintness, weakness, sleeplessness, depression and even indigestion. Lydia couldn't find a thing on Mother's Helper specifically, since it didn't appear to have been produced by any of the larger companies of the time.

Lydia always found the history behind the item being researched was just as valuable as the item itself. In this instance Lydia learned that there had been a whole battle over the advertising of patent medicines with an attempt by the government to regulate them. She was also amazed to learn that lobbying was definitely not a modern day process.

Lydia discovered that the United States government, as young as it was, wanted to have a way to monitor the ingredients that went into the patent medicines. The medicine makers of course were against such controls and began to put pressure on newspapers across the country to have this legislation squashed; primarily because the newspapers made big bucks from the advertising, thousands of dollars and by today's standards that was a huge chunk of change.

If those companies had been regulated and therefore possibly put out of business (most of the stuff that went in the bottle was scurrilous) that revenue to the newspapers would cease to exist. Most papers could not survive on the circulation fees alone. Lydia also learned it took many years for the government to win its case. The legislation that came from those regulations formed the Pure Food and Drug act, as well as the Meat Inspection act; two early forms of what was known today as the FDA and the USDA. Towards the end of the first decade of the twentieth century patent medicine started to make a decline. There were still some available into the 1930s but by then the popularity had died.

Mother's Helper, from what Lydia could discern, was composed pretty much of what the other patent medicines were composed of. The base was usually some kind of vegetable extract. The next major ingredient was a ton of alcohol and in some cases things like morphine, opium and cocaine were added to the mix. Lydia decided that must be why people immediately felt so much better, they didn't feel anything else. The ingredients were always ambiguous and not required to be listed on the bottle. The closest to a description of the ingredients was located either on the label, or in the title of the medicine: honey, vegetable extract, cherry extract, swamp root and so on. They were produced by companies whose names told an even better tale: Duffy's Malt Whisky Company, the Liquizone Company and a number of private individuals like Pinkham, Ayers, Pierce and Warner. Some of these individuals touted themselves as doctors but the majority of them weren't.

The liquid was packaged in glass bottles and obviously were not sealed and protected like they were now, so anything could have been put inside of them

That was when the mental light went on. Lydia rolled her chair over to the file cabinet, where she had started storing the family charts and documentation she had been collecting on the Captain and company.

Now she just had to find what she needed.

❖

How could she have been so stupid? How could she have forgotten? How could she have let something like that slip right through her fingers?

There it was the inquiry papers—right in the Captain and Silla's testimony. She plopped herself back in the chair and took a deep breath. She didn't want to get so excited that she read too fast and missed it. After some slow, focused reading, she found what she was looking for.

It was in the Captain's testimony but Silla was the one who had suggested it to him and Lydia's guess was, had supplemented its contents as well.

"...But the more she complained he thought there might really be something wrong so he asked Silla, the clerk who worked for him what she would recommend. She suggested the tonic that his previous wife Amelia had taken off and on, reminding him how well it worked for her. So that is what he brought home—Mothers Helper. She started feeling better right away and he was pleased."

Lydia reminded herself that's what had started her on the whole Internet search, the premise of spiking something that had been consumed by the wives. She had decided to try the patent medicines because the mercantile had supplied them to the public. The other light bulb that went on was that Silla's brother, according to Uncle Daniel, had also partaken of the stuff when he was low on alcohol. Had it affected him in any way?

It certainly put a whole different spin on things. There was no safety packaging back then. No laws governing the purity of a product. People didn't really worry about things like that. Lydia realized she needed to call the girls but she wanted to wrap up those last few things before she did.

She wanted this to be presented to them as tight as could be.

❖

Lydia didn't say a word to Faye about her theories the next morning as they made their way to the library. She wanted to check on two important things before she did. It wasn't that she didn't trust Faye to be impartial and it wasn't that she wanted to be the one to solve the mystery (maybe she did a little) it was she didn't want to look like a fool. No it was more than that. Just once, she wanted to be the *cop* that solved the crime. Deep down inside she wanted to walk in Faye's shoes for just a little while—even if it was vicariously.

But on the other hand, Lydia didn't want to make someone look like a murderer if they weren't, even if the other girls had also leaned in that direction. She felt strongly about this since those they were accusing of the crime were dead. They couldn't defend themselves.

So the conversation on the drive up to the Family History Center revolved around Faye's stepsons and their antics during summer vacation. They were both in trouble in school during the year more often than Faye's husband Scott would have liked but as Lydia the mother of a son told her—boys will be boys.

She'd had her share of Lucas getting into trouble since he'd started kindergarten. It took many years for her to simply back off somewhat, realizing a good deal of it was his own free will. You could only beat something into someone for so long and they either figured it out on their own or they didn't.

Lucas was getting there slowly and as she told Faye, as long as they aren't running around in black coats and carrying guns she should be thankful. In Lucas' case, both Lance and Lydia knew who his friends were and they trusted him to make relatively good decisions, most of the time. They had a semi open door policy at home, there was private time but if Mom and Dad wanted in, they were in.

Lydia felt the teen years for boys were the worst. As Lydia explained to Faye, who was child challenged, the parent had to be on them but not on top of them. Faye seemed to understand, nodding as she listened. Lydia remembered Faye as being the one to torture her brother mercilessly and he turned out all right. She just had to remember her boundaries as a stepparent and then work from there. The kids truly seemed to like her and listened to her, so that was a start in the right direction.

The conversation came to and end as they pulled through the gates. It was one of those lucky days where there was plenty of parking near the entrance to the Family History Center, so no long treks were required. There were days that they would arrive and have a terrible time parking. Occasionally, Faye would circle for a good ten to fifteen minutes for a close spot, or they would end up in the very back parking lot and then have the long walk to the entrance lugging their stuff behind them. Lydia found the walk, even to the north forty parking lot much nicer since she had upgraded to a wheeled computer case. No longer did her hand and shoulder throb from lugging the bag. Now she could immediately roll that film and not have to wait for the feeling to come back to her extremities.

"So what's up for today?" Faye asked as they headed through the doors and towards the elevator.

"Well I'm finally going to see where Lissa was during Mildred's time in the household. Then I am going to check and see about Charlie, Silla's brother. And finally I am going to check and see where Amelia's children were living after her death," she replied as she pushed the down button.

"Charlie? Why?" Faye asked cocking her head to the side. Lydia realized that she hadn't fully filled Faye in on the conversation with Uncle Daniel. Not because she was holding anything back but because there had been so much to remember. And at the time Charlie and the possible timing of his death, didn't mean anything to her. It did now.

"Well, according to Julia's Uncle Daniel, Charlie was a lush. He was so bad, that he would dip into the stock of patent medicines at the mercantile when he ran out of his regular alcohol. It's just a feeling but I want to make sure that he died of natural causes, or somewhat natural like liver disease or alcohol poisoning."

"I get it. It might be that the patent medicine was tampered with. That would then make it Silla then right?" Faye said excitedly. Lydia was trying not to show her disappointment. How did Faye do it?

"Maybe," Lydia said softly. "But I don't have any real concrete proof yet."

"You aren't holding out on me are you?" Faye asked giving Lydia the cop look.

"Not totally." Lydia hedged. "Look, I just want to clear up some things in my mind before I throw anything out there. You're the one that said it looked like a female murderer and we speculated it might be Silla. I'm simply following up on that," Lydia said defensively. She hated when Faye got into her "mode" as Lydia called it. She wasn't a criminal; she was Faye's best friend. So Lydia decided to turn it back around. "Anyway you promised to go through those journals for me. And I got a ton of stuff on at least two possibilities for the poison and you never offered to follow up on it." There, Lydia thought, two can play at this game.

"Oops, I did say we would talk about it, didn't I?" Faye conceded. "I'm sorry. I was being an ass wasn't I? How about I stop in after we finish and we can sit down and go through them." Faye sounded just a little apologetic. It was a start.

"That would be nice. Sarah would like to see you too and then Beth will be free to take off and go out with her boyfriend."

"When you're ready will you tell me your theory before the others?"

"Always."

Chapter Seventeen

For Lydia it was a crap shoot as to which to try first, the 1910 census, or just go straight to the marriage records looking for Lissa. If Lissa married in 1910 or after, she should be on the census married but that would be like looking for a needle in a haystack. So Lydia decided to go straight for the marriages. After getting settled at the film reader, she went to the rental cabinet, pulled out the marriage record roll and loaded it up. Lydia knew that Lissa would have married after Katherine died in December 1904 since she was still at home when it happened.

The roll of film covered all the marriages from 1863 to 1909. Lydia needed volume four of the marriage record books so she rolled the film to the index at the beginning of that volume. There were three marriages listed under Bower in the fourth volume, which covered 1904-1909. Lydia was pleased to see that the index was a Bride/Groom combination. Some indexes were by bride only, which could be very limiting, as well as time consuming under different circumstances.

She wrote down the appropriate page numbers and then rolled right to the three records. The first one was on 5 March 1905 and that was the marriage for the Captain and Mildred, which Lydia already had so she crossed it off her list. The second one was pay dirt. Melissa Jane Bower married on 7 June 1906 to William Towers. The Reverend Johnson was the minister of the Saylesville Methodist Church at the time of the marriage. Lissa's parents were listed as Melissa Stewart and Andrew Bower. So Lissa was married and out of the house by 1907. That proved she lacked the opportunity to put poison in anything, least of all a patent medicine, unless she spent a great deal of time with Mildred. And as Lydia knew from personal experience, a young woman starting her own family didn't have the time to just go over and hang out. She decided to double check the city directory for their address and then the 1910 census to see how the family had progressed.

Since she was already there, Lydia copied the marriage for Elias and Dorcas Peterson. She thought at some point when all the finger pointing was done she would have to come back and finish filling in the blanks to make the family whole but for now she had what she needed.

Lydia moved on to task number two, which was checking the 1910 census for the children in the household of the Captain. Amelia had died after the census was taken in 1900 on 2 November, so the 1910 census was the next available for Lydia to check. Emma would have been about twelve and her sister Mollie ten or eleven, both still young enough to be living at home.

She pulled the roll she needed, double-checking the enumeration district and page number. It took her right to Saylesville where the Captain was living with Silla and Daniel. No other children were listed living with them. Lydia thought briefly about confirming it by checking the grandparents dwelling but time was getting short and there were other things that needed to be done. It confirmed Uncle Daniel's recollection and that was all that was important.

Task number three, the death entry for Charlie Drake. Lydia knew it was doubtful that he died in or before 1909, simply because Uncle Daniel remembered him and Daniel would only have been three in 1909. But Lydia figured it still wouldn't hurt to look and if it wasn't there, she could send to the Ohio Historical Society for it later. The Historical Society was usually pretty quick when ordering records and she ought to have it in about ten days to two weeks. Lydia figured that would give her time to thoroughly go through the journals and letters and then sit down with Faye and see what she had before presenting it to the ladies.

Muriel had really gotten into the mystery aspect of it all. She had been asking Lydia when she saw her, how it was going, or simply calling just to chat and then taking the conversation around to the topic. Lydia told her that she was still working on some ideas and that once they were presentable, she would definitely have her over to share what she'd found. Those calls were then followed by Julia's.

Lydia could see her impatience, even though she was always nice about it when they talked. It had been over a month and except for speculation and family stories, nothing was nailed down yet. Julia wanted to get together too, to go over the information again, in the hopes she might see something she had missed before.

Since it was so hard making everyone happy, Lydia decided to make a pecking order instead. First Faye to evaluate the evidence since that's what cops and detectives in training do, then Muriel to show her what she had found in order to get a second opinion, or in some cases third opinion; and then finally Julia to present the evidence and discuss the case. It really was starting to become more and more, like a Nancy Drew mystery.

As expected there wasn't a death listed for Charles Drake, which confirmed he died after 1909, or at least not in the town of Saylesville, which from Uncle Daniel's recollections was unlikely. Lydia would get on ordering that right away when she got home. She then went to the directory for 1909 and 1910, since the film was still there and looked at where the Towers family lived. Their house was on a county road, so from the sounds of it she had married a farmer. Probably someone she had met at the mercantile when she worked there, at school, or maybe at church.

Lydia then popped the 1910 census on the reader where she located Lissa with her new family. They were on a farm as expected and according to the census were renting their dwelling. Enumerated next door was the Peter Towers family. Peter was forty-nine, just about the right age to be William's father. Most likely the young couple was living in a separate dwelling on Peter Tower's farm. Lydia knew for a fact that, that type of arrangement was pretty common back then. A number of her ancestors had done exactly the same thing after marriage. Lydia figured it not only helped out the parent who owned the farm since the child stayed to help with the crops but it also helped the young couple save money to get their own place.

By 1910, Lissa and William had two small children, Melissa Jane age 3 and Kate Emma age 1. So Lissa didn't have a problem naming at least one of her children after two stepmothers. Kate Emma looked to be a derivative of

An Old Fashioned Murder

Katherine Amelia and of course her first-born daughter was after her mother Melissa. Lydia calculated, based on the dates of the children's births, that Lissa became pregnant right away after marrying. That information added to the theory that Lissa would have very little time to go and hang with Mildred.

Lydia decided once she got home, she was going to take a look at the plat map. She wasn't looking for any revelations, she just wanted to see where these people lived and worked and worshiped. Like the pictures it would give Lydia a better feel for their lives and how they lived.

"Find anything?" Faye asked cautiously.

Lydia felt bad that she had jumped on her best friend but they had known each other for over twenty years and were more like sisters than friends. They had always been straightforward with each other through the years but Lydia had found herself backing down more often lately as Faye started becoming more cop like. It wasn't that she didn't approve of Faye becoming more assertive, she knew Faye needed it to survive on the street but sometimes though she just wished that Faye would leave the attitude at work.

"I found Melissa married in June of 1906 and giving birth in the spring of 1907. So the opportunity to mess with Mildred's food, drink or medicine wasn't that easy. She was establishing her own home about the time that Mildred died. Also the marriage of Mildred to her father may have spurred Lissa on to marry as well. It looks like she married a farmer and by 1910 they had two little girls. I noticed that Uncle Daniel was born a month before she married. I'm thinking maybe that was her cue to get out of the house, since none of them could "seem" to cut the marriage, kids and the mercantile. Simply put Lissa didn't want to get stuck raising her half-brother."

"But she ended up with kids of her own right away, what would the difference be?" Faye asked questioning the theory.

"They would have been *her* children. She would be the one to set their discipline and form their personalities," Lydia explained.

"But that still doesn't necessarily let her off the hook for Amelia or Katherine," Faye proposed.

"No it doesn't." Lydia conceded reluctantly.

"Okay, what about the other kids from Amelia?" Faye asked leaning over to look at the notes Lydia had taken.

"They were taken away right after Amy and Cyrus." Lydia explained.

"No." Faye looked as surprised as Julia had. "For the same reason?"

"Yes. According to Uncle Daniel the grandparents must have gotten together after the inquiry and started talking. They decided to follow the Stowe's example."

"Sad isn't it?" Faye said thinking out loud. "I've never had to remove children from a household yet but I've heard it's not a picnic either. No matter how rotten the parents might be they are still the child's parents."

Lydia nodded absently and then she looked up at Faye. "I haven't talked to you for a while have I?" Now Lydia realized it wasn't just Faye who had been out of touch, it was her as well. She hadn't ever sat down and shared with Faye all the stuff they had learned that day. She had just given her the nutshell version, and apparently not even that, from the look on Faye's face.

"No you haven't," she said quietly. "…but then I've been really busy, it's partly my fault."

"Well let's talk about the visit with Uncle Daniel at lunch and then we'll go over everything after we get back."

"Sounds good to me."

After lunch they settled back into routine and for once, Lydia actually squeezed in a little bit of time to do her own research. Faye then got a call from Scott, who told her that his sister's party had been cancelled due to the flu. Scott had then called one of the guys at work, who had been offering Dodger tickets to see if they were still available. Since they were he decided to take the boys to the game instead. Faye was relieved because she hadn't really wanted to go to the party and with them busy at the game she and Lydia could stay a little longer. Lydia then called Beth to make sure that staying until closing would be all right. Since there had been no blood or broken bones reported she'd been free to stay.

Since Faye couldn't seem to wait to hear what Lydia's theory was until they left for home, they took a short break at three for a soda.

"...So what you're saying is...if Silla was tainting the bottles with some kind of poison, as we previously discussed, then that explains how the women got sick?" Faye simplified.

"Yes. And if what Uncle Daniel said was true, there's a chance maybe that Charles could have gotten some of the poison by accident too. But a lot of that depends upon when he died. Since it looks to be after 1909, the chance is minimal he was poisoned by anything other than just plain old alcohol."

"You know, he could still have gotten some of the stuff before she stopped doing it. It may have taken him longer to feel, or notice the effects because of his drinking, as you suggested. He could have had liver disease in addition to all sorts of other things and the poison's effects just fell in with the other symptoms," Faye added.

"The other terrible thought I had was that some of those bottles could have been accidentally sold to customers. I only hope that if Silla did do it, and I know this might sound awful, she kept it to the bottles that she sent home with the Captain. Think about it. She could have been poisoning more than just the Bower women." Lydia felt shivers down her spine.

"If it was her, she was truly a piece of work, wasn't she?" Faye asked appalled.

"Yes, she was." Lydia nodded in agreement. "Well then, I guess I'll need to pay more attention to the information in those journals. I should see if there are any notes on Charles being out sick regularly," Lydia contemplated.

"What if Silla and Lissa were working together?" Faye tossed out.

"Boy, that's a scary thought. We should know for sure when Lissa was working by the employee records. Although with her being family who knows, maybe they didn't keep track. Moreover, I can't see her father starting her off in the store until at least sixteen. It's not like they lived in a New York tenement where the kids started working, practically at the age of five. That would only give her a three year window to do the deed and we know this was planned and carried out for a much longer period of time."

"So how would Silla get the poison into the bottle? Wouldn't she have had to make it into a liquid somehow?" Faye asked. She actually seemed to be getting interested in Lydia's theory and not shooting it down, which gave Lydia the confidence to continue with the thread she was following.

"If we take Katherine's minimally described symptoms and compare it to the effects of foxglove poisoning, the herb, flower, whatever you want to call it, could be dried and then the leaves later made into a tea."

"So, the being thirsty, feeling tired, the heart palpitations and the speeding of the heart when the doctor got there, could all be symptoms of the poisoning." Faye clarified.

"Can be...yes." Lydia gave Faye a brief run down of the results from her Internet search. "...In any form it is poisonous to animals and humans, even in small quantities. Since foxglove was on the list we created from the journal, as being one of the herbs that was being supplied by the mercantile, it fit. At first I thought it was unusual, since from what I read it had to be carefully used when treating someone. I really expected the distribution to be handled by the doctor but then I realized it wasn't present day and no such regulations existed back then. It was probably being used by others privately within the community and the mercantile supplied it as a service."

"Or...could she have been getting it for herself and then funneling it through the mercantile?" Faye suggested eagerly. Lydia could see where Faye was going with the thought and it was a sound one.

"Alright, since we know the Captain didn't run the place and Silla apparently did, that could be a very real possibility. I wouldn't put it past her to have the mercantile order it, pay for it and she would have unlimited use without question" Lydia agreed.

"Forensic science back then was nothing like today but if someone had eventually figured out what they died of and traced it to the mercantile, it wouldn't have been too difficult for her to lie and say the Captain ordered it since it was his store." Faye added.

"You're right. Unless outsiders had knowledge of the running of the mercantile, he would be the first one suspected. When she did request it, from whatever farm produced it, she could have said a number of things so it didn't look like she was specifically requesting it for *herself*." Lydia added eagerly. "The best part is, as I did the research, I found that there aren't very many places that can grow foxglove. I was able to locate one spot near where the Captain lived in nearby Athens County Ohio, just a hop and a skip from Saylesville. So the farmer who supplied it had to be local," Lydia said. "I think I will still order Charles' death certificate first thing Monday, just to see what it says. You never know, there's always the chance she grew tired of him too."

"She sounds like a serial killer to me. A very subtle one," Faye whistled softly.

"That's what I am afraid of," Lydia said softly. "I'm just hoping there'll be something more in those letters to help us out."

"Okay, when we get back to your house, you hit the letters and I promise to double check the journals since we have all three. If we crack the whip, maybe we'll find something tonight."

"I sure hope so."

Chapter Eighteen

Before arriving at Lydia's, she and Faye stopped off for pizza at the place on the corner. They ordered two, one just cheese and another with everything on it. Faye, Lydia and Beth dived into the one with everything, Lucas and Sarah devoured the cheese. Once the dinner table was cleared and the plates put into the dishwasher, everyone went back to what they were doing. Beth went to get ready for her date, Lucas returned to his battle to the death on the computer and Sarah followed her sister to the bathroom to keep her company as she got ready for her date.

Faye and Lydia spread out in the living room, which was becoming their hang out and shut the doors. They had some time alone to read and work quietly, before Sarah came back downstairs. Once Sarah came down, Lydia would have to open the door to keep an ear out. She knew there would be drinks to get and television channels to change. If Sarah was switching between Noggin, Disney and Nickelodeon, she was fine. But sometimes she hit the wrong button and ended up with the Home Shopping Network, or old Jerry Springer reruns.

On the way home, they had discussed calling Muriel and Julia to see if they wanted to join the fact-finding fest. Lydia had called Muriel on Faye's cell phone as they were sitting in traffic on the freeway. Muriel was practically bubbling over the phone, even suggesting she could pick Julia up and bring her. Next Lydia called Julia who agreed to the arrangement. They were due to arrive closer to seven.

Faye reminded Lydia, that working as a team would not only speed up the investigative process; but since people tended to see things differently, Muriel or Julia might see something that Lydia or Faye may have previously missed, or had not even thought of. Lydia agreed. They were all getting something from working on this project and she didn't mean to be the one to exclude anyone. As Beth would say "get over it."

Lydia pulled out the stack of letters that appeared to be the Captains. She was getting tired of Silla's sense of propriety and self-importance. Maybe the Captains letters would be a little more entertaining. She would ask Muriel to take the other letters. A fresh, unbiased eye might see something that even Lydia and Julia had missed.

Faye removed the flower arrangement from the coffee table, laid out the notes she had previously taken, as well as the journals themselves. Faye planned to give Julia the personnel journal to peruse. Mainly to see what Silla and, or the Captain had noted for each worker, assuming there was more than two and if they were paid, how much. Both Lydia and Faye figured that would keep her occupied and not so troubled by Silla's behavior.

Beth had finished up and was getting ready to leave.

"Make sure you have your key. I'll leave the porch light on for you," Lydia said as Beth started to open the front door. Kyle her boyfriend was driving, so she wouldn't be coming in through the garage like normal.

"No problem. They want to stop after and get hamburgers but we shouldn't be too late since I work tomorrow," Beth said as she ran back over and gave her mother a kiss on the cheek. "You guys have fun now…"

Just as Beth opened the door a hand popped through. It was Muriel and Julia. Lydia figured they must have just been about to knock when Beth opened the door.

"And where are you off to young lady?" Muriel asked in her best grandmotherly tone.

Beth smiled knowingly. She had known Muriel since before her head could reach the counter at the Tri-Cities library. Most of the older ladies in the genealogical society had nothing but good things to say about Beth and lots of dating advice as well. Beth was always graceful about accepting their hints, and tips.

"Movies. As a matter of fact my boyfriend just pulled up. The movie starts in forty-five and we're meeting a bunch of people, so we need to get running." Beth said as she gave Muriel a quick hug and ran down the steps. "You have fun!" she called as they watched her retreating back.

"How old is that child again?" Muriel asked as she watched them drive away.

"A mature nineteen. Now get in here and let's get going," Lydia said, laughing as she shut the door behind them. She knew it was hard to see little ones grow and understood Muriel's lament. "They don't stay little for long do they?"

"No they don't," Muriel replied, with a wistful look on her face. "Let's get down to business."

❖

The assignments were distributed and the room grew silent as each person became absorbed in the task handed to them. Faye was bent over, intently focused on the journals and notes in front of her. Lydia could tell she was taking additional notes as she went, since every now and then a scribble would break the silence. They would all look over at her briefly and then go back to what they were doing.

Lydia settled down with the Captains letters. Some of them appeared to be from business acquaintances asking when the next time the Captain would be in Chillicothe. There were price quotes included for items such as: wheat, heating oil and salt. Lydia figured he had kept them in order to compare prices over time, reminding him of what suppliers had charged him in the past. Most of the other business letters were all rather innocuous.

She picked up the next stack that was tied together. The first one on top was a love note from Melissa to the Captain. It was written on engraved stationary in a beautiful flowing hand. It described how their life would be once he was settled and on his feet. Melissa promised to be the best wife possible and to support him in all his endeavors. She then asked him why it was taking so long for him to announce their engagement. Melissa reminded him that even though he

An Old Fashioned Murder

wasn't established they could still surely do that. She also mentioned that many of her friends had been engaged for three, or four years, so it wasn't something bad. She signed it affectionately yours, Melissa.

Lydia felt sort of sad for her. Melissa was on the edge of spinsterhood, her friends were marrying and Lydia was pretty sure she was probably feeling heat from her mother. Didn't all daughters at some point in their life?

The next letter wasn't from Melissa, Amelia, Katherine, Mildred, or Silla. It was from Rebecca Cox, according to the return name on the envelope. One of the few envelopes he had not discarded.

Lydia stopped in mid read and looked up. Her perplexed face must have caught Muriel's eyel, because she looked up from her task, cocking her head to the side inquisitively.

She held up one finger to hold off the question. Faye and Julia hadn't noticed. Muriel simply nodded and went back to her job.

Rebecca Cox had also written a love note, one that seemed far more mature than Melissa's had. Not so dream-like in how it was written.

My Dearest Andrew,

My father has insisted I write and see how you are, since it has been so long since we talked. Chillicothe has been hot these past few days and I have been spending much of my time either at father's store or down at the stream cooling my feet.

It is so hard to believe it has been a month since you were last here and proposed. I know that it was hard for you to do, especially on bended knee and in front of my parents, but they were so pleased. They truly love you as their own son.

I know you are busy with building your store and will be up to see us soon. I cannot wait to be with you. Whatever you ask of me I will do.

Yours Always,

Becca

❖

"Oh my." Lydia's mouth dropped open. They were all looking at her.

"Lydia?" Julia said softly from the corner of the room. "What did you find?"

"Apparently the Captain was engaged…and not just to Melissa."

❖

Lydia looked at three faces, which looked back at her in disbelief. No, shock would have been a more accurate description. From everything they had learned, there had only been one sweetheart and that was Melissa. But according to what Lydia had just read, it seemed as if the Captain had been leading a double life. He had two sweethearts.

"Say that again?" Faye asked, still looking dumbfounded. It was so unlike Faye that Lydia almost laughed out loud.

"You heard me right. The Captain was engaged to a woman, or a girl named Rebecca Cox. The date on the note is March of 1882, a year and a half before he married Melissa."

"Rebecca Cox. The name doesn't a ring a bell, so no one in the family talked about her, at least that I remember," Julia replied shaking her head. She stood and stretched and then sat back down. "He was engaged before he committed to Melissa." It was more of a statement than a question. "Were there any letters from Melissa to him?"

"As a matter of fact the one at the top of the pile was from Melissa and it was dated April of the same year. So the reason why he hadn't committed to Melissa is that he had gotten engaged to Rebecca."

"What a tangled web…" Muriel began then abruptly stopped. "Why did he change his mind?"

"Good question. I'm going to continue reading. I normally would have but I was so shocked I couldn't hold it in," Lydia explained. "Maybe somewhere he'll allude to it. I only have the letters he received, not the ones he sent, so this may prove to be a very one sided view—an interesting one at that," she remarked, waving the rest of the stack in the air. There were at least 30 or more to go.

Lydia had to admit she felt awkward delving into someone's privacy like that. But then on the other hand, maybe the Captain had saved them to be read someday. Perhaps he hoped to provide his descendants with a better view of him, other than that shown through the gossip and innuendo of a small town. Possibly even a chance to someday clear his name?

What better way to find out than to just keep on reading?

Moments later Faye slapped the table with her hand and shouted. "Bingo!" Her brisk action made the ladies jump, as well as the cats, who had been asleep on the carpet. One cat flew up the stairs and the other one flew onto the couch in the family room landing beside Sarah, who then started cooing "here kitty."

"That just took ten years off of my life," Muriel remarked sourly. She didn't mean to sound cross, Lydia knew but she hated loud noises of any kind. Lydia could remember a time when a car backfired as it drove down the street in front of the library and Lydia thought Muriel was going to jump out of her skin.

Faye looked apologetic. "Sorry, I just got excited," she said as she rolled on to her knees. She pointed at the page in the journal she had been reading. "I found a pattern. There were purchases from a farmer named Stevens for five pounds of foxglove, exactly six months before each of the deaths, from Amelia through Mildred. It says here ....'Dried leaves for medicinal purposes. One pound sold to Dr. MacKay for one dollar.'"

"Can you tell if it is a man, or woman's handwriting?" Julia asked trying to help. Lydia thought it was an excellent question. She had found through doing her own genealogical research, that sometimes by the style and shape of the letters it was possible to tell the sex of the writer. Also thanks to the letters, they had a sample of Silla and the Captain's writing, which could help identify the recorder. She realized the only other one that could have possibly kept the early books would have been Charles and they didn't have a sample of his handwriting at all.

"I would guess female and the same on all of them," Faye commented as she leaned over squinting at the cursive writing.

Lydia reached into the box of letters that she had been working with and pulled out one that Silla had written to the Captain describing some concerns with the mercantile. Lydia had wanted to look at it closer but decided to save it for later. The Captain had placed it in the bundle of business letters that Lydia had looked at earlier. She passed the letter over to Faye, who then took the letter, opened it fully and laid it beside the journal. Lydia then grabbed one the Captain had written and passed that over to her too. Faye then asked for a magnifying glass and Lydia ran up the stairs to get one from the study. Lucas was in the middle of a game and simply grunted as she entered the room and didn't blink when she exited moments later.

Back downstairs she eagerly handed it to Faye who sat there close-mouthed for a good five minutes. All three of them were leaning over her, their breath beating on her neck.

"Okay, to me it looks like it could be Silla's but the style is much tighter than the flow in the letter. I faintly remember from that cursory handwriting training we got at the academy that a person's style can change through the years and depending on mood."

"That's true, Lance's signature used to be legible, now it looks very different," Lydia interjected. "A doctor couldn't compete with him."

"Exactly," Faye agreed. "This handwriting is very precise, much like an accountants. Looking at these two letters, her handwriting is small and precise, whereas the Captains writing is much larger, and fluid. So my guess is it very well could be Silla. But to be sure, I have a *friend* who does consulting work on the side for the department, who happens to be handwriting analyst. He also owes me a favor. I'll call and ask him Monday to look at these and see if the person could be the same."

"Fantastic." Lydia was very pleased that they'd had such a productive night. It was getting late and Muriel and Julia needed to head home. Muriel asked if she could take the rest of the Captains letters, so she could read them at her leisure.

"Take all the time you want," Julia said quietly, she had been pretty silent most of the night. Lydia was worried that this might be taking a toll on her.

"Shall we meet again when I get the death certificate for Charles?" Lydia asked the assembled group. They all looked a little weary but each of them had a satisfied grin on their face nonetheless.

"Works for me," Faye said as she picked up the journal and the letters. "I should hear back from the analyst by then too."

"I'm game," Muriel chimed in. "I like coming over here too, it's a nice change from my hovel that I call home. I'll even bring muffins next time."

"Okay and I'll make some tea or coffee. Do you want to do it earlier in the day, so we aren't so weary when we go to bed?" Lydia asked them.

"That would be nice. Plus, I'm on days for a while, so I have Sundays off starting next week. Would Sunday be okay?" Faye asked as she started to head for the door.

"After the library closes? Say two-ish?" Lydia looked at Muriel and Muriel nodded excitedly. "We can try and meet there but if it isn't available for some reason we can come here like normal."

"Julia?" Muriel looked over at the woman who seemed to have aged almost a decade since this whole thing had started. Lydia prayed they were right and it was Silla. Everything seemed to point that way. Lydia knew that it would certainly ease Julia's mind to know her grandfather was in the clear.

"Sounds fine," Julia said as she gently cleared her throat. Lydia thought she was about to cry. Muriel put her arm around her tiny shoulders and hugged her. "Thank you all for everything. I can't tell you how much your kindness and friendship means to me. I just wish my mother could be here too. This would have put her mind at ease."

"Don't worry Julia, we'll know what happened soon," Faye said gently.

"I think so too," Lydia agreed as she said a small prayer inside.

Chapter Nineteen

The week flew by, faster than Lydia would have liked. The end of summer was approaching and in a week it would be time to start thinking about school again. She was noticing, more and more, that time just seemed go so quickly; maybe it was because the kids were growing so fast or maybe because she was getting older. Whatever it was, sometimes she wished time would just slow down, if only for a little while.

On Monday Lydia had called the Ohio Historical Society to check on Charles' death record. They were able to find him in the death index in 1918, two years before the Captain. It seemed that her theory—that he had died from the same poison as the others—was most likely off base but she ordered it anyway.

Lydia finally made time to sit down with the pages from the plat map. She had photocopied it in sections, making sure that all the townships for the county were included. She spread them out on the dinning room table, which was large enough to accommodate the eventual size. She carefully pieced it together with tape, using a ruler to make sure all the lines were even and that the roads lined up.

She located the farms for the Browns' and the Stowes' and then moved into Saylesville proper, where she pinpointed the Stewart Hay and Feed, as well as their permanent place of residence. Lydia then found the Wells family on Clark, the mercantile on Main, the Bower house on peach, the boarding house that Charles and Silla had started off in and finally the cemeteries and churches. She hadn't expected it to shed light on anything special, it was just interesting to see where everyone was living in retrospect to the mercantile and churches.

An Old Fashioned Murder

The one thing Lydia did check on was the location of the local school. There was one elementary marked (probably a one room schoolhouse) and one called an upper school that was next door on (go figure) School Street. Lydia surmised that was where Charles, Silla, Andrew and Melissa attended and probably where they met.

Faye called and said that she was still waiting on a response from her friend at the police department. Without the others around, Faye had the opportunity to fill Lydia in on who this guy was and how she had actually met him.

The date happened right after Faye had joined the police department and right before she had started seriously dating Scott. The two of them went out a few times and on one of those occasions, he'd gotten very intoxicated, so much so, she'd had to take him home. When she suggested dropping him off he became quite edgy and nervous. After a bit of prodding and a few threats, by Faye, he finally admitted that she needed to do it before his wife got home.

For Faye, that pretty much sealed the deal on him. She didn't have a clue he was married and not one of the other cops had been willing to warn her either. As Lydia had learned through the years, it was wise not to tick Faye off—ever. So one day at shift change Faye cornered him outside the building. She politely explained in very to easy to understand terms, that in order to keep her silence he owed her a favor and she would definitely be calling on it at later time.

She told Lydia that she had wanted to tell his wife in the worst way but she had been advised that their date had not been the first one and sadly the wife knew he cheated. She simply put up with it hoping someday he would change. Faye could never understand women like that but decided that if that was her decision so be it.

Shortly after Faye met Scott, Faye and the guy's wife Tracy, met at a police fundraiser. Faye described her as small and mousy, someone beaten down, who had given up on life. All Faye had wanted to do at that point was hug the poor woman and then find her a good lawyer. They talked for quite some time, and Faye subtly put a bug in Tracy's ear.

Faye heard through the grapevine a couple months later, that his wife had left him. She'd taken the kids, the car and the house and had gone back to work as a nurse at a local hospital. He on the other hand, had to get a new car, a place to live and still owed Faye the favor whether he liked it or not. It also helped that he never knew Faye was the one who got his wife out of "prison." So it was a double bonus in Faye's favor.

Personally Lydia didn't care how they were able to cash in, as long as the end result was worth the cause. So she waited patiently for both pieces of the puzzle to materialize. If neither crucial piece of information arrived before Friday, she had one more idea up her sleeve.

That was trying to track down the children, or grandchildren of one Rebecca Cox.

❖

Lydia in the meantime continued to read the Captain's letters. There were several more from Rebecca and two more from Melissa. She found it interesting that Melissa wrote him letters when she supposedly lived in the same town. Lydia thought maybe with the Victorian Age morality Melissa may have felt uncomfortable expressing herself when they were together in person. It was also highly possible they were never left alone.

The age difference, the lack of commitment on the Captain's part, whatever his problem had been—it was obvious he had strung Melissa along. Could that have been because he had met Rebecca?

The letters from Rebecca (three years worth) actually pointed to indecision. He was at a crossroads and didn't know which way to go. From those letters written before the engagement and two soon after, it sounded as if he really did love her. So why did he propose and then back out? Guilt over Melissa? His parents maybe? She knew it wasn't Rebecca's parents since according to her they thought of him as a son.

Lydia decided this soap opera could run into a whole other direction if she wasn't careful. How deep did she want to dig into the love life of Andrew Bower? Did it really make any difference to the goal at hand—proving whether he killed his wives or not? But her curiosity was piqued and whether it was relevant or not, Lydia Proctor wanted to know. She wanted to see a human side to this man who had constantly seemed to disappoint his granddaughter.

Inspiration hit her on Wednesday. Lydia had taken Sarah to the doctor for a well check so it was an early day. With Lance out of town Beth had access to the other car so there was no need for additional chauffeuring. As a reward for her being good at the doctor's, Lydia and Sarah stopped for a snack before heading home.

It was barely three when they walked in the door. Lydia pounced on her computer and did a quick search on the Internet for the Chillicothe Historical Society. According to the schedule on the website, their hours for summer were from ten to five, so they would be just about fifteen minutes to closing.

She dialed quickly, crossing her fingers.

"Chillicothe Historical Society, how can I help you?" Lydia noticed that the voice on the other end was female. Although the woman sounded professional, she didn't sound very sincere. Lydia decided to make the best of it.

"My name's Lydia Proctor and I live in California. I'm working on a genealogy for a friend and she just recently found out that her grandfather was engaged to a resident in your area."

"This was a pretty big town you know." Lydia caught the ice in the woman's voice.

Lydia tried to be sympathetic—to a point. She acknowledged that if they were locking up the last thing this woman wanted was a search and find at ten to five. But then on the other hand, it was ten to five and if they hadn't wanted to help, they shouldn't have answered the phone.

"I realize that but the family name was Cox and the father owned some businesses in the Chillicothe area. I just wondered if it might ring a bell?"

"Hold on a minute," she responded. Lydia got a nice dose of elevator music in the receiver and patiently waited.

"Hello?" This time it was another voice, one that sounded even older and not as formal. It was husky like a smokers voice.

"Hi, this is Lydia Proctor from California and I'm looking into the Cox family…"

"What do you want?" she asked grudgingly. Gee just bite my head off Lydia thought. Here she thought the other woman was bad acting like the ice queen. Lydia kept her cool because she really needed the information.

"My friend Julia Franklin's grandfather, Andrew Bower was briefly engaged to a Rebecca Cox about 1882 and I wanted to learn a little more about the family." Lydia responded as pleasantly as she could. She was starting to think this was a bad idea.

"Oh." There was a long pause. "Would you mind if I called you back? I can't talk here…" She began to whisper and Lydia could hardly hear her. "…Too many gossips."

Lydia almost started to laugh. "No problem." She rattled off her number. "Can you help me?" she asked hesitantly.

"Yes, I can. Rebecca was my grandmother."

❖

When the phone rang ten minutes later Lydia didn't even give Lucas a chance to pick it up. She was pleased to find it was the mystery woman, who about thirty seconds into the conversation became Mary Stark. Lydia also found out quickly that Mary was one of those who people who took a breath only if they had to. She had dealt with many people like her before, so she let her ramble a bit before she jumped in.

"So why are you asking again?" Mary asked. Here we go Lydia thought, one more time. Couldn't people just pay attention the first time and listen, instead of having to make people repeat themselves? So for the third time Lydia started again.

"My friend Julia Franklin is the granddaughter of Andrew Bower and his third wife, Katherine Stowe. Melissa Stewart was her grandfather's first wife. I've been helping Julia put a family history together and while doing, so we came across some letters that belonged to Andrew. Several of those were from Rebecca Cox, of Chillicothe Ohio who was, as I am sure you know, the daughter of a merchant in the city. I really just want to learn more about Rebecca's life, learn why Andrew and Rebecca didn't follow through to marriage?" Maybe Mary would get the gist of what Lydia was after, without another explanation.

A deluge of coughing preceded the next segment of non-stop talking. Lydia figured that she was either currently, or formerly, a chain smoker. She recognized the cough because her mother had the same kind before she died. Mary probably figured the faster she talked, the less likely she might start coughing again.

"My grandmother kept all his letters. My sister has them all now. We talked about burning them when she died but they were a part of her none of us had ever known and to be honest we were just plain nosy," she stated congenially. Lydia could tell she was trying to justify her curiosity. As far as Lydia was concerned, she had no need to do that with her. She totally understood the concept of nosy. "She married my grandfather about three years after the engagement ended and had nine children. Only five lived, my dad being one of them. He passed six years ago. My mother passed ten years ago and I just lost a sister last year…"

Quickly Lydia cut her off. "Do you know if the letters explained why the marriage didn't happen?" Lydia asked again. It was nice of this woman to share the information with her but Lydia really didn't need their whole family history, she had enough of the one she was working on.

"Oh yes. I remember reading that his parents threatened him out of it." Taking a deep rattled breath Mary continued. "From what we were told, he had also been courting another girl in his hometown. My grandmother was twenty at the time of the engagement, quite a bit younger than him and a little too trusting it seems." There was silence on the phone and Lydia could hear her inhale. She also knew that sound well. Mary was smoking as they were talking, that certainly answered the does she, or doesn't she question.

"That would probably be Melissa the woman he married," Lydia clarified for Mary.

"Probably. He wrote my grandmother that one of her school friends had told his parents what he was planning and they confronted him. His parents were good friends with this girl's parents and had pretty much expected the two of them to marry. Kinda' like an arranged marriage I guess. So when he insisted he wanted to marry my grandmother, they threatened to disown him and take his business away. If you consider those days, he had very little choice. There weren't too many jobs back then. I remember my grandmother saying he came to the house crying and apologizing…just beside himself." Finally there was a pause. "She said he told her he just felt like his world was ending."

"So he broke it off instead of becoming penniless?"

"Seems so." She took another puff and then continued. "He had met her visiting my great-grandfather's store and they became friends. She was young then like sixteen or seventeen. Every time he came to town he made sure he visited her." She could hear Mary take a deep breath and then she continued. "They corresponded for many years after the engagement broke off, remaining friends. I give my grandmother credit for that, I don't know if I could have done the same." Mary stated flatly. "Even years later, when he was in Chillicothe on business, he continued to stop and see her, talking over old times. I really think he was still in love with her but too many years had passed. I remember her telling me he'd had a number of tragedies in his life and had changed a great deal. According to my grandmother, he'd become very hard hearted and sad but when he was around her he softened up some."

"How old were you when your grandmother shared this with you?" Lydia asked, making sure the information wasn't second or third hand, which would put doubt on its reliability.

"I guess I was about sixteen or so, it was like 1946, because she died the following year." Mary explained.

"What did your grandfather think about the visits?" Lydia asked curious. She also wondered if Silla, or any of the other wives knew about the spurned love.

An Old Fashioned Murder

"My grandfather didn't mind much. He knew that my grandmother loved him but she still had a softness for Andrew. He used to say as long as she didn't go home with him he was just fine." A hacking laughter echoed over the phone line.

"Did he ever mention to your grandmother in any of the letters a woman named Silla?"

"You'd have to ask my sister Martha that. Like I said, she currently has them. Let me call her and pass your number on. Hopefully you can get more out of her. All depends on her mood."

Lydia believed immensely in serendipity and thought it awfully coincidental that Mary happened to be at the historical society when she called. She just had to ask, "Do you volunteer regularly at the historical society?"

"I volunteer there twice a month and this was one of my days. My great-grandfather as you know was a prominent merchant and my father was a local doctor. We just feel a bond with the city and to keep our family's memory alive we volunteer. Our ancestors were one of the first settlers of the area, actually. So we have a lot of history here."

❖

Lydia waited patiently for the phone to ring—again.

How long could it take for two sisters to call each other and pass on a phone number? She prepared dinner, which consisted of chicken and dumplings and continued glancing at the clock. It was going on to close to ten o'clock on the East Coast. Just as she was about to give up the phone rang. Lydia decided if it were Lance, she would have him call back. She needed to talk to this woman desperately.

This time Lucas beat her to the phone. Moments later he flew down the stairs at his usual clip holding the phone out. One day, Lydia knew, he was going to slip and fall on his bottom. She was just waiting for it.

She figured by the phone being shoved into her hand it was for her.

"Hello?"

"Hello?" the voice reminded her of a parrot, high and screechy. "This is Martha Clark, my sister Mary called and said you were interested in my grandmother's letters?" she sounded a little more elderly than Mary. Older sister maybe?.

"Yes. I'm trying to learn why the Captain...I mean Andrew Bower didn't follow through with his marriage to Rebecca. Your sister said it was because his parents interfered due to a tip they got from one of his friends. She said you would know more about it?"

"Well I don't mean to talk ill of the dead..." Uh oh, Lydia thought, Martha's one of those.

It was very possible the whole lead could die, depending upon the whim of this woman. Even though Mary was willing to share the contents of the letters, they were in Martha's possession after all. Lydia worried that she might be one of those family members whose ultimate goal is to protect the family reputation no matter what. To get what she needed, Lydia decided to tread lightly; placating Martha being her main objective.

"I'm not asking you to." Lydia assured her. "This relationship involved my friend's grandfather, and she was just curious as to what happened. I don't want to read the letters. I just want to ask some questions." She paused and then decided to try a fishing expedition. "You know, the Captain kept her letters too."

"He did? Well then, I suppose it would be all right to talk about it. Mary gets really excited and sometimes isn't too clear. I just wanted to make sure that your motive for knowing was proper."

Dear God, Lydia thought. It was a hundred years too late, to sell it to the tabloids. What would Lydia and or Julia do with some love letters from the 1880s?

"Really we just want a few questions answered. I assure you that's all." Lydia found her tone getting edgy, which was mostly from frustration. She reminded herself of the old saying that you could get more bees with honey than vinegar...well something like that.

"It's fine, go ahead dear," Martha cooed. Well at least Lydia had been promoted to dear.

"First off, Mary told me that she remembered the engagement was called off because the Captain…I'm sorry, Andrew's parents forced him to call it off."

"That's right. There was this nosy woman, who was the sister of this man that Mr. Bower had gone to upper school with. She was a friend of the girl that his parents wanted him to marry. Somehow she got wind of the engagement to my grandmother and blew the whistle…so to speak." Her voice seemed to slightly rise in pitch. Lydia wondered if there wasn't actually a bit of a gossip monger inside that little old lady after all.

"Do you happen to know who this woman was?" Lydia asked as she crossed her fingers and held her breath.

"Yes. Her name was Silla Drake."

Chapter Twenty

Lydia could hardly contain herself. She sat for a moment taking it all in. Silla just seemed to be everywhere, her tentacles reaching out from beyond the grave. She couldn't seem to stop melding in people's lives, especially the Captain's. If she buttered Margaret up who knew what else she might learn.

"You're grandmother gave you her name?"

"Oh, no. It's in the final letters between them, right before Mr. Bower died. He would come to visit when he was in town, as well as write my grandmother every few months. Apparently about a year before he died, he found out it was that Silla woman that told his parents what he was doing. Her brother Charles, I believe, worked for him and one day he asked Mr. Bower why he was going to Chillicothe so much. Mr. Bower told the brother that he was seeing a wonderful girl and that he planned to break his ties with the girl he was seeing and then propose to my grandmother. I guess he proposed before he got to tell the girl (…as an aside I think he was a bit of a romantic…) and then this Charles told his sister Silla, who was friends with the girl he was seeing and then she went right to the parents. Seems odd he wouldn't have figured it out before hand, don't you think?" Martha pondered out loud.

"Was this all revealed in one letter?'

"Yes. It was almost like a deathbed confession, although he wasn't on his deathbed. My grandmother was a widow then. My grandfather had been killed in a horse accident on the way back from a house call (the horse got spooked and threw him). I think if Mr. Bower had been free he would have come for my grandmother." Lydia realized that there wasn't any way that the Captain could have left Silla even if he had wanted to, she would have stopped him cold.

Maybe she did.

"Martha, I know the letters are personal and I wouldn't normally ask this but would you be willing to copy just that one and send it to me? I promise to pass it on to my friend. I think this would answer a lot of questions she has on her mind." Lydia hated to renege on her promise but the letter really was a major piece to the puzzle. Plus it was documentation, who could say no to that?

There was a moment of silence before Martha responded.

"I guess that would be alright…" Martha hesitated. "But in good conscience, I should mention that there was another letter that came later, that your friend might also be interested in. Mr. Bower wrote my grandmother telling her he had learned something just awful and didn't know what to do about it. He wanted to see her on his next trip to talk with her about it. I guess he wanted to take her into his confidence."

"He trusted her." Lydia remarked matter-of-factly.

"Yes."

"When was that letter sent?" Lydia asked curiously.

"February of 1920."

❖

Lydia chatted a little longer with Martha, which proved fruitful. She ended up sharing a recollection of the Captain from one of his visits to her grandmother's home.

About a year after the birth of Martha's baby brother her mother had become very ill and Rebecca had taken in the older children while she recuperated. Martha thought it was about 1918 or 1919 right after the Swine Flu epidemic had blown through town. She remembered while they were at their grandmother's Andrew had stopped for a visit. He gave each of the children some candy and then Rebecca shooed them out to play. To her he seemed like a very sad man, even though he laughed as the children fought over the candy he gave out. To Martha it was almost like he worked at trying to be happy.

Even for being five, the memory of the day had remained with her. Here was a ninety year old woman recounting the sadness she felt from a man she hardly knew, a man who was still in love with her grandmother and could do absolutely nothing about it.

Before they hung up, Martha promised she would have one of her grandchildren copy the letters and get them in the mail as soon as possible.

As soon as Lydia hit the disconnect button, she immediately hit number three on her autodial. Julia answered on the first ring, almost as if she had been waiting for the call. Lydia knew this was something had to share with her first, before all the others.

"What's the scoop?" she asked excited. Lydia almost laughed out loud. Julia sounded so cute when she was in detective mode

"I just got off the phone with Rebecca Cox's granddaughters…"

"You what?" she blurted out, sounding absolutely awed.

"That's right…I'll explain how I found them later. One of them is mailing two letters to us that are rather important to our theory. It appears that Silla was the one that orchestrated the break-up of the engagement between Rebecca and the Captain."

"No. Really?" Julia sounded dumbfounded.

"Yep. It seems that she was a master manipulator early on. I suppose she did it out of loyalty to Melissa, who apparently the Captain had some misgivings about marrying," Lydia remarked. "It also makes me wonder then what she told the Captain about the behavior of his wives. How much was truth and how much was total fabrication. He most likely based his opinions of them from what he was told."

"Not surprised," Julia said.

"It also makes me wonder where he was, if he wasn't at the store and he avoided home."

"Good points. Maybe hiding in the park? Or, he had another lady friend on the side," Julia remarked.

"Don't even go there." Lydia began to laugh. "But this bit of information is even more telling I think."

"Go ahead," Julia said hesitating just a bit. Lydia got the feeling she was expecting the other shoe to drop and to be honest Lydia felt the same.

"The Captain wrote one last letter to Rebecca before he died, telling her he had learned something very significant and didn't know what to do about it. He wanted to see her to discuss what she thought he should do."

"Did he?"

"No, he never made it. He died," Lydia said.

"When was that letter written?" Julia asked hesitantly. Lydia could feel that Julia knew.

"February of 1920."

"He died March of the same year." Julia said.

"Yes Julia, he did."

❖

The next day Lydia contacted Ohio again to order the Captain's death certificate. Both she and Julia agreed that it wouldn't hurt to have it, especially with the contents of the letters casting a shadow over the last days of his life.

Lance called later on that afternoon to say his trip had been extended due to an emergency stop over in Houston, which would add another whole week to their separation. Lydia couldn't get mad at him since it was his job but she wasn't happy about it either. She assured him it was fine, keeping her true feelings to herself. That rotten news was tempered though by the arrival of the mail, where Lydia was excited to find a letter from the Saylesville Methodist Church.

Lydia sat down at the kitchen table and looked out the back door into the yard. Sarah was busily playing with her kitchen. She and her imaginary friends had all the food scattered around. Earlier Lucas had gone with his friend David to youth group and Beth was off at work. Beth had promised Lydia she would pick him up when he was finished, sometime around seven. Lydia knew she needed to fix something for dinner but at that moment nothing sounded appealing. She decided she would cook when Sarah was hungry. There was nothing like procrastinating.

She reached behind her, took the letter opener from the drawer in the cabinet and slit the letter open. The clerk who wrote it started off with an apology. It seemed that she had been on vacation and the person filling in had not known what to do with the request; so she had set it in a to-do pile, which of course never got done. When the clerk returned from vacation and went through the pile of papers, she found the letter.

It began:

Dear Ms. Proctor,

...This letter is a response to your query about the Bower family. They were one of the first members of this church back at its founding in 1842. Captain Andrew Bower's grandfather was a regular Sunday attendee according to the history "Saylesville Methodist Church, a History." They had two sons, one died young and the other was Andrew's father.

Andrew married three times in the church as you mentioned. All three marriages were arranged by the brides. There was a note by the minister at the time of Andrew Bower's first marriage. Mr. Bower was not active and the bride was of a different faith. This apparently did not hold up the nuptials since according to your letter and the burial entry, they married at the home of the bride.

All of his children were baptized here though and all his wives were buried in the cemetery. There is an entry noted that he had looked into another marriage sometime around 1907 but he never returned to confirm the arrangements. I assume that was his fifth wife?

In regards to the wives he did marry here. All of their families were very active in the church. The Stewart family, as previously mentioned was not members of this congregation. They were members of the Baptist Church at the end of town. If you need additional information, I would look there.

At the time of Mr. Bower's last wife's death, there was a note made by Reverend Harris that there had been some re-arranging of

An Old Fashioned Murder

the graves which he vehemently discouraged. After much debate he decided that in order to keep harmony amongst family members he reluctantly gave the go-ahead.

Other than that there is nothing truly notable mentioned. I hope some of this helps. Enclosed are copies of the marriage and baptismal entries for those you inquired on.

Sincerely,

Patricia Smith

❖

The clerk, bless her, had included copies of the marriage and death entries with the letter. Lydia knew she would have to send her a donation and an nice box of candy as a thank you.

As expected there hadn't been anything earth shattering in the letter. It had been interesting to learn though that Melissa had been Baptist. That explained the marriage being at her home and not at either of the couple's churches. If they had two very strong parental factions, it would have been too hard for them to choose without offending one set of parents or the other.

With those letters it looked like they might have a case against Silla after all. Even though most of their evidence was circumstantial, there was enough of it to form a conclusion that maybe Julia and her family could live with.

Lydia just wished they had the final nail for the coffin.

❖

What Lydia felt could be that final nail came via Muriel who called the next day. She had been through all of Silla's letters and felt that she had come across something that might be of interest to Lydia. The main question Lydia had for Muriel was do they meet now, or wait for the additional outstanding information?

Muriel assured Lydia that the letter definitely supported their theory but if Lydia wanted to wait they could.

Deep down, Lydia did want to wait until everything was in hand. She wanted to call the courthouse and see of there were any additional records pertaining to the custody of the Bower children. She knew some kind of custodial decision had been made, since the Sheriff had posted that blurb in the newspaper, after the inquiry into Katherine's death. She also wanted Charlie and the Captain's death certificates.

And as far as Lydia was concerned, without those last pieces to the puzzle, the conclusion wouldn't be nearly as clear-cut as it could be.

To make it fair, Lydia offered to call Faye and Julia to see how they felt about meeting sooner than planned, then promised to call Muriel back with the decision.

Lydia called Faye first because her schedule was the most difficult to work around. "Muriel wouldn't tell you what it was?" Faye asked suspiciously.

"No. But it must be something significant, or she wouldn't want to meet so soon. I told her *I* preferred to wait for the items that were still in limbo, that way we would have the complete picture. She just didn't seem to want to."

"How much longer do you think before everything arrives?" Faye inquired.

"Well, Charlie's death certificate should have been here by now but they've been having some nasty weather so it could have been delayed. And then I just sent off for the Captain's. I'm not sure how long that will take, Saturday maybe, if all goes well. Also I would still like to call the courthouse and ask about those custody records too."

"Well I have to work Saturday for sure and Sunday afternoon too. Could we meet at the library early Sunday morning?" Faye asked trying to find options.

"That's bad because they're spraying for insects and we've been asked to close that day. The city is paying the bill, so I can't tell them no. If you didn't have to work Sunday, we could have met at my house again and started as soon as I picked Lance up from the airport around noon." This was getting to become a chore. How hard could it be to get four women together to talk?

An Old Fashioned Murder

"I am totally free Monday. We could meet Monday night. I know you wanted to meet earlier but that's my only free day."

Lydia was getting frustrated. It wasn't Faye's fault. It was just so hard to work out the details to everyone's satisfaction. "I would really like to wait and since you can't get off before next Sunday…But… if what she found does indeed have the piece we have been looking for…" Lydia didn't want to sound whiny but she couldn't help it. There were so many decisions: meet or not meet. Suffer or not to suffer. They were so close to finishing this!

"Say, you know I still need to contact my friend and see if he's done with that analysis yet. I haven't heard a thing from him and he hasn't been on my shift for the last couple weeks. I would like to make sure that's included in the final examination as well. I think it is really pertinent to all of this. Would that buy you some more time with Muriel? That analysis is pretty crucial after all." Faye clicked her tongue on her teeth. The wheels were turning in her head.

"She might…" Lydia began.

"Let me try this too…I'll see if I can switch shifts from Sunday to Monday. I might be able to find someone. Would that make everything better?" Faye soothed.

That would work Lydia thought. "Sounds like a plan. That will give me time to tie up those loose ends. Let me call Julia and if she agrees then I will call Muriel back and set it up."

"Okay. So if all goes well we will have two death certificates, one court record, one report on handwriting analysis and whatever Muriel found in that letter."

"Sounds right," Lydia said.

"I'll bring a white board and pens. We can each share what we've found and then go from there." Faye volunteered.

"Do you think we're close? I'm getting awfully tired of so many loose ends." Lydia sighed. She was getting worn out from everything. A vacation was starting to look really good.

"And that statement came from the mouth of a genealogist?" Faye chided her good-naturedly. "Remember when I told you that we would know when we had it? We just didn't know what it was yet?"

"Faintly." Lydia opened the refrigerator. Staring inside she started to contemplate what she could make for dinner. She was getting tired of making that too. Yeah, a vacation was starting to look really good. "As I recall you said that it was *you* that would know it, when you saw it," Lydia reminded her distractedly.

"That could have been what I said but that's really neither here nor there," Faye said dismissively.

So?" Lydia retorted, waiting for Faye to get to the point.

"I think we will know what *it* is on Sunday," she encouraged.

"I sure hope so."

❖

First thing Monday morning before Lydia headed off to work, she pulled out her *Handybook for Genealogists* and looked up the county courthouse phone number. She thought about just looking it up on the Internet but that would mean breaking out the laptop, logging on and then taking time to surf the net and she just didn't feel like it. Besides she had just bought the new edition with money she had earned from giving a talk to another local genealogical society.

By Lydia's clock it was the crack of dawn her time and nine in the morning back east. She needed to make the call quick, since she still had to get Sarah up and ready for preschool. She figured someone should be in by nine-fifteen their time, so she tried calling as soon as she hopped out of the shower. By the second ring the phone was picked up by one of those automated machines: press one for this, press two for that, requests of the probate court was choice number three. She pressed three and low and behold a real human being answered.

"Probate court, how may I help you?" The person sounded much more chipper than Lydia felt at that moment.

"Yes, I'm looking for some old custody records from the turn of the century...twentieth century that is, 1905 or 1906?" Lydia asked the person on the receiving end of the phone. She

An Old Fashioned Murder

had to remind herself, to distinguish between which century now.

"Oh I'm so sorry but those were destroyed in a flood about twenty years ago. We had a horrible storm that year. The office was overcrowded at the time, so many of our records were stored in the basement. When everything flooded, the crates also flooded and the papers disintegrated. We couldn't salvage a thing."

Lydia let out a whoosh. "I was afraid something like that might happen. We 've been so lucky lately," Lydia told the clerk.

"If I may ask, what were you after?"

"Well I'm helping a descendant of Andrew Bower look into some family dynamics and we were hoping that the court case on the custody of his children from Katherine Stowe might shed some light on a family situation. But I guess that won't be happening now."

"You mean Andrew Bower of the mercantile?" the woman asked.

"Yes," Lydia responded, with a small amount of hope starting to bubble up.

"Well there was a big court case in 1905. His wife's family took him to court for wrongful death."

"Oh…" Lydia said quickly. She was right not to get too encouraged. "We have that record, including the letters to the court and the testimony."

"Are you associated with that nice young woman from California?"

"Yes, she was there primarily for her grandmother but I'm the one who asked her to get another copy of the inquiry," Lydia remarked.

"Well there was one packet she didn't get and it was partially my fault. We have the main record in a box on the shelf here in the office, along with the probate records and some of the older superior court papers that they didn't have space for when they moved out and a file cabinet with loose papers. After she left I realized that I'd forgotten to pull out the file that had the correspondence between the Stowe's, Andrew Bower and the judge who had presided. There was a researcher in here a few years ago looking into unusual court cases and he thought this one was quite an example. I later heard he died and never finished his book."

Lydia got really excited at the thought that something had been left out. But her time was running out to get them before the meeting. She decided to take a stab in the dark.

Would it be possible for me to have those copied and then faxed or Fed-Exed to me?" Lydia began eagerly. "I would be willing to pay for both the copies and the mailing."

"I'm not supposed to do research for other people since I am a clerk of the court. We actually have another person who comes in once, or twice a month who handles the mail requests for me but since it was my fault that she missed those letters, I'll do it for you at no charge. Unfortunately our fax is down right now but I can send the information to you if you want. It will probably take me a day or two to get it all together and I'll need reimbursement at least for the Fed-Ex," she explained. "Is that alright?"

"More than. Would I be able to pay with my credit card?" Lydia asked hopeful.

"We don't do that over the phone. But since you were willing to call, at what, six your time for this, I'll trust you to reimburse the court. We have a small slush fund for emergencies that I can borrow from."

If Lydia had been in the same room with the woman she would have kissed her. "That's more than fine. How much do you estimate the cost might be?"

"Under ten. Even though the correspondence is extensive, it shouldn't weigh too much," she said. Lydia would love to deal with more clerks like her. Most of them couldn't give a person, especially genealogists, the time of day. "I'll slip in the receipt for the package when they pick it up. Just mail the reimbursement it to me before the end of the month. That's when they count the change in the slush fund."

"Sounds fantastic!" Lydia enthused. "We've been talking all this time and I never asked your name, I'm sorry."

"Betty Robeson," she replied.

"Any relation to Blanche Robeson?" Lydia asked only half joking. She figured the odds this woman was related to a long ago neighbor of the Captain practically impossible.

"Actually, my husband is her great-grandson. We've lived here all our lives."

Chapter Twenty-One

Things started to happen on Saturday. Lydia greeted the day with the arrival of the Fed-Ex truck at the crack of dawn, with the package from the courthouse, including a bill for twelve dollars. Lydia knew that requests of a genealogical nature were not a part of Betty Robeson's job but bless her, she had gone above and beyond the call of duty.

Later in the day the mailman delivered both Charlie Drake and the Captain's death certificates, both in separate envelopes but at the same time. Who could figure out the post office?

In the same mail delivery were the letters from Martha. Lydia found the envelope to be a little fuller than she had expected. That envelope was open before she even got into the house. Dear Martha had included a bonus letter, one that Lydia thought they would all be very interested in.

Faye called later in the day with the good news that she had not only been able to switch her Sunday and Monday but she had found an envelope in her mail slot at work on Friday. As anticipated it contained the long awaited handwriting analysis. She assured Lydia that both the letter and the journal were safe and sound in her hands. Since they had received all of the things they were waiting on Lydia considered it a good sign.

Also," Faye started. "I've been a very good girl."

"You have? How so?" Lydia asked.

"I finally got the chance to check over the employee records." Faye announced proudly. "From what I can tell, Lissa didn't start working in the store until after Katherine died."

"I hope that was because her father was a firm believer in educating women."

"Whatever...That just explains why she was home with the other kids that day." Faye said dismissing Lydia's observation. "I'll bring the white board and my notes over on my way to work this afternoon too. If that's okay?"

"Sounds awesome," Lydia said. "See you then."

After she hung up with Faye, Lydia called Muriel and then Julia, to let them know they were still on for Sunday. The biggest relief came when Lance called to announce he would be home on time. Lydia had just a few loose ends left to tie up on the home front and then she could relax. That would get taken care of at dinner when she passed out the kid's assignments for the next day.

She sat the dish of chicken and noodles in front of the kids and started to dish out Sarah's portion.

"I don't want that," Sarah protested.

"You've had it before," Lydia said as she dished two small scoops into her bowl.

"What's that?" Sarah asked pointing at the green parsley flakes and black pepper in the sauce. It always amazed Lydia how that child could pick anything apart if she had to.

"Pepper and green spices," Lydia said, as she sat down in her chair. Lucas rolled his eyes at his sister's protests. Beth leaned over and looked into Sarah's bowl. She knew Mom needed help. It had been a long two weeks.

"Look Sarah...see...I have the same thing. It's really good. It's the white sauce that Mommy always makes us when Daddy's gone."

Sarah poked her finger into the sauce and then into her mouth. "Oh yeah," she said finally. A collective sigh escaped as she took her first bite, chewing with deliberation.

"So...Sarah has a birthday party tomorrow at the Pizza Factory. Would you mind taking her?" Lydia asked Beth point blank.

"Is cake involved?" Beth asked. Lydia could tell she was thinking about the proposition. She was never one to turn down good pizza or cake if she could help it.

"Yes." Lydia nodded. "We're meeting tomorrow all day and Dad will be tired from the trip so he won't want to take her. We won't be starting until after one and the party starts at one."

"I guess so," Beth agreed. "Can I take the car next Saturday then to that concert?"

Lydia figured it was a fair trade. "Deal," she said as she took a bite of the garlic bread she had made from scratch.

"Remember I'm going to that baseball game with Dave," Lucas volunteered. Lydia was more surprised he had spoken, than actually volunteered the information. Usually he would eat as fast as he could and then run back upstairs, never uttering one word the whole time.

"I remember. Need a ride?" Lydia offered. She figured she could always drop him off when she went to get Lance.

"Nah, Dave's Mom'll pick us up."

Well that went well, Lydia thought. She was very pleased to see that they would be set without interruption for pretty much the whole day. Why couldn't every meal be that easy?

❖

Muriel called after dinner to remind Lydia that she was bringing muffins. Lydia wanted to do something special for them in return for all their hard work, so she decided to make finger sandwiches, which she hadn't done for a really long time. In addition to the sandwiches, she also planned to whip up a Waldorf salad and a nice pot of tea. It would be like a real old fashioned luncheon, something to go with a real old fashioned murder.

❖

Bright and early Sunday morning Lydia set up the living room. She took all the documentation they had acquired and placed into a three ring binder with tabs for easy reference. On the wall behind the couch, she placed a poster that showed a timeline of events. Lastly she set up the white board Faye had

An Old Fashioned Murder

dropped off the day before. Faye had also brought a set of different colored markers which Lydia put up high where Sarah couldn't get at them. Sarah was a budding artist and anything that she could write with was up for grabs. Since they were the police department's markers, Lydia didn't want the tips ruined like most of her own scrapbooking pens had been.

Lydia then headed into the kitchen where she started to prepare the sandwich fixings. With Beth's help, they spread the mixture onto the bread, cut them into fours and bagged them to chill in the refrigerator. She then mixed up the Waldorf salad and put that in to chill too.

She had just about an hour before she needed to leave to pick Lance up at the airport, so she snuck upstairs, locking herself in her bedroom for a half hour. Lydia wanted a good look at the letters and the additional court information before the meeting. She found the exchange between the judge, the Stowe's and the Captain very interesting. She couldn't wait to see the other's reactions when they reviewed it.

Before she knew it, the bright red numbers on the clock told her it was time to pick Lance up, so she called to Beth as a reminder to watch Sarah while she was gone. With the party at one she knew they would probably be gone by the time she returned.

Lance was arriving at Los Angeles International Airport, her absolutely least favorite place in the world. But fortunately for her, she didn't have to pick him up there. A shuttle would take him from the airport to his office, which was just South of the airport. She would wait by the parking structure of his building and grab him there. Lydia made sure she had his parking pass and headed out the door.

❖

The wait wasn't long. The shuttle dropped him off at the parking structure at a quarter past twelve and he was in the car by half past. Lance leaned over, kissed her cheek, then slid into the drivers' seat. "Thanks. I know you have the girls coming over. We'll get back on time right?"

215

"Oh yeah. I have everything pretty much ready anyway," Lydia assured him. "You'll be surprised at how much we have accomplished over the past couple weeks."

"I can only imagine. You've been working hard on this all summer—all of you. Was it worth it?" Lance asked as he merged onto the freeway.

"From a genealogical standpoint, we didn't accomplish much but from an investigative view point, we really got a lot done. I mean...we gathered the documentation to prove the Captain's true culpability. But I guess the real surprise was when we discovered that we had the opportunity to prove that someone else actually did it."

Lydia knew that Lance knew most of this already. It was the adrenaline pumping through her veins that made her so hyper; she simply couldn't help prattling on. The constant flow of words really did help clear her mind and calm her down, sort of like the Energizer Bunny losing steam. Lance had been married to her long enough to know what she was doing and let her do it. No matter how much it drove him nuts.

Lydia continued, "After this, Julia and I will go back to do the clean-up work—really help make the Bower's stand out—apart from the tragedy." She shook her head at the thought of all the work yet to come.

"After everything else, that'll be the easy part," Lance assured her as he gave her hand a squeeze. "And I'm glad that there has been some kind of a conclusion, especially for Julia." Lance added.

For the rest of the ride home Lydia was lost in thought. She watched the scenery as it passed by, thinking about how things happened, whether you liked it or not. Lydia felt that they had done the best that they could and this afternoon would hopefully give Julia the closure she needed.

❖

Just as Lydia and Lance walked in the door, Faye called asking if Scott could come with her. Lydia was fine with it when Faye originally explained Scott just wanted to hang with Lance but as the conversation progressed, Faye hinted that Scott's real motive was curiosity. He wanted to see what the girls had been up to.

This revelation made Lydia somewhat nervous. Even though Scott was a nice guy and Lydia had always gotten on well with him, she wasn't so sure how he would react to "amateurs" trying to play detective. She didn't want anyone's feelings hurt by unwanted criticism either. But if he was coming along, they would just have to cross that bridge when they came to it. Knowing Faye, she would put him in his place if he said or did anything he shouldn't.

When Faye and Scott arrived, Scott joined Lance on the back patio until the girls were ready for them. Muriel and Julia arrived not too long after and Lydia ushered them into the living room. She warned them about their impending audience so they wouldn't get a shock later when the two of them came in and sat down. Muriel and Julia simply smiled, nodding in understanding. Faye on the other hand, looked like a deer-in-the-headlights. Lydia thought it odd that Faye hadn't considered Scott a liability until that very moment.

After a bit of chit-chat they settled down. Over time each of them had staked out a spot in the room and that's where they headed. Muriel sat in the rocking chair by the window, Julia in the wing-backed chair, opposite Muriel, Lydia on the couch and for the moment Faye was standing. Normally she either sat next to Lydia, or on the floor in front of the coffee table. But Faye had asked if she could be in charge of the white board and since Lydia wanted to guide the flow of the discussion, she had no problem with it.

For fun, Lydia decided to use her mother's teacart for its intended purpose. It was the absolute first time it had ever been used as such. It had always just been a piece of furniture in her mother's house, to put things on when there was no other place for them. When she had inherited it at her mother's death, it became the spot where she put important family items: the kids baby books, scrapbooks and the family bible. For today, she had taken those items and placed them up in the study for safe keeping. She gently sat the cups on the pull out tray, the salad on the bottom shelf and the sandwiches and teapot on the top. She was actually enjoying this more than she ever thought she would.

They decided to eat first. Lydia passed around the sandwiches and salad. She filled her grandmother's teapot with hot water and then pulled out the cups and saucers. She had them pick from a variety of different tea bags and then they all dived into the food.

"Yummy," Muriel exclaimed between bites. "These are the best sandwiches I've eaten in a long time." If she could and still be ladylike, Lydia thought for sure Muriel would lick her fingers.

"This tea is good too, where did you find it?" Julia asked as she finished taking a sip.

"Trader Smiths. Someone got me hooked on it at work and that is the only place I buy my tea now."

"I'm more of a coffee and donut person..." Faye started.

"No, really?" Lydia interjected laughing

"Stop right now or I am leaving," Faye stuck out her tongue. "I don't need that kind of abuse."

"Get over yourself." Lydia said as she got up to re-fill Julia's teacup with fresh hot water.

"Now girls..." Julia chided them good-naturedly.

When Julia first encountered the two of them together she thought Faye and Lydia were really mad at each other. It took other meetings for her to figure it out. Now she laughed with them, playing the scolding grandmother. Muriel sat there watching in silent amusement.

"So are we ready to bring them in. Apparently they want to see what we've done." Lydia asked.

"Scott isn't going to be overly critical is he?" Muriel asked growing concerned. "I mean we are only amateurs and not a professional like he is."

"Oh please, if he even opens his mouth to say anything remotely offensive he knows where he will be sleeping tonight," Faye responded smiling smugly.

"Faye!" Muriel said mockingly. "You wouldn't *really* do that would you?"

An Old Fashioned Murder

"Hell...I mean heck yea!" She stuck her hands on her hips trying to look tough.

"This should prove to be entertaining," Lydia said as she got up and headed out back.

❖

Scott and Lance pulled the dining room chairs up to the living room entrance and settled down. Faye announced that their input was not needed or wanted and that there would be dire consequences if they interrupted the summit. Lydia thought her pronouncement to be a bit over the top but then when both guys looked at each other, suppressing a chuckle, she decided maybe it hadn't been such a bad idea.

It seemed they had all dressed up for the occasion; even Lydia was trying for comfy casual. Faye was in a nice set of beige slacks and a burgundy silk button down shirt. Muriel was wearing a high end jogging suit in blue with yellow piping. Lydia could tell this one was not for the gym, but for out on the town. Julia always dressed nice but today she was in a pair of linen slacks and a sleeveless cotton blouse. It was cool looking and she seemed comfortable. She had topped that off with her signature pearl necklace and earrings. Lydia had on her purple ankle length straight skirt and her white snap tee that had been a hand me down from Beth. It had still been like new when she inherited it. She decided there had to be some perks of having a post teen-ager in the house; so what if hand me downs were one of them.

In contrast the guys were in t-shirts and shorts, both holding bottles of beer. Lydia felt it detracted from their charmed ambiance. But oh well, they *were* guys after all.

All eyes were on her as Lydia stood. She felt like she was in grade school all over again. She hadn't been this nervous, even when she had done the genealogy lecture for the society a few months back.

What wasn't helping was the whispering emanating from the dining room and the occasional guffaw. Lydia wasn't sure what they were talking about but she was pretty sure it was about them and not good.

She decided to address them first, "Okay boys…you're the ones who wanted to sit in on this. If you're going to kibbutz, then just leave, because we're taking this very seriously and apparently you're not." The ladies applauded Lydia's forthrighted ness.

"You go girl," Lydia heard Faye cheer her on from behind.

Scott cleared his throat; Lydia thought he was going to apologize. "If you're not prepared for this yet and if we are making you nervous, we can come back later and then get the nutshell version. It's up to you." He smiled, as he leaned back into his chair.

Smug was the term Lydia would have used to describe the look on his face. Lance sat there not saying anything. He was beginning to look enormously uncomfortable. Lydia knew Lance was more supportive of her than that and was pretty sure Scott was the ringleader for their bad behavior. Not only wasn't he taking them seriously, it was pretty apparent his intent was to tick Faye off. Lydia was starting to get seriously miffed.

"Maybe you should then," she stated flatly. Lydia noticed after her declaration their faces changed. Lance looked even more uncomfortable and Scott looked offended. If he thought his comment would be a challenge, he was sorely wrong. She was pretty sure he wanted them to beg him to stay and give them advice on their technique; but that wasn't going to happen. Not today.

"Lydia…" Muriel scolded. Muriel hated to see any kind of confrontation, unless of course she initiated it.

Lydia figured if they left that was their choice. No, actually Lydia realized it was Scott's choice, since he was originally the one who wanted to stay and watch. "If you aren't going to take us seriously, there's a TV waiting in the family room with your names on it."

Muriel was starting to purse her lips, which in Muriel terms meant she was getting peeved with Lydia, Scott and Lance too, for starting the whole thing.

An Old Fashioned Murder

Lydia leaned over, picking up the first group of papers that they were going to review. "We've worked way too hard on all of this, to be shot down by one borderline male chauvinist."

All of a sudden Lydia realized those words had come from her mouth and it was too late to take them back. The look on Scott's face was priceless.

Faye looked at Lydia like she had never seen her before. It was a look of awe and respect. Muriel was taken aback, her eyes looking up toward heaven; Julia pretended she had lint on her sweater.

"I'm sorry." Scott was actually apologizing. Lydia looked wary. "Lance didn't have a thing to do with the heckling. I promise I'll be quiet and listen."

"We will even move our chairs back to the dining room table and listen from there, if you like." Lance said giving a nod to Scott. He knew the farther away they were at that moment, the better.

The crisis was over.

"Thank You. That would be nice," Lydia said amiably. "It's just we are used to working alone and we hadn't expected an audience." She looked pointedly at Faye who grimaced.

Lance walked over, took her hand and squeezed it. Then the two rabble rousers moved to the table as promised. The girls never heard another peep.

"Let's get busy ladies…"

Chapter Twenty-Two

"**F**irst let's list the evidence we have for both the Captain and Silla." Lydia could see the other three starting to protest. "Trust me the Captain isn't even in the running anymore. I just want to bring out what little we know, that *might* look like it could be him, just for the sake of the experiment. Is that okay?" Murmured nods of agreement filtered through the room.

Faye drew two columns on the board. One she listed as CAB and the other Silla. "I really wish I could make her column longer," Faye commented, as she stepped back to look at her somewhat straight line.

"You can always divide the Captain in half if needed, or just print really small," Lydia suggested.

"But then I won't be able to read it girls," Muriel said, as she took another sandwich from the plate on the cart. "I see pretty well with my glasses but I'm waiting for my new prescription and my vision just isn't one-hundred percent. So can't we just skip him and Faye can print bigger?"

"Don't worry we'll deal with it," Lydia retorted blowing her bangs from her eyes with her breath. She of all people understood not being able to see. If it got bad she would read each line back to them if needed.

"Okay, what do we have for the Captain?" Lydia asked the group. Notepads were pulled out of bags and laptop cases. They were finally on their way.

"I guess I should ask if we want to discuss the additional information at this point," Lydia said in an aside to Faye.

"Probably should, then we will have everything out in the open," she agreed.

An Old Fashioned Murder

"Let's ask Muriel and Julia first," Lydia suggested. "She may want to keep hers for the end."

"We could call it the grand finale," Faye threw her hands in the air in a dramatic pose.

"Cute," Lydia turned to face her groupies. "Would you like all the evidence presented first, or would you like to add them as we work through each scenario? Or go through the known facts and then add the coup d'gras at the end?"

"That's a tough one," Julia said as she looked at Muriel for guidance. "I would like to have it all but that's just because I'm greedy. I've had to wait over seventy years after all."

"How big is your discovery?" Muriel asked Lydia.

"Please…we're not playing poker. We don't have to hold all our cards in front of us." Lydia regretted saying it once she saw the look of hurt on Muriel's face.

"I'm sorry. Blame PMS and a husband who is perpetually out of town." Lydia glanced over at Lance. Lance smiled back apologetically. "I didn't want this to become a competition, but apparently I've led the way in that department. I only suggested those options because in the end they will all have the same conclusion, it's just whether we want a surprise at the end or not. Think of it as the option of reading the end of a book first."

"I understand," Muriel acknowledged Lydia with a smile. "Let's put all of it on the table but leave those two for last. Let's keep a little of the surprise, just for fun."

"That sounds fine with me," Julia said eagerly. At least she was ready to go. "Shall we start?"

"Okay but if the time is right and something should be added, I'm going to toss it into the ring instead of waiting. Knowing me I will forget what it was if I don't. So…" Lydia began. "…The Captain. We know he was neglectful and he had a low threshold for screw-ups, or those that he perceived that way. Are we in agreement with that statement?" They all nodded their heads. Julia flipped through her note pad and then made a mark. Lydia apparently had scored on one of Julia's points.

"He was a temperamental man," Faye said, as she wrote down the prior point on the board. Her printing wasn't big but it wasn't so small, it wasn't readable either.

"True. But that also went along with his need for control," Muriel added as she grabbed another scoop of salad.

"Next. The Captain did not like spending money and his wives, Amelia and Katherine especially, suffered for it," Lydia continued with the train of thought.

"Ah, but did that contribute to their demise?" Faye asked as she carefully erased a word she had written and then re-wrote it.

"That's up for debate," Lydia said. "There have been and still are many men who are inconsiderate…" she glanced across the room at Tweedle Dee and Tweedle Dum. "But that does not mean that neglect, or ignorance killed them, directly or indirectly."

"True… true…" Julia remarked as she poured some more hot water for her tea. She then settled in the spot Lydia had vacated on the couch. Lydia knew the chair Julia had been sitting in could be hard on the bottom but she figured it was more like Julia was excited and wanted to sit as close to the action as possible. "…But does that absolve him from neglecting his wives medical conditions? I mean you can ignore someone and be inconsiderate but he refused to pay for medical treatment when it appeared to be warranted and fed her cheap over the counter medicines," Lydia could tell that Julia was feeling compassion for her grandmother. Even though her tone was changing and so was her posture, Lydia let her go. She had every right to be indignant in her grandmother's memory. Hopefully once this was done, she would never have to dwell on it again.

"Remember, they weren't the only ones during that period in our history that took patent medicines in the hopes of feeling better. There were tons of people who thought the stuff could cure them. So although I agree with your statement about his care towards his wives, we are talking murder by means, not by omission," Lydia explained calmly, as she tried to keep the mission on target.

"Sorry," Julia apologized.

An Old Fashioned Murder

"Not at all. It's a valid point," Lydia assured her.

"But then didn't he get it when three of his wives were physically in the same boat?" Faye asked stretching. "I mean come on…"

"We don't know for sure that Mildred had the same symptoms. We can only assume so. Hers is the only death we couldn't get anything on—unfortunately." Lydia sighed.

"Maybe not," Muriel began.

"Is that part of your discovery?" Julia asked Muriel as she sat her cup down on the tray.

"Yes. But for now it's all right, we can add it once we get to Silla," Muriel said.

"From various accounts, we know the Captain spent very little time at the mercantile. Thanks to Faye we now have a better handle on what he did do, at least when he was there."

Lydia turned the discussion over to Faye for a few moments so she could take a small break. All the talking was making her parched. On the bright side, at least she wasn't nervous anymore.

"From the employee entries there were only two permanent employees, Charles Drake and his sister Silla. In addition to the permanent employees though, there was a revolving door with family members. Elias was working in the store by age twelve. His sister Lissa was a late bloomer, she didn't start there until she was nineteen, just after Katherine's death and then later on Daniel started. Now I figure that you're all wondering why Lissa wasn't home with the younger children after Katherine's death?"

"Because he married Mildred?" Muriel interjected.

"Because according to Julia's Uncle Daniel and verified by the census, the household was quite small by then. After the Stowe's took Amy and Cyrus, Amelia's parents came and took the little girls. That meant there were no children to take care of."

A whistle issued from Muriel. "So the other set of grandparent's jumped on the bandwagon too huh?'

"Appears so," Lydia began. "I can't see where a young girl would willingly kill a step-parent, knowing that they themselves were old enough to take on the burden of raising their siblings if anything happened. And at that time the wait between the new step-parent was brief, especially in the Captain's case. That's why we eliminated Lissa. She was married and likely expecting her first child when the Captain married Mildred."

"She got out while she could," Julia said thoughtfully folding her hands.

"Exactly, Lissa didn't work in the store long enough to have poisoned anyone. More on her as a suspect later," Lydia added as she turned back to Faye.

"Remind me in a little bit to share with you the information I got from the courthouse. It makes the Captain look a whole lot more compassionate than any of us could have imagined," Lydia said.

"Why not now?" Faye asked. "It's a good place."

"I want you to finish this thought first," Lydia encouraged.

"Okay then…the Captain rarely showed up at work except once a week, to check the books, count the cash in the safe and then deposit that cash into the First Bank of Saylesville. The only other time I could find him in the store, was when larger items were being delivered, or when he returned with those that he went into Chillicothe for personally."

"So he kept his time there limited but expected his wives to be there when they weren't tending to babies, or cleaning house," Julia sounded incredulous. "Where was he the rest of the time?"

"We could never get a real handle on that. Lydia found some references to him being in the Rotary Club, the Masons, on the road commission,—town stuff," Faye gestured to Lydia to continue.

"I was looking for information put in the paper at the time of the wives deaths and came across some little tidbits as I went," Lydia explained. "I don't know, maybe he spent more time there when Melissa was alive since they had such a partnership but there wasn't anything that either Faye or I could find to confirm that. I thought maybe the store being her domain, created too many memories and he just opted to stay away doing "guy" stuff."

"We know he didn't train the wives at the store, Silla did. Looking back at her malicious tendencies, we can assume she fabricated much of what she told the Captain about their progress, just so they would look bad," Faye offered. "We can talk more about that when we get to the queen bee herself."

"What else do we have on the Captain?" Muriel asked looking though her note pad.

"These letters," Lydia picked them up. "They contain information that the Captain was engaged to another woman."

"Sweetie, we know that already," Muriel looked at Lydia with great sympathy. From the tone of her voice, it sounded like she really thought Lydia was losing it.

"I'm not mental," Lydia laughed. "There was one additional letter that came along with this one, which helps to clear the Captain."

"I'm wounded!" Muriel said mockingly. "You never told me about that one?"

"She told me, because it shed some light on my grandfather. It made me see him more human—not so much a tyrant."

"Fine then, spill," Muriel sat forward. Any closer to the edge and she would fall off the chair.

"To be honest I only got them yesterday. I called Julia to prepare her for what was enclosed," she couldn't wait for the reaction to this one. It had shocked her to the core. A box of Sees Candy was going to be on its way back to Ohio by the end of the following week. She had to remember to send one to Betty Robeson too in addition to the check for the Fed-Ex delivery. "Alright then…we know that he told Rebecca why the engagement was called off and that he had wanted to visit her before his death to discuss something of dire importance but the third letter was mailed the day before his death. It was postmarked from Saylesville and reached Rebecca less than a week later, which by mail standards back then was darn good…"

"Just tell us already!" Muriel could hardly contain herself.

"The Captain wrote Rebecca, predicting his own demise."

❖

Her announcement seemed to get the attention of the boys in the dining room as well. There was not a peep in the room, just jaws hanging slack and teacups on the edge of spilling.

"How?" Faye asked, coming out of her trance.

"This will require reading for the full effect. As I said I read it to Julia first so she would be prepared," Lydia took another sip of tea and cleared her throat.

My Dearest Rebecca,

I had hoped to come and see you before this, I actually had hoped to be there now but things are not working as planned. I have been feeling ill the last few days. Dizzy, thirsty and my heart can't seem to make up its mind what it is doing. I eat and feel better but the medicine the doctor sent over seems to make me feel worse. I called him and he assured me that I should be feeling better in a day or two.

I am constantly thirsty and cannot keep my glass of water filled. I want to sleep all the time. Maybe I am being re-paid for all those times I did not attend to my wives illnesses dismissing them in my ignorance. I remember Katherine, the one who reminded me so much of you and how ill she was. The cold comfort I provided was a bottle of tonic to ease her pain.

I do not think any tonic will help me. I am sure I know how this began but I cannot prove it. That was what I wanted to share with you. There are some in this house I do not fully trust with my life but until I am feeling better I can do nothing to prove it.

Please my dearest Rebecca, if too much time passes before you hear from me again, make sure my letters to you are safely hidden. I have loved you from the moment I saw you in your father's store. I had hoped to share the rest of my life with you but fate gave me an alternative end instead. I wanted to re-create that feeling that I had— have for you but it never came, not even with Katherine and definitely not with the current one.

With each of their deaths I lost a little more of my desire for life but never for you.

Remember me fondly,

Yours, Andrew

Lydia picked up the box of tissue from the end table and passed it around the room after taking one herself. If anything the letter had given Julia something that Lydia never could, not even putting her family history together, warts and all; a sense that her grandfather had been a good man, not perfect, just good. The Captain had tried and failed but at least he had tried. And the most important thing of all was he had loved her grandmother almost as much as the woman he had given up.

"Wow," said Muriel in between blowing her nose. "He wasn't as rotten as we thought."

"No, just used and manipulated, by his parents, his sweetheart and the woman he left a widow."

"From the tone of the letter he knew something was wrong and he knew it was too late to do anything about it," Faye said wiping her eyes. It was rare that Lydia had ever seen her best friend cry. The first time was at her stepfather's funeral; the second was at her wedding to Scott and then just at this moment.

"How did he get that letter out?" Muriel asked in awe.

"I guess we'll never know. Let me share with you one more item and then we can safely say the Captain is finished and move on to the suspect at hand."

"Go on..." Muriel said as she sat back in the chair, taking a big sip of tea.

"The other thing I want to share is the fact that the Captain *did* fight for his children. It seems that when the Stowe's asked for the inquiry, the Captain wrote a letter to the Sheriff protesting his innocence. He said that he had brought no harm to his children, or his wives and that the Stowe's couldn't be more wrong in their suspicions of him. He asked that he be allowed to speak to the judge presiding over the case, to make his plea. It looks like the judge was very concerned about the circumstances surrounding the Bower household regardless of the Captain's assurances. He sent an order to the Sheriff and some of the town elders to check things out."

"You're kidding?" Muriel said. She looked quite shocked at the thought of the town coming in to examine someone's household and lifestyle.

"Nope. It also looks like the Stowe's…I've already warned Julia about this too…started spreading rumors, through letters to the court, about the Captain and guess who?"

"No way!" Faye exclaimed looking at Lydia with surprise.

"Yes, way—Silla. It seems the Stowe's didn't like her much either and I think I know why. It was because she defended him so vehemently. They thought something must be up. So between the mysterious death investigation and the rumors abounding about his having an affair, the judge decided that it was no place for the younger children to be raised, so he gave them to their grandparents. In the last letter the Captain wrote to the judge, he basically stated that they had taken away everything he had and that he had nothing left to live for."

"So Silla's meanness towards the children was because she knew how much the Captain truly cared for his family and she was jealous," Julia stated bluntly.

"Yes. Her cruelty was driven from that jealousy," Lydia agreed, "But honestly, I think the jealousy had turned to pure hate—for both those alive and dead."

Silence over took the room, as each of them thought about Lydia's statement. Finally Faye broke the quiet.

"So are we ready to move on?" Faye asked in her most authoritative voice.

Besides the silence, Lydia noticed the room had grown cold. Instead of an omen, she saw it more as a sign of the work ahead of them; the leads for all those years had grown cold. The Captain had lost his children and at least three wives and no one even cared until now. But now the lead was fresh and they would see it to a successful conclusion and then hopefully *all* of the Bower's could rest in peace.

"Yeah, but can we take a break first?" Lydia asked.

Chapter Twenty-Three

Lydia was thankful for the fifteen-minute break. She used the time to tidy up the room by taking out the sandwich plates and silverware.

It had been obvious from Faye's posturing during the discussion, as well as the fact she avoided looking directly toward Scott, that she was still mad at him. As Lydia passed them on the way to the kitchen she was pleased to see that they had called a truce, since a hug was involved. The war must be over—for now anyway.

As she sat the dishes on the counter she waved to Muriel and Julia who were on the back patio getting some fresh air. Moments later, Lance joined Lydia in the kitchen carrying the empty salad bowl and sandwich platter.

He leaned over and gave her a kiss on the forehead. "Never saw you do that to Scott before. You really cut him down to size. He was really pushing your buttons, wasn't he?"

"Oh, Yeah. True it isn't a modern day crime where you have DNA and forensic evidence. I mean we aren't *CSI* or anything but for what we had, I think we did a damn good job."

"You know a lot of it is the police thing and egging Faye on is part of it. Even though he is her husband he still sees her as a rookie cop."

"Maybe. But they aren't at the police station and she isn't on the clock. This is something that Faye enjoys…no we all enjoy, and to make light of it was wrong. I really like him and normally he isn't like this at all. It was purely competition that didn't need to be," Lydia said as she put the dishtowel down and looked out the window. "Yes, we're amateurs and yes, our "big in" with criminal science is a rookie cop of two years but you know Faye's eye and instinct are invaluable. She's the one who first zoned in on it being a female murderer and I dismissed her. I made a mistake by not really giving her opinion more consideration. I would hope in the future Scott will not make the same mistake."

"And I apologize too," Lance said sheepishly. "You were right I went along with it because it was a guy thing to do and I made you feel bad. I'm sorry." He gave her a big hug. "Can I make it up to you later?"

"We'll see how you behave for the rest of the time." She smiled at him. "At this point there is a high possibility you will have that chance," she said as she swatted him with the dishtowel. Slowly Lydia proceeded to re-assemble the group back into the living room.

Once they were all back into position, Faye's hand moved back into place over the Silla column on the white board. It reminded Lydia of a jockey anticipating a horse race. And Lydia couldn't blame her one bit. She only hoped that all the evidence would point where it should. If anything they could honestly say that the Captain was innocent but Lydia didn't want to leave without making sure they knew who did. And by looking at all the faces in the room neither did they.

"I didn't introduce the Captain's death certificate during his presentation, because evidence wise, it's more appropriate being submitted under Silla. When we get to that point I'll go over what I have. I also received Charlie Drake's as well. While it doesn't specifically point to our hypothesis, it does have some interesting revelations I didn't expect," Lydia explained.

"I found letters that help shine some light on Silla's early background. Can I add that now, sort of give a background on the embittered soul?" Muriel asked.

"That's great...go for it. Then I can sit for a while too!" Lydia said as she plopped herself onto the couch next to Julia, who had decided to forgo the chair by the window, for the comfort of the couch. Muriel pulled out her reading glasses, put them on and then unfolded the letter she had in her hand.

"Now mind you this isn't my bombshell, it's mostly for background information. I thought it might help explain why Silla did what she did to people," Julia started to say something and Muriel gently put her hand over Julia's. "I am not condoning what she did, or what we think she did but people do things for a reason, or reasons. How one person reacts to a situation and how it forms their being is really random. I truly think killers think differently than the average person does. They rationalize what they're doing so they can live with it. I also think sometimes there's something in a person that snaps for whatever reason and it changes them forever. True there might be some people who could be inherently evil but that can't be the case with everyone. We can make that final judgment with Silla when all the evidence is in."

"Did you ever think about being a lawyer?" Scott asked from the other side of the partition between the dining room and the living area. "You're good."

"Thank you. Actually I did briefly in college but decided to get married instead," Muriel replied pleased that she had helped Scott to perhaps take them a little more seriously, for now. "Let me read you the letter and then you will get a feel for her life."

"My Dear Cousin Silla,

I cannot believe it has been almost fifty years since we have seen each other and over twenty since we have written each other. We are both old women now aren't we? I was saddened to hear about Charlie. I find it hard to think of him as anything other than Frank. He always did like the name Charlie, didn't he? He was such a free spirit but that was broken while you lived with us. Father could be so hard on him. We took father's discipline in stride and avoided it when we could but he could never get Charlie to bend like we did. I remember you defending him to Father before each beating and you my poor dear ended up with the same fate as your brother.

Your parent's death was such a tragedy. I know that fires can start anywhere but how sad that you all could not have escaped the flames. If it hadn't been for Charlie carrying you out of the house in time you would have met the same fate as your dear parents. Then you came to us and I am not sure if your life was any better.

I was sad but relieved when you left. It was best for all. But I thought of you as a sister for those five years you lived with us. And I had hoped that your life would be better than it would have been here.

Since Charlie was older, you were lucky to have someone take care of you. I was most glad to know that you finished school and secured a good job. Your choice was unusual though, since most women prefer marriage to working.

I was sorry to hear you had been recently widowed. I remember that you had married a widower, who had been fated with such bad luck, in regards to his wives. I also remember you writing how much trouble his children gave you when you decided to wed, boycotting the ceremony and all. You did say that it was a lovely wedding at your home anyway, after much debate upon a church. Being a Baptist is who you are. We must not compromise on our beliefs.

I found it such a tragedy for you to finally marry at such an advanced age and then to be widowed after only a few years. You were very brave also to take on raising such a small child which was not your own. You should be very proud.

Please come and see us. We would love to have you if only for a few days…"

"And that's where that portion ends," said Muriel as she pulled off her reading glasses. "The rest centers on the other members of the family and what they are doing. It was signed Grace Pearce Dennis." Muriel sat for a minute, gathering thoughts. "If you can give her a reason for her cruelness, it may have come from the fact she and her brother were apparently raised for a short while by a very cruel man, who from the sounds of it, beat them on a fairly regular basis. Maybe whatever her uncle did, it taught her that she wanted out and in turn wanted things that she couldn't have. It may sound like pop psychology but I think her uncle took an already tortured soul and made it into a monster."

"Hold on a minute!" Lydia exclaimed as she ran from the room and flew up the stairs. She pulled open the closet door and inside safely sat the two boxes of items Uncle Daniel had given Julia. Julia had let Lydia hang on to them for safe keeping while the project was going, in case she found or needed something more from the box, while she was doing the research.

In the bottom of the box, Lydia found the tiny black leather New Testament that she needed. It was the one she had come across briefly when scrambling through the box after they had first got them. She quickly flipped through it, looking for the newspaper clipping that had been tucked inside. When she first found it, it didn't mean anything—but it did now.

The clipping had talked about a couple, Thomas and Blanche Ward in West Virginia, who had perished in a fire near Wheeling. Their bodies had been charred so bad, that no funeral had been planned and their remains were to be interred in a crypt at the local cemetery. They had left two children; a boy Franklin C. and a daughter Jane P., who were sent to relatives in Ohio. The attendees for the private service included the mother's brother Joseph Pearce and his wife Emily.

Lydia laid it gently on to the copier and ran it off. The original was very old, very brittle and very rare. Lydia assumed because it was such an unusual death that was why it made the paper. There were fires in homes all the time back then but maybe because the children survived, it made for important news. Most times the entire family perished before any help could arrive.

If Silla was born around 1855, then the fire probably happened closer to 1865. If she had gone to school with Melissa and Charles with Andrew, then they would have had to have settled in Saylesville sometime before 1870 or so, which fit.

Lydia took the copy downstairs where she found the girls in a huddle. She figured they were wondering what had set her off. Lance and Scott looked curiously at her too. She passed the page to Faye first, motioned for her to read it and to pass it along.

Faye looked up at her with recognition. "They changed their names?"

"Sort of. The last name for sure, which the cousin probably didn't even know about, since from the sounds of it Silla hadn't contacted her for many years. Didn't you catch the reference in the letter when the cousin referred to Charles as Frank?" Lydia asked breathlessly. "I thought when I saw the article briefly the first time that the P probably referred to Pearce since that was the mother's maiden name. But now I can see she was Jane Priscilla and like my grandmother growing up probably preferred Silla over Jane. When they ran and relocated, she kept the name she preferred and Charles did the same sort of thing by using his middle name too." Lydia said as she watched the article pass from Muriel to Julia.

"So Jane is Silla and they picked up Drake somewhere as a new last name," Julia stated. Lydia noticed it was more of a declaration than a question. Like Lydia, Julia liked to think things through out loud. Sometimes it helped to clarify something that was wrong but not caught right away. "The two of them fled and altered their names in case the uncle came looking for them. Charles had to have looked older than what…the sixteen he was. Otherwise wouldn't someone wonder?" Julia asked as she finished reading.

"Maybe not," Lydia began. "The boarding house landlord could have taken one look at them, saw they needed a safe place to live and just ignored their ages, or they knew someone in town and that person helped to arrange a safe haven. We'll never know. They may have lived in that boarding house for sometime before the Captain hired them and took them in to manage the store."

"How could they have afforded to live there?" Muriel asked, astounded at the thought of two children living on their own, in a strange place.

"Odd jobs for Charles, at first probably. If he did enough as a farm hand that would support them, spring through fall at least; or maybe Silla found a job with someone else in the town after school or on the weekends. Together they could have done it, at least for a while. The landlord could have taken pity on them and took whatever they could pay too."

"Could Silla have confided in Melissa after a while about their circumstances and she arranged for them to have some stability by getting them jobs at the mercantile?" Faye asked as she continued to make notes.

"Quite likely," Lydia said. "And that may be why Silla was so loyal to Melissa. It explains Silla's intervention and assistance, in the demise of the engagement between the Captain and Rebecca. She felt she owed Melissa because of the jobs and secondly she was probably afraid they would lose those same jobs if he didn't marry Melissa."

"She would have lost her champion," Muriel remarked.

"Now, that fire...just being devils advocate and all," Faye began as she leaned over and borrowed the article back from Julia. "Could one of them have started it?"

"Charlie? When I actually looked at it upstairs I thought about that. If he carried Silla out of the house, that's possible. He wouldn't have had a lot of time to get them out though. Those old places would burn in a flash; which would make one wonder if he was awake when the fire started," Lydia said.

"Or he had a really good sense of smell," Muriel added, not sounding terribly convinced. Lydia noticed the mocking tone right away. Muriel had the same thought as Faye. Ugh! Lydia groaned to herself.

"That might explain the drinking problem too," Julia said softly.

"If it wasn't Charlie, then that leaves Silla. And from what we now know, that wasn't her method of operation at all," Lydia remarked.

"So was it deliberate, or accidental?" Muriel asked thoughtfully.

"Now we don't know that for sure. As we know from history, Fires happened in homes all the time. They could have left the fireplace going, a lamp could have tipped over and caught the bedding on fire—it could have been anything. We can't assume that either of them did it. All we do know is that they both got out alive and unscathed," Lydia harrumphed. "We are not starting another murder investigation!" They all laughed at her pronouncement. "I just brought the clipping down because the letter Muriel read, reminded me of it. When I went through everything I dismissed it because it had no bearing on what we were looking for."

"Lots of tragedy for one person," Julia remarked sadly as she hung her head.

Chapter Twenty-Four

"All right, now that we have established that Charles and Silla had a rotten childhood, which may have accounted for his drinking problem and her being a serial killer, lets get to the evidence that actually points her in that direction," Faye said as she got back into position by the white board.

"At this point, just throw out what each of you remembered from past discussions, or from the information you looked over. We may not remember everything individually but collectively we should be able to get everything," Lydia said, as she started the ball rolling. "Okay, we know Silla worked for the mercantile for close to forty years if not longer. We get this from the city directory and from the employment journals that the Captain kept. After Silla was hired and for sure after Melissa died, she slowly took over the books and the ordering of some of the merchandise as needed."

Faye took over for Lydia from there. "The Captain only handled the larger items and things that he could pick-up in Chillicothe, probably to save on transportation fees. Since we now know that was just an excuse to visit Rebecca, he had to come home with something to justify his going into the city."

"Exactly," Lydia agreed.

"Silla had full run of the store and Charles was probably still there only because of her. His drinking problem may have started very early and just progressed. Charles may have originally been the manager but Silla took over as time passed to keep them employed and housed," Muriel added.

"We know that the Captain and Melissa lived behind the store first. It wasn't until the pending birth of their third child that she got him to build her a house, still in town but not attached to the store. According to the town directory, after

Melissa and the Captain moved out, Silla and Charles moved in, probably as permanent managers. It was a great arrangement for the Captain. It kept the store safe, the mercantile running; and he didn't have to spend every waking moment there." Lydia explained.

"Not that he did to begin with," Julia interjected.

"That's true. It was his store, he was the owner, he didn't have to be there, that's what the clerks were for." Lydia shrugged.

"I suppose," Julia conceded.

Lydia continued, "At some point it must have gotten bad for Silla living with Charles that is, so she got a place of her own. How she was able to afford this is anyone's guess but she did and was living there when Katherine died."

She figured when they went back to do the clean-up work on the Bower family, they could check the land records for that lot in town and see who the owner was. It could have been a home owned by the Bower's and then rented out, or Silla really had saved her money all those years and was able to buy the house outright. As they all knew, Silla had a will strong enough to do just about anything she wanted. Why would home ownership be any different?

"That was where Lissa took the children the day my grandmother died, correct?" Julia reaffirmed.

"Yes. Why they simply didn't go next door to Mrs. Robeson is unknown."

"What about our theory that she did all of this to get the Captain?" Muriel asked.

"Okay let's address that," Lydia said, changing gears. "We can assume that since she helped nix the engagement between the Captain and Rebecca she wasn't interested in the Captain, at least at that point in time. She was simply protecting the person who had saved her from living on the street."

"How melodramatic," Faye teased. Chuckles emitted from the dining room. The boys had been so quiet, Lydia had completely forgotten they were there.

"It's true though. Who's to say anyone would have hired two strangers, children yet, who wandered into town, accepting the charity of the people who lived there. Someone did help protect them and if we are correct in our assumptions, Melissa was probably number one, if not a close second."

"Sorry," Faye apologized.

"Not necessary, I suppose it was a little over the top…but effective in setting the mood," Lydia emphasized. Lydia caught Faye rolling her eyes heavenward but continued anyway. "I think that she nursed him through the death of Melissa and fell in love with him. Or, Silla expected some kind of payment in return for all of her support, which she probably saw as marriage."

"That did happen back then," Muriel concurred. "I had an uncle who was married and when his first wife died the neighbor next door would come help with the children and cook meals. A year later he married her."

"That just said he liked her cooking skills, not necessarily that he loved her," Faye commented.

"Funny as I recall she couldn't cook worth beans," Muriel said smiling at Faye.

"Back to the topic at hand," Lydia said trying to get them back on track, whatever that had been.

"Whether he loved her or not, she must have loved him, if our suspicions are correct," Muriel said. "So if she had fallen in love with him either before or after Melissa died is mute, she did and she didn't like any kind of competition, so she eliminated it."

"Now we get into the how portion," Faye said, reminding them that she was still standing there, pen poised over the board, just itching to write something. "It all started with the journals. Lydia noticed that the items Silla had purchased to use for her dirty deeds were listed but in an odd shorthand…"

Lydia cut Faye off with an additional tidbit. "Actually *everything* in those journals was in an odd shorthand."

Kibitzing was one of Faye's biggest pet peeves but Lydia figured tough. The fact that Silla went to all that trouble to create a code to hide her deeds and then put everything in those journals into that same code, was kind of interesting. She could have been selling bootleg whiskey out the back door and no one would have been the wiser.

"So, the handwriting...I finally got the results of the analysis," Faye said ignoring the interruption. Lydia noticed that Faye had avoided all reference as to where she had gotten the analysis done. True the girls already knew, so there was no point in explaining again but the guys didn't. Lydia wondered if the omission had to do with how much Faye had told Scott about that disastrous date. By skirting the issue, she didn't have to worry about explanations, later, at home.

Faye cleared her throat before continuing. "According to the report, the handwriting in the letter and the journals are one in the same. They're Silla's," Faye announced jubilantly. They all nodded and then waited for her to continue. It wasn't that big of a revelation since they kind of already knew what the answer was going to be. They just needed the confirmation. Lydia felt bad for Faye so she decided to smooth over her obvious disappointment at their reaction with heaps of praise

"Thanks to the diligence of our cop in residence," Lydia gestured over to Faye. "The source of the poison has been tracked." She smiled at Faye as an indication it was back in her court.

"From what I could decipher, she purchased the base for the weapon from farmer Stevens, out on one of the rural routes. He delivered five pounds to the mercantile three confirmed times with one pound pre-sold to the doctor in town. Now I had two problems with that. One was that they were a mercantile. They did carry some other herbs and herbal remedies—which we will get into more later on—but none of them were blatantly poisonous. I mean everything can be poisonous to some extent but many not quite as volatile as foxglove. The second thing that came to mind was why would the doctor buy from the mercantile when the farmer could just go down the road and sell it to the doctor himself. Now in this day and age we buy in bulk to save money but I don't think that was the case here. She set up an alibi, just in case. Silla kept the pound but made it look like the doctor had it. And if approached of course the doctor would deny receiving it and who would be next? She didn't own the mercantile, so they would look to the Captain. That's of course if she was caught and they could break her code."

"She didn't?" Julia asked stunned.

"Yes, she did. Silla wanted to make sure that if anything happened, the Captain would be blamed." Faye started writing her own thoughts onto the board.

"So she loved him, but used him as a scapegoat. How screwed up can you be?" Muriel remarked.

"Did she really sell the other four?" Julia asked.

"Actually, yes she did. There was a woman named Sinah Meyer who bought three pounds of it. On one of my days off I ran up to the Family History Center and used the film Lydia had rented and looked at the town directory. From what I could gather, Sinah Meyer was a midwife and healer. She practiced what we now call alternative medicine and she had this little ad in the city directory that was geared to women only. She advertised that she was there for all rites of a woman's passage, from birth to the change. So my guess is some of the rural women who couldn't afford the doctor saw her for their health needs. Remember foxglove had been around for hundreds of years and people like Sinah were trained in its proper use, like many other herbal remedies," Faye said nodding to Lydia who then picked up the trail.

"My guess is that Silla was trained in using foxglove leaves as a tea for treating heart trouble, because that's its primary purpose—digitalis," Lydia passed around copies of the information she had found on the internet. "So Silla just added the poison to the patent medicine *she* recommended and since the women took doses according to how they felt, which then determined how often, it took longer for some to get sicker than others."

"Foxglove. You can find it out here but it is really rare," Julia said. She knew a poison was involved but Lydia didn't want to tell her which one until she knew for sure herself. Faye cinched it with the journals.

"The missing pound?" Scott asked from the dinning room. All their heads turned to look his way. It was the first sentence he had uttered and to both Faye and Lydia's delight it was a good question. He was getting it.

"It was sold to someone who was not a regular buyer, maybe someone from another town, or another neighbor. If the doctor did prescribe it for some of the patients in town, like one leaf boiled and drank every other day kind of thing and he was out, they probably went to the mercantile. Especially if word had gotten out that they were selling it. Things don't stay quiet for long in a small town," Lydia replied.

"So let me get this straight," Muriel began. "She bought the leaves from the farmer and then boiled them to make the tea. Then she transferred some of it into the patent medicine that the Captain was picking up at the store and taking home to his wives? What a…"

"That she was," Faye said cutting off the rest of the remark as Sarah walked into the dinning room, holding a goodie-bag and sporting a crown on her head.

"We're done," Beth announced. They all turned abruptly and looked at them.

"Can we have another hour?" Lydia asked Beth. Lydia felt awful when she saw the look on Beth's face. Lance glanced up too and like the trooper he was (always was, Lydia had to admit), offered to take Sarah. He suggested that they would go to the pool for a while. That was one of the things that had sold them on the house and complex. They had a nice community pool that was gated and used it fairly often, especially when the weather was nice. When Sarah was born she wasn't much of a water baby, but that had changed in the last year. Any opportunity to go into the water was numero uno.

"May I stay?" Scott asked. He reminded Lydia of a child who was being bodily removed from a candy store, kicking and screaming all the way. Lydia felt bad for Lance but it wasn't like she couldn't fill him in later and he was only present because Scott was. Lance had originally planned to be watching the world poker tournament upstairs while they were sleuthing.

"Yes, you can," Lydia said to him.

"Let's take a ten minute break while they get settled and then we'll resume," Lydia suggested.

"Sounds good. I need a stretch," Scott announced, acting as if he was doing all the work.

Chapter Twenty-Five

Lydia got Lance and Sarah off to the pool. Beth made her escape upstairs to use the computer, since her brother wasn't on it for a change. Lydia got a pitcher of water, added crushed ice, pulled out Muriel's muffin's and then took everything into the living room. She passed Muriel who was admiring some of her antique music boxes and leaned over, "So when's the bombshell?"

"I am saving it for last. You asked for the nail in the coffin and I have it."

"Would it save some time if we just went right to it?" Lydia asked. Why, Lydia asked herself, go through all the trouble of this little exercise if Muriel had the key the whole time.

"This is fun and a good work out for the brain. Let's continue. The more evidence we present, the more convincing it will be to Julia. She really is the jury on this whole thing."

"But she already thinks its Silla anyway," Lydia protested.

"Yes, but she wants to see it in black and white, or blue and white—whatever color Faye is using on the board in there."

"Alright then, let's get back to it," Lydia said as she led the way into the living room.

Faye took her position once again at the board and they dove in.

"I'm going to quickly go over the timeline...throw everything out in the open and then we can save questions and comments for after..." Lydia was getting tired. It was getting late, almost five o'clock and she felt it was time to start wrapping it up. She pointed to the poster above the couch. "...We know that Silla and Charles came to Saylesville as teenagers and found a place to live and work. We know by the letters, that Charles worked at the mercantile and that Melissa and Silla attended school together. We know that the Captain was engaged to someone else and thanks to Charles telling Silla, that situation was revealed to and ended by his parents. They felt he had a made a good choice in Melissa, who came from another prominent family in town even though she was Baptist." Lydia took a big sip of water and then continued.

"There was that disinheriting thing too. Nothing talks like money," Muriel grumbled.

Lydia had to agree with Muriel on that one. "I have to admit that Muriel's right. If he had truly felt that passionate toward Rebecca he could have left home and just married her. If her parents cared for him as much as she touted, they probably would have taken him in, someday passing their business on to him. But his parent's didn't necessarily expect him to work it, just manage it. It was income without all the fuss. He had limited options and he made his choice. Money over love."

It was such a sad statement that no one commented on it.

"We've already talked about the pecking order as far as who lived where and when, so there's no need to review that again. The Captain married Melissa, had kids. Grew out of their abode and moved to bigger quarters on Peach. Melissa and her son died a few years later and the Captain went into a terrible phase of grief. Silla took advantage of the situation making the store her own. We agree that she must have fallen in love with the Captain about this time..." They all nodded in agreement. "...because she expounded all over the place about him, to the point of trashing his wives to their own children."

"Keep going..." Julia said placidly. She had been waiting for this almost her whole life. Julia's mother had wanted to know the truth till the day she died. She wanted her grandfather to be innocent.

Lydia took another sip of water, smiled and then continued. Her voice was getting tired. "So the Captain upon recommendation from someone, probably his parents—obviously not Silla as we've seen by her comments—starts attending his own church, becomes engaged and marries a spinster of twenty-five. They're married long enough to produce two girls. According to his neighbor's testimony, the Captain is gruff and unyielding. He works his wives to the bone having them take care of the house, children and then assisting at the mercantile. We know Silla trained them. How did that make her feel?"

"Like an employee but very superior," Faye interjected as she sat down in Lydia's spot. Keeping up with Lydia was no longer a viable option. They were on their own.

"Exactly. She saw him as a lover, he saw her as a worker bee. At some point she gave up waiting for him and decided in order to have him, *she* needed to speed up the process."

"But explain to me why she treated them so nasty? I know this sounds weird...but she was just going to kill them off anyhow, she could have been nicer to them. Couldn't she?" Faye tossed out. Lydia had never thought about it like that.

Muriel had the comeback to the question. "I think the circumstances of her early life made her cruel. I think that goes back once again to her uncle and his beatings, her life on the road and ultimately her desires. She liked treating them like dirt, it made her feel superior. Something she never had growing up.

"Superiority is a whole other topic of discussion. We can save that for a later time," Lydia recommended.

"What was the defining moment then?" Julia asked.

"Well, this is only my theory. But after reviewing Silla's testimony, the letters and the journals, I came to a conclusion as to how Silla made her decision. My guess is, the Captain came in to do his bi-weekly book keeping and Silla asked him how things were going. She had been his dead wife's friend after all so he felt comfortable enough to spill his guts. He shared with her how his wife—Amelia—wasn't Melissa. How she complained about being tired and she had so much to do. Silla of course fed him her observations too, since she worked with her and he was in the right frame of mind to eat it all up. He then asked the typical male question 'What do I do?' Silla didn't answer right away. It took some thought and planning. How she chose the Foxglove is anyone's guess...but she did. She boiled her tea, added it to the patent medicine in the store and the next time he came in she recommended he try taking some home to see if it might help. Back then just about everyone had taken some at some point in time and he agreed.

"He never stopped to think that they were just exhausted?" Muriel asked incredulous.

"Obviously not. I'm also pretty sure that Silla would never have brought it to his attention. It defeated her purpose. And too, there is absolutely no way that she would've ever admitted that she and her brother left his wife—who had little to no experience—and their child alone to run that store. She made it as difficult as possible for them. She *wanted* them to fail," Lydia said.

"And it worked," Muriel said flatly.

"That it did. He took the medicine home and the poor thing started taking it. At first it probably did help because the alcohol and any other drug that was in there made them happy as a clam. But at some point the poison started to build in the system. I'm not a doctor but I would guess there was probably some adverse interaction between the poison and the other ingredients already in the bottle. Simply put, she started feeling worse and her symptoms changed: thirsty, tired, faint, weak…"

"Dear God," Julia said putting her hand on her heart.

"Eventually Amelia went to the barn for something and didn't return. Since she was found on the ground with no sign of trauma one can assume it was probably because her heart just gave out."

"To add to this," Faye picked up. "I also spotted that the ordering of the leaves dropped to one shipment, every couple months and then just the three pounds that Sinah required."

"The pattern repeated. He married Katherine, same thing…same church, good farming family. The Captain married her and not the one right in front of him—Silla. She produces two more children for him and then she's run into the ground feeling poorly. Silla strikes again. She reminds him of the tonic that Amelia took and how much better she'd felt…"

"She died!" Muriel said astounded.

"Yes, she did..." Lydia nodded. "This time though Katherine died in the house while cooking dinner. The doctor arrived just in time to catch her heart doing ninety miles an hour. He barely had a chance to examine her. No sign of trauma, just her heart racing. Of course he's puzzled and later the mortician is puzzled. The Captain is now quietly hysterical, because even though he wasn't demonstrative, he actually loved Katherine."

"Then Silla tries to make him feel better by trashing his wife," Faye said angry.

"Yes, she was a bitch wasn't she?" Lydia responded. Lydia tried not to use expletives too often—kids had a way of curbing that bad habit—but this time certainly called for it and Lydia wasn't going to be a prude about it. Faye nodded in agreement, along with Julia and Muriel. "As we know Katherine's parents decided that the Bower household wasn't such a safe place for their grandchildren. One wife dying without symptoms was one thing but two was too many. I also think they probably had concerns that the Captain would work the grandchildren like he had Katherine and that wasn't going to happen. So they went to the Sheriff and requested a hearing in order to take custody of their grandchildren. They made a circumstantial case but it wasn't good enough. They needed more."

Lydia took a sip of water and collected her thoughts. She was almost done.

"Stir the pot was their motto," Lydia smiled apologetically to Julia. If Lydia had been in the same situation, losing a child like that without a known cause, she probably would have done exactly what the Stowe's did. She couldn't fault them for their extreme measures considering what they were thinking.

"The Stowe's used who they considered the enemy. They took examples of Silla at her best: making herself a spectacle by standing up for and fawning over the Captain; her publicly trashing his wives during the inquiry; her self-importance. Her abhorrent behavior was perfect for what they wanted. They started spreading rumors that there was something going on between the Captain and Silla—not just in court but in the parlors, kitchens and church hallways. And it worked. In the end the judge sided with the Stowe's. No old boys school in this case! Amelia's parent's also church members and probably acquaintances with the Stowe's decide maybe it wasn't such a bad idea and do the same thing. By the time the Captain marries Mildred there aren't any children left to care for, other than the one she will eventually be carrying. Uncle Daniel."

"And the pattern repeats again," Julia said lost in her own thoughts. "She didn't wait as long did she?"

"No. Mildred was fast. Maybe her heart couldn't take it, or she may have had some kind of a heart condition already that was triggered by the 'medication'. For sure though Silla wasn't waiting for anymore children to be born, especially if there was a chance she was going to raise them. This time she acted swiftly and won," Lydia said flopping down in the chair. She was totally drained.

"So how did she convince him to marry her?" Julia asked, wiping her forehead with her hanky. Lydia walked over and opened the window slightly. It was getting late, almost five and the evening was getting cool. She knew that Julia wasn't warm because of the house but the air outside might make her feel better. Lydia also re-filled her glass of water.

"That's where I come in," Muriel replied from the chair by the window.

"About time!" Faye exclaimed.

Chapter Twenty-Six

"First off I want to thank Faye for bringing up the sale of the foxglove, which later became tea leaves. When I was reading through Silla's letters, I came across one that now makes perfect sense. I wanted to wait before I shared it, only because I wasn't sure if, or when, it would fit into the picture without all of our discussion first. With the natural ebb and flow, it found its moment to come out," Muriel explained.

"Really quick...can we discuss Charles and the Captain's deaths first and then move on to that," Faye asked Muriel. Faye was as curious about what Muriel had to share as the rest of them but she knew that they needed to know the cause of death for the two males, before they could continue.

"Since those two are mine, I'll explain and promise to be brief," Lydia said as she stood back up and stretched. "As you all know, Charles was an alcoholic and drank pretty much like a fish. When he was out of his own "cure," as they used to call it, he would go into the mercantile and start taking the patent medicines off the shelf and consume them. From what Faye and I could tell as we examined the journals, was that they had a lot of patent medicine bottles in inventory but by the end of the month they had dwindled considerably, probably because of Charles." Lydia shook her head thinking about what a sad life Charles had led. If it had been her, she probably would have been a drinker too.

"But there was always a big peak in ordering about the time that the foxglove arrived in the store. So not only do we suspect that Silla was replacing what Charles drank, she was making sure she had plenty to send to the Bower house," Lydia explained. "So what I thought might have happened was: she filled a bunch of bottles and then Charles came in and helped himself to some of the spiked ones, which then hastened his demise. But then we learned that Charles died in 1918 *after* Silla had married the Captain. It was pretty unlikely that she was still doing anything anymore, since her competition had been eliminated…"

Muriel jumped in, "Which then meant… if he did die from the poison, he was consuming it in a different fashion."

"But she had no motive anymore," Faye began to protest.

"That's what I thought too and maybe I'm reading more into their deaths than what actually existed. I can't be one-hundred percent sure on Charles but as far as the Captain…once I got those two letters in the mail from Rebecca's granddaughter; it sort of did it for me." Lydia explained.

"Go ahead," Muriel encouraged.

"The first letter had the Captain wanting to talk to Rebecca in confidence about something that was happening at home that he felt was 'dire'. The second letter was where he wrote her to tell her he was too ill to travel, showing similar symptoms as his wife Katherine. I submitted them under the Captain to clear his name but I also want to use them now to make another point. I think Silla poisoned the Captain and maybe Charles too and I'll tell you why…I firmly believe Charles some how found out what she'd done and he told the Captain. It was because of that knowledge, neither one of them made it."

"Interesting," Muriel said.

"The only other option is more specific to the Captain and a bit more plausible. Silla found out he was still seeing Rebecca and was done with the deception. She learned from his letters that he had been seeing her on the QT for years. That couldn't have set well with Silla." Lydia explained.

"She snooped," Julia said.

"Wouldn't put it past her," Lydia said.

"Either of those would be hard to prove without real proof but you know what? I agree. Either scenario would work," Faye concurred. "Going back through my criminal and psych books from the academy, she screams psychopath. Silla reminds me of that old lady who was renting out the room back east to lonely old men who had no family, taking their Social Security checks and then killing them and burying them in the basement." Faye visibly shivered.

"You know, if she actually did poison Charles, it may have had absolutely nothing to do with the Captain at all. It was simply another selfish act on her part." Muriel shook her head in disgust. "She'd pretty much taken care of him all her life. They lived in separate homes for a reason. Maybe when Elias was put in charge, he made sweeping changes. Charles may have been ousted and then Silla was stuck with him on a daily basis, and she just couldn't handle it."

"God." Faye uttered under her breath.

"She resorted to her old ways to take care of another unpleasant situation," Julia said.

"Like I said, there's nothing concrete. It's totally conjecture," Lydia reminded them.

"So what was the cause of death for the Captain?" Muriel asked.

"A weak heart. It was a different doctor than the one who treated his wives and he probably didn't know the history of the family. He wrote that it had been sudden, with the Captain feeling bad only in the last month or two. His heart apparently gave out." Lydia took another sip of water. "As for Charles—his 'official' cause of death was cirrhosis of the liver but here the doctor wrote that he also had recent symptoms of heart trouble. Now we can't prove his heart trouble stemmed from the poison. But for both of them to experience sudden heart trouble and then death within months if not weeks, although not uncommon, seems odd. There are always symptoms of some kind when long term; it's just that most people ignore them until it is too late. We know that the Captain must have thought his symptoms were out of the ordinary, or he wouldn't have visited the doctor and then expressed his concern in writing to Rebecca. As for Charles he was simply too out of it to notice."

"She would have had to slip it into their food or drink, right?" Julia asked. "It would be easier for her since she was probably taking care of both of them at that point."

"Bingo," Lydia said.

"So then how does yours fit in Muriel?" Julia asked softly.

Muriel started reading,

"Silla,

Just a quick note to ask you to visit soon. We are close to finishing your training in medicinal herbs and I want to get it done before I go to Indiana. You only have two more lessons left. I know you're busy with the store since Melissa died but I want to know how your practice in making the foxglove tea is going. Remember to have Dr. MacKay take some to try out on his patients. He will know the proper dosage. Remember also it is only to be used in small quantities and only by people who really need it. Any living soul who ingests it, even a small amount, can become gravely ill. When I return I want you to accompany me on a delivery too, maybe someday you can become my assistant; you are such a wonderful learner…"

"Who signed it?" Faye asked.

"The second page was missing, so I have no idea. But the first page was kept for a reason. You're thinking Sinah Meyer?" Muriel asked Faye.

"That was my thought exactly," Faye nodded. "But that still doesn't answer how she got him to marry her."

"I guess we'll never know now," Julia said sadly. "It will remain lost with the two of them."

"So that's it…she was trained in the use of the medicine," Lydia said flatly. "The funny thing is…all this time…we never even considered her being trained. We knew she used the foxglove but we never thought that someone had shown her what to do with it. We looked at Lissa as being the one, since she was young and they tended to train young women."

"Remember, we didn't have a full grasp of Silla's background either. There were gaps in her life, this was in one of those gaps," Muriel defended. "We saw her as an older woman with issues, not someone who had been working on a second career. One that obviously only she knew about."

Lydia plopped down on the couch with a whoosh. All of a sudden she felt so sad, so deflated. After all the detective work; all the frustration of not finding what they were looking for—the answer had been in that box all along. "If we had found that first, would all of our hard work have been needed?"

"Oh Lydia, don't go there! Without everything else we wouldn't have put two and two together," Julia looked right at Lydia, the others nodded in agreement. "We would still have thought the Captain did it, or that maybe she even helped him do it. But knowing her character, where she came from, what she wanted in life...what she would sacrifice in order to have it; made us see that it was all her and no one else!" Julia chided her. "This was the final piece you were looking for Lydia. The piece we needed to clear my grandfather."

Lydia sat and thought quietly. Scott slowly stood and walked over to the doorframe where he leaned against it. Lydia caught the grin on his face.

"Ladies, I have never seen such a team effort in my life. I don't even think the detectives at work know how to work together, to get such results, like you all do. I owe all of you an apology." He smiled, as he pulled Faye over beside him, placing his arms around her shoulders. "I underestimated all of you. I guess when I heard Faye call you the Nancy Drew Crew, I took it as a joke and I was wrong. You presented a fine case, even though most of it was circumstantial. And I also have to give you credit...you certainly dug though a lot of crap to find the things you needed."

"Thank you Scott," Faye said beaming at him.

"So what do we do now?" Lydia asked. They had worked with this family for such a long time, to the point they had almost become Lydia's own. The feeling she was experiencing was almost as if a piece of her had been taken away.

Julia and Muriel both rose from their chairs and walked over to where Lydia was sitting. Muriel then gently pulled Lydia to her feet and they both hugged her.

"Well...let's find another one and start over!" Muriel declared.

"Ugh!" Lydia groaned. They all started to laugh.

Chapter Twenty-Seven

Several weeks later Lydia packed all of Julia's family items into a couple empty computer paper boxes. She had entered the Bower family information into her genealogy computer program, filling in all the blanks, including the events and sources for those events. She looked at the timeline and smiled to herself. They *had* done a good job.

The clean up work had gone quickly with Julia pitching in like a pro. Lydia introduced Julia to the Family History Center, where they spent several days rolling microfilm until they were cross-eyed. Census', wills, land records—whatever they could document, they did. It turned out to be a very full family tree.

Sitting on the floor with the boxes, Lydia wondered how different the Captain's life would have been if he had married Rebecca Cox instead of Melissa Stewart. Lydia was positive that if his parent's hadn't interfered, there would have been no Silla.

Since Rebecca had been the child of a merchant, she would have immediately been comfortable with running a store. She would also have been content to raise a family in that little house off the back; it reminding her of her own childhood home. But Melissa who was raised in a large home and used to getting whatever she wanted, expected a bit more than that. She sought a successful husband, a big house, a status in the community. Andrew fit all her requirements. She eventually adapted to working in the store, making it a success—making her husband proud.

On the flip side; the Captain probably figured as long as Melissa and Silla kept the store running and sound, he was free to do whatever he wanted. This included the monthly visits to his old flame.

An Old Fashioned Murder

Then Melissa and Clarkson died. It was then he realized how much he had loved, or at least relied on Melissa and became lost in his grief. Waiting in the wings there had been someone to take care of him, help him through the death of his wife, the death of someone they both cared for. But instead of rewarding her with marriage, he spurned her for a younger girl.

Once again he couldn't marry the woman he truly wanted because she was married with a large family of her own. So he went back to church, probably at the insistence of his parents and found a girl who he felt wouldn't care so much about the trappings—someone more like Rebecca.

But Silla never forgave him for passing her up, so when the complaining started, she helped stir the pot by reaffirming his convictions, true or not. Eventually she saw the solution to both their "problems" was by removing the problem; always with the hope that he would see Silla was just like Melissa.

And then finally after three times at bat, Silla finally got her wish—but why? That was one question they had never been able to answer. It was just as Julia said, the real truth had died with Silla and the Captain.

Lydia figured at some point, after their marriage, Silla discovered he was still in contact with Rebecca. It was a given that Silla would have felt betrayed, which then gave her the excuse to resort to her former methods. Lydia didn't think that deep down Silla's main intent was to kill him—since he had been the entire focus of her adult life—but by making him ill, Silla was assured that he would *need* her again.

Then there was Charles, her brother, the one who saved her life; the poor soul, who for whatever reason couldn't function in daily life. Whether Faye and Muriel were right and he started the fire, deliberately or accidentally, who knew. But whatever those demons had been, they had driven him to drink. For years Silla had protected him; then one day she simply stopped.

Silla had to have known he was sneaking the bottles of Mother's Helper. If she had grown tired of taking care of him, she probably figured those bottles she had tainted—the ones that he was snatching—would eventually catch up with him. After all who would think anything of a dead alcoholic?

But, what if the Captain's final illness had nothing to do with Rebecca? What if Charles really had tipped him off to Silla's path of destruction; or, with Elias in charge of the mercantile the Captain finally got a good look at the books and put two and two together; or, unfortunately it wasn't until he started getting sick that he truly clued in. No matter what, something happened and he didn't live long enough to tell anyone what he finally knew.

But it didn't end there. Silla made sure she got her way to the bitter end. After the Captain died she had the opportunity to move his wives out of their assigned burial spots so she could be beside the one person, probably the only person, she actually loved beyond all rationale. Because of her the Captain lost three wives and four children. And now, knowing Silla Drake Bower, Lydia knew there was absolutely no remorse whatsoever attached to any of her actions. The woman had simply done what she felt she had to do.

But in the end, Silla hadn't really won, because Lydia had done what she had to do and that was to help Julia find closure. That was the greatest revenge of all.

Before Lydia closed the last box, she picked up the small leather New Testament and opened the book to the page in Psalms that had held that tiny cut out article from over a hundred years ago.

What had started with death—had ended with death.

❖

Another three weeks had passed since Lydia had delivered the boxes to Julia. She had been meaning to call her but getting the kids ready to go back to school, the new semester starting at work, with all the chores that came at the start of a new year; she hadn't had time for much of anything. She meant to e-mail Julia, now that Karen had started teaching her how to use the tool but Lydia's laptop had been having technical difficulties and she had been unable to log on. Getting on the family computer was like trying to swim the Atlantic and in Lucas' case, he would rather drown than give up his online time. Plus, as he explained to Lydia his virtual soldier would

An Old Fashioned Murder

die if he stopped playing, even for a second. Lydia decided she and Lance needed to re-think parental controls and soon.

After a bit of cussing and finagling, Lance was able to determine that the problem was with their home computer network, not the laptop itself. He discovered that Lucas, in an attempt at playing computer technician, had changed some settings which then threw everything out of whack. With that minor repair made, she was back in cyberspace.

Her volunteer Sunday at Tri-Cities rolled around. She knew her day would be spent indoors from twelve to two. The other members of her family though, headed to the beach for a big end of summer blow-out. She planned to meet them there after her shift ended, just so she could get a few rays in before the sun went down.

Lydia found it to be one of those peaceful Sundays at library. Since she had gotten back into the swing of things with her own genealogy, she knew the quiet would allow her some time to make a game plan for the research trip she and Faye had planned for the upcoming Saturday.

There was only one patron in the library and that was reliable old Mr. Smith, a retired theater director. His wife had recently passed, so he decided as a Christmas present to his children, he would attempt to finish the genealogy his wife had started. Mr. Smith had his son, daughter-in-law and three grandchildren living with him. As he explained to Lydia, they were there to keep an eye on him, mainly because he didn't want to be in a nursing home when his time came. But sometimes he found the house too noisy, so he would take the bus to the library to work in peace. He and Lydia would share the antics of small children and laugh and then he would settle down to work.

She was just getting up to take a stretch when a young brunette teenager walked into the room. Lydia looked at her knowing that she knew her but couldn't place where. Then she smiled and Lydia remembered the shy lost girl who had come in at the end of the school year to finish her project on her family tree.

"Mrs. Proctor, I don't know if you remember me," she began.

"Amber right?" Lydia was proud of herself since she tended to be very poor with names.

"Yep. I wanted to come in and thank you for helping me work out that situation with my Dad. I was able to get the information I needed, for the assignment."

"Good for you, how did you do?" Lydia asked excitedly.

"I got an A-minus, mainly because of my punctuation, I'm just awful. But the teacher said I did a good job and the best part was I'm talking with my Dad again," Amber said beaming.

"I'm really glad. I figured since your Mom didn't come after me, it must have worked out," Lydia said, good-naturedly. Amber laughed.

"Actually, that was why I hadn't come in sooner. My Dad sent for my sister and I and Mom let us go. His girlfriend was visiting her own children, so we spent three weeks alone with him. She got back right before we left for home. She seems alright," Amber twirled her hair again, just like she did the day she had come in. "At least my parents are communicating again. Oh and my Mom didn't get *really* mad. I did tell her the truth as you suggested and she admitted feeling bad for putting us in the middle."

"Well I am glad it worked out," Lydia said as she gently patted Amber on the back. She seemed much more relaxed than the last time she had been in.

"What I wanted to know was…could I volunteer to help here? I really would like to learn more about building family histories and I really want to do more on my own. Would you mind?" Amber asked cautiously.

"No, I wouldn't mind at all, we would love to have you. Maybe you could bring in your Mom and sister someday too."

"That would be cool!" Amber exclaimed. Lydia took her over to her desk and had her fill out a volunteer information sheet and then handed her a calendar. Lydia figured with school starting she would probably be volunteering on Sunday's only.

Just as she had gotten Amber settled the phone rang.

An Old Fashioned Murder

"Lydia?" It was a very familiar voice, one she hadn't heard from for several weeks and missed hearing.

"Julia, I've been meaning to call you but I haven't had the chance!" Lydia explained apologetically.

"Have you checked your e-mail?" Julia asked. Lydia noticed the connection wasn't clear.

"No our network at home was down and my computer at work is too slow to log in. I'm back up though why?" Lydia asked curiously, the connection was breaking up. "Where are you? You sound like you're in a tunnel."

"I'm in Ohio. I have all kinds of wonderful things to tell and show you. Karen and I have e-mailed some stuff to you, so when you get home tonight I want you to logon and look at them. I'll try and call again in a few days," Julia said hurriedly. Lydia got the feeling she was afraid the phone might cut out on her.

"Are you in Saylesville?" Lydia asked.

"Yes. I would have called to tell you but Karen got sent to Cincinnati again on a whim. It's been almost two weeks ago now. She asked if I wanted to tag along. Since Saylesville is only about three hours or so away from Cincinnati and then with Chillicothe on the way to Athens County too, I jumped at the chance," Lydia could hear the phone breaking up. They were probably out in the middle of nowhere. "I e-mailed with Karen's help as soon as we got here and then got worried when you didn't respond."

"I'll log on as soon as I get home," Lydia told her.

"I'll call you when we get home!" Julia said as the phone finally broke up.

❖

That night Lydia called Muriel, to tell her about Julia's trip. She promised to forward the e-mails to Muriel so she could share in Julia's adventure. Muriel was as pleased as Lydia that Julia finally got to "go home" without such terrible rancor tearing at her.

She then played back the few messages they had on the answering machine: two were from Lucas' friend David and the other was from Faye. She wanted to let Lydia know she was back on nights for a while, so she might not hear from her until Saturday morning. The message reminded Lydia that she would needed to tell Faye about Julia's adventure when she called. She might even forward the e-mails to Faye too.

After cleaning up the dinner mess, Lydia settled herself on the couch and turned her laptop on. Lance was sitting next to her doing that guy-flipping-the-channels thing, which Lydia found terribly distracting. After a few minutes of his irritating indecision, she moved into the living room where she could check her e-mail and think in silence.

She successfully logged in and saw that there were several messages but three specifically from Julia:

Dear Lydia,

I am so excited. Karen called from work a few days ago, to tell me that she had to go on business to Ohio again. She asked if I wanted to go this time and I simply jumped at the chance. I hadn't been on a plane in years and was a little nervous but the flight really wasn't that bad and I was just so happy to get here! I have all the information you put together with me so that will guide me around town. I am so excited! Karen says she will help me e-mail while we are gone, as often as I want (I'm starting to get the hang of it). I promise to share all the exciting things that I find...

Always,

Julia.

P.S. Sad news...I hoped to tell you in person but maybe this is alright. Uncle Daniel passed in his sleep last week. I had called him right before it happened and told him what we discovered about Silla. He told me it confirmed everything he'd thought all those years ago. He assured me that knowing gave him some peace. I wanted to call you right away when I found out but we left the next day for Ohio. I will share the whole conversation with you when I see you...

The second e-mail was sent a few days later had a number of attachments with it. They were marked: mercantile.jpg;

An Old Fashioned Murder

house.jpg;   graves.jpg;   mortuary.jpg;   saylesville.jpg.; cemetery.jpg

Lydia opened the e-mail and read the brief note Julia had sent to accompany the pictures.

Dear Lydia,

Karen took these for me as we drove and walked through the town. I stopped in the ice cream parlor my Dad took us to when we were here for Silla's funeral. I went to the cemetery where they are all buried, except for Mildred, who I found in the Saylesville cemetery which is at the other end of the town as you know. We went to the mercantile and the new owners showed us around. It has changed little since the Bowers' owned it. Of course there are lots of items that they no longer sell there (foxglove being one of them). The store itself is laid out pretty much the same as it was back then.

The little house attached to the mercantile was a two bedroom, with a kitchen and parlor. No wonder Melissa wanted to move, especially with a third child on the way. There was one wall in the mercantile that had a set of engraved initials. They were Uncle Daniel's. I wish he had been there to see us find them...but then maybe he was.

We stopped at the mortuary and met that nice young man Brad that had helped you over the phone. We visited with him and his Dad and let his father know again how kind it was of them to help us with our quest. We had our picture taken with him in front of the mortuary. Then we walked a few doors down to the Methodist Church and I had a nice visit with the minister there.

Finally I found the house that the Captain had built for Melissa. It is just as beautiful as I imagined and the new owners have taken great care of it. They actually bought it during the estate sale when Silla died. I should say their grandfather bought it when Silla died. They have worked very hard at restoring the rooms to what they were in the 1880s.

We hunted down the Stowe farm since I wanted to see where my mother grew up again. I hadn't been there since my Grandpa Stowe died and I thought it would be a nice pilgrimage. The Stowe family plot is there also, so I left some flowers for my great-grandparents. I think now maybe Jack and Carrie may not have been totally convinced that the Captain was guilty, otherwise why didn't they have Katherine moved to their family plot when they brought the children to live with them? They may have just despised Silla so much, they lost all judgment.

And lastly I wanted to tell you I learned the secret of why the Captain was called the Captain. He had served briefly in the Civil War at the very end as a flag bearer—since he was just fourteen, for one of the last companies drafted for the war. He had marched to the edge of the border between Ohio and West Virginia just as the war ended. He was really a private but no one remembers things like that. So for his three weeks of service he went from a private to a captain, at least with the general populace here anyway.

Enjoy the pictures. I will send more later,

Julia

Lydia looked at the pictures and almost cried. Actually by the time she was done looking at them and being particularly envious, she was. The town was small and clean, similar to the one where her grandparents had grow up, which was just a few miles north of Saylesville.

The pictures of the cemetery were similar to the ones that Karen had taken but then Lydia noticed something strange in the arrangement—Katherine was back at the top beside Amelia, who was next to the Captain with Melissa on the other side. Silla was nowhere to be seen.

Lydia didn't need to be a rocket scientist to figure that one out.

The church cemetery seemed enormous in relationship with the town but then as Lydia recalled there were only the two churches, Baptist and Methodist for the whole township, so they had to hold quite a few people.

The shot of the mercantile was wonderful. It was bigger than Lydia had expected, with a long porch in front that had ornately carved posts supporting the roof. It was white with dark green shutters, reminding Lydia of the dry goods store in *Hello Dolly*.

The picture of the house showed Karen and Julia posing on the porch. It had been taken on a clear day. The house was pea green with light brown shutters, a truly Victorian home. It was then Lydia realized why it looked so familiar. It was the same house in the picture that they found in the box from Uncle Daniel. There had been a large group posed on that same porch. When Julia returned they would have to go back and try to identify all the people posed.

The last picture sent was of Karen, Julia and Brad in front of a pretty garden that looked to be in front of the mortuary. They were all beaming proudly. Lydia guessed his dad had taken the picture.

She opened the last e-mail.

Lydia,

Just a quick note before we start to pack and head to the airport. I hope that you heard me okay and that you've gotten to see the pictures. There are lots more on Karen's camera. We'll show them to you when we get home.

You probably noticed that the headstones were rearranged. I had to throw a hissy fit with the town clerk (not the nice lady that helped you but her supervisor) and even brought the mayor into it, because with all the bureaucratic red tape it would have normally taken months to do. But thanks to Brad and his family, the mortuary stood right behind us and so did the church. It took three full days but I had everyone put back where they were, except for Mildred who I felt really should remain with her parents as they wished. I learned from church records (ones they neglected to send us…) that when Silla had her booted, Mildred's parents arranged to have her moved to their family plot. Since she had been buried with them for so long, I couldn't see moving her back. I think they would have agreed.

Then the kind minister at the church came out and blessed the new graves. I didn't know what to do with Silla, especially after all we had learned about her. I didn't exactly share everything with the minister. I just told him that Silla had been a severely disturbed woman, who had brought a great deal of pain and suffering to my family, as well as experiencing a great deal of pain herself. He told me that I had two choices: I could leave her in the cemetery with the family, or I could have her moved to the city lot. I thought long and hard and decided that although she had been treated poorly and may have been mentally ill, I could not in good conscience leave her with the people she so wronged. I had her moved at my own expense to the city cemetery, which is just as nice. I even moved the headstone.

While I was there I did inquire about poor Charles. I didn't want to abandon him. Even though his death certificate said he was buried in the city lot, they had no record of him. I even tried his birth name too. Just to be sure I checked with the Methodist and Baptist cemeteries as well and there was no record of him there either.

Maybe someday you and I can figure out that one. I said a prayer for him anyway.

Karen is giving me the eye, so I must hurry. I promise to call and come by as soon as I get home. So much to tell you!

Love,

Julia

P.S. Karen is getting married to that nice young man with the BMW. I knew she had the right one!

Lydia sighed contentedly as she wiped her eyes on her sleeve. It was on that happy note that she shut down her computer and began closing up for the night.